CANDLELIGHT

CANDLELIGHT

Part 4 of
The Four Lights Quartet

FERGUS
O'CONNELL

THAMES RIVER PRESS

Candlelight

THAMES RIVER PRESS
An imprint of Wimbledon Publishing Company Limited (WPC)
Another imprint of WPC is Anthem Press (www.anthempress.com)
First published in the United Kingdom in 2014 by
THAMES RIVER PRESS
75–76 Blackfriars Road
London SE1 8HA

www.thamesriverpress.com

All the characters and events described in this novel are imaginary
and any similarity with real people or events is purely coincidental.

A CIP record for this book is available from the British Library.

ISBN 978-1-78308-201-8

This title is also available as an eBook

For Kim Shotola

"If in this book harsh words are spoken about some of the greatest among the intellectual leaders of mankind, my motive is not, I hope, the wish to belittle them. It springs rather from my conviction that, if our civilization is to survive, we must break with the habit of deference to great men. Great men may make great mistakes"

—Karl Popper, *The Open Society and Its Enemies* (1945)

Author's Note

In 1914 in Central Europe, there was a political entity known as the Austro-Hungarian Empire. Today's Austria was a part of that empire. For simplicity, throughout this book, I have referred to the Austro-Hungarian Empire as simply 'Austria' and anything related to it as being 'Austrian'.

Chapter 1
Wednesday 23 December 1914

It has been a hundred and seventy three days since Clara Kenton, née Jordan, last had sex. That's if you mean sex with somebody other than herself – which is what *she* means.

She hurries through a dark, smoky, bitingly cold, November evening to her assignation. The bitter and acrid London air makes her eyes water. And that is not the only part of her that is wet. Clara is damp with excitement. She wears her heavy winter coat, a thick scarf, gloves and boots and these are just about enough to keep out the cold. She carries an overnight bag because she is going to stay at a hotel. She hasn't stayed at a hotel since her honeymoon.

It has all been arranged very hurriedly. And messily. Not the way Clara likes her life to be, at all. She hopes it won't come back to haunt her. James' telegram arrived yesterday evening just after Mrs Parsons, the housekeeper, had left. It said that James would have a twenty four hour pass and asked if she could meet him. He could be in London by late afternoon.

Clara didn't hesitate. She bundled up the girls in their coats and went round to Mrs Parsons. An old friend from Clara's schooldays was going to be in London for just one night and Clara wanted to meet up with her, staying overnight in London. Could Mrs Parsons stay with the girls?

It was such a thin story. But mainly it was so out of character for Clara. She could see that Mrs Parsons didn't believe her. But the older woman was happy to oblige nonetheless. Mrs Parsons loved the girls and took any opportunity to be with them.

A combination of guilt and trying to demonstrate that the story was true had kept Clara at home until the first smell of dusk was in the air but then she couldn't restrain herself any longer. Kissing and hugging each of the girls and with a 'see you in the morning' to Mrs Parsons, Clara took her overnight bag and was soon walking down Horn Lane in the gathering gloom.

She feels a bit like a prostitute. There is something of a Jack the Ripperish air about what she is doing and this causes her to shiver and feel excited at the same time. She doesn't know, but she imagines there must be prostitutes who do as she is doing right now. Of course she knows about the thousands of women who ply their trade on the streets but it has to be true, she reasons, that there is another class of woman. A sort-of upper class. These are women – she imagines – who charge an awful lot of money for their services and who are incredibly confident about what they do.

Clara reckons that *she* is incredibly competent at sex. Even though it has been such a long time and even though sex with her husband has been anything but extraordinary, Clara remembers how self-confident she was on her wedding night. It was as though all her assurance, her self-esteem, her view of herself got channelled down to that one act. To her surprise, rather than thrilling her new husband Henry, it unmanned him so much that it took him several months before he was able to achieve an erection.

She feels that same self-assurance now, and she has no fears about the effect it will have this time. She is confident about her lover, James. She has seen how joining the Army has brought that quiet self-confidence he always possessed out into the open. How she wishes with all her heart that there was no war and that he didn't have to go. But she can't help thinking how there seem to be very few things in life that are all bad – that don't bring with them some element of good. Of course, Clara knows that it is because she is so happy that she *would* think this.

Clara has long loved the paintings of Atkinson Grimshaw and tonight, not for the first time, she feels she is the woman in such a painting. The dark cold air that she moves through feels almost liquid rather than gaseous. It is tobacco-coloured, so that the points or slabs of golden lamplight look warm and inviting. But nowhere near as inviting as what she pictures is waiting for her when she gets to Claridge's.

James is in the lobby, eyes fixed on the front door and his face breaks into a smile when he sees her. He stubs out his cigarette in the nearest ashtray and hurries to her as she comes towards him. He had offered to meet her at the Bond Street Tube station but she hadn't been sure what time she would get away and she didn't want to miss him in the evening crowds. This had seemed like a more sensible choice.

James is about five foot ten with brown hair and green eyes. She thinks he looks terribly handsome in uniform.

'Have you eaten?' he asks.

She shakes her head. Her face and eyes are tingling from the cold.

'I'm not that hungry,' she replies. 'Maybe later.'

Clara *is* hungry. But not for food.

She is quite overwhelmed by the sumptuous interior of the hotel, but doesn't say anything, trying to give the impression that she is quite used to this kind of thing.

'So let's go upstairs and you can unpack,' says James, catching her eye and smiling.

'Unpack *this*?' she laughs, holding up the tiny weekend case that was part of a set her father gave her when she got married. Clara sometimes thinks ruefully about that present. He must have thought she'd travel the world.

Their room has a vast bed, a wardrobe and a dressing table. The gas lamps are turned low so that the room has a honey tinge. The yellow and coral of a fire burns brightly in the grate. All the fittings and furnishings look far more expensive than anything Clara has ever seen before. She had wondered what would happen once they got to the room and I too, have been wondering, dear reader – because it is my intention that this book begin – just as did its predecessor – with a sex scene.

There are a number of problems with this. The most obvious one is the number of bad sex scenes that get written. But there are other problems. A fairly standard approach is that the scene begins with the participants undressing each other. If the writer is a man – as in this case – the focus is generally on how the woman undresses or is undressed. And with a book set in modern times then, there is no great problem. To put it simply – everybody knows what lies beneath.

So – the outer clothing is generally dispensed with fairly quickly. It's cursory – or is that perfunctory, as Clara wondered (and never successfully resolved) on the night of 27 June 1914? After that, the next decision to be made is probably whether there are stockings or no stockings. If it's stockings, then they can stay on or come off à la Anne Bancroft in *The Graduate*. And then it's a pretty straightforward bra first and then panties or (the slightly kinkier) leave the bra on and take the panties off.

With a story set in 1914, things are far less clear. Bras have only just been invented. That piece of brilliance is generally credited to Sigmund Lindauer, a German, who developed a bra for mass production in 1912 and patented it in 1913. Corsets had been the thing up until then but as soon as the First World War began, metal was needed for munitions and weapons and so Herr Lindauer was one of those lucky entrepreneurs who 'caught the wave'. (And proving once again Clara's theory: nothing is totally bad, not even World War One.)

Sorry – I digress. My digression could have been worse though. I could have also spoken about the myth that it was a man called Otto Titzling ('tit sling' – gettit?) who developed the bra and who is commemorated in that great Bette Midler song in the movie, *Beaches*. However, I'm not going to do that because I really need to get back to the issues confronting both myself and Clara as she finds herself in the room that James has booked for their night together. (I would also hope that my wanderings may have heightened the sense of anticipation we are all hopefully feeling – James, Clara, you, dear reader, and myself, who is trying to work out what is going to happen next.)

Essentially, what is going to happen next boils down to what lies beneath and how shall these items be removed.

As it turns out, Clara is a thoroughly modern woman and has begun to experiment with bras. To be more specific, she is the owner of one. Up until then, she wore bodices, and mainly still does. But tonight she is wearing brand new knickers that come down to her knees, a bra and stockings. Clara has also brought with her the nightdress she changed into after sex with Henry on the night of 27 June 1914.

So now the big question. What are our lovers to do? In a modern setting, as we have said, it would be pretty straightforward – Clara would either do a striptease or James would do the undressing. But in 1914, the conventions (for the novelist and the participants) are not so clear. So Clara makes the decision.

James has helped her off with her coat so now she excuses herself with a smile that she intends to be coy – and which seems to have the desired effect – and goes into the bathroom. There she strips naked, goes to the toilet and washes herself – even though she did so just before she left home. Then she changes into the nightdress. She brushes her hair and applies fresh lipstick and a dash of perfume.

What kind of perfume is it? Well, since you asked, dear reader, it's *Shem-el-Nessim* by Grossmith – 'The Scent of Araby' as it says on the bottle.

Finally after carefully folding her clothes and putting her underwear into the overnight bag, she emerges. Two glasses of champagne stand waiting by a bottle nestling in an ice bucket. James sweeps up the glasses and hands her one.

'You look so beautiful, Clara,' he says, as they clink glasses.

'Do I?' she replies.

Clara likes compliments.

'The most beautiful woman I've ever seen.'

Now at this point, in a conventional love scene of the period, you might be anticipating, my expectant reader, that Clara and James would engage in rather conventional sex. The missionary position springs to mind. After all, the Victorian age – a byword for prudery – ended only a dozen or so years previously. At this stage, you don't know a lot about James other than that he works at the Foreign Office and Clara – whom you know quite a lot about – has fallen in love with him. The thought that he's a civil servant might have led you to believe that he is a somewhat unexciting character. Maybe you've been a little afraid for Clara – afraid that she is about to make the same mistake twice, by becoming involved with a man who turns out to be not what she expected.

But I actually have a surprise in store for you because, whatever else we will learn about the other parts of James' life, when it comes to sex, he is anything but dull. And in this he and Clara are going to find themselves perfectly matched. Given the right circumstances, Clara is openly, wildly passionate – even predatorily so. James, on the other hand, is happy to be led but sometimes will take the lead. Both people in their own ways are prepared to test limits.

And while Clara has only known (in a biblical sense) one other man – her husband – James, apart from his ex-wife, also had a love affair – before he was married – with a French woman he met while on holiday in France. She was a couple of years older than him and had determined to educate him. After all, that would heighten her pleasure too. And indeed it did. One of the greatest compliments James was ever paid in his life was when she said that what he was lacking in *expérience* he more than made up for in *enthusiasm*.

And so Clara stands opposite him. She is in her nightdress but he is still fully dressed. (He is in shirtsleeves and has removed his tie.) Clara steps past him and climbs onto the bed. (The covers have already been pulled back.)

'Aren't you joining me?' she asks coquettishly.

'Are you cold?'

This is one of the things that Clara likes about James. She has liked it from the first time she met him. She's never quite sure what he's going to say and sometimes what he does say is not at all what she was expecting. She looks at him, puzzled.

'No, the room is lovely and warm,' she says.

'Then you won't mind taking your nightdress off, will you?'

'Why should I?' says Clara teasingly.

'I'll make it worth your while,' says James.

'And what about you, Private Walters – are you going to undress as well?'

(You may have been wondering, curious reader, why James is not an officer – in particular, a second lieutenant, as this would be the conventional thing for an author to do with an upper-middle class male character of this period. However, you will have to wait a few chapters before you get the answer to that question.)

'I am, but not just yet.'

'So it's just me?' she says in surprise.

'It's just you.'

Clara does as she is told. She slips off the bed, her feet landing on a deep, warm, fluffy rug. She lifts the nightdress off over her head so that she stands naked in front of him. A memory of the statue in the park comes into her head. A dream she had soon after she met James and when her world had not yet been turned upside down. She knows she looks beautiful. She *feels* beautiful. She finds she is not at all anxious or fearful about what he will think. She trusts him completely. She looks up at him. (He is a good six or seven inches taller than her.)

'You are so, so beautiful,' he says, his voice soft, almost a whisper.

'I'm glad you like it.'

'Are you sure you're not cold?' he asks.

'I am a little now.'

'So hop into bed and cover yourself up. Lie across it.'

The bed is so wide that she can do that. Her head rests near the far side and her feet protrude slightly over this side. She pulls up the heavy bedclothes over herself. They are wonderfully warm.

James kneels on this side of the bed and puts his head in under the covers. Next moment Clara feels her legs parted gently and then there is a kiss on her thigh. The effect is electric. There is a surge of moisture in her vagina. She has never known a feeling like it before. James proceeds to kiss his way up her thigh. Then he does the same on the other thigh, starting near her knee and working his way slowly upwards. James pauses.

Clara finds that she is whimpering. Why he is not kissing her *there*? Her legs are parted. She is open, waiting for him. She pushes her groin towards him but he withdraws a fraction. Impatiently she throws off the covers and at that moment, he strokes her with his tongue. With this single movement she feels herself opening. He begins to kiss her and lick her and tongue her. She climaxes within a couple of minutes.

Ever since she discovered it, when she was in her teens, Clara has loved sex. Her experience of sex with other people has been limited to Henry and this, her first night with James. Clara knows that the most important sex organ is not the penis or the vagina or the breasts or anything else. It is the head, the brain, the imagination. She has often imagined the conversation she will have with her girls on this very subject once they grow up. Unlike most mothers, Clara would feel no compunction about discussing this with her children.

Clara's imagination has been fertile indeed in anticipation of this night. She met James on Monday June 29th last. She was in love with him by the 29th of July – if not before that. She has spent many hours imagining her and James together. The result has been that since the telegram yesterday, Clara has been like a gun with a hair trigger or, as she's thought of it, a barrel of gunpowder with a short fuse. Tonight, James lit the fuse and shortly after that, Clara exploded.

Clara's orgasm lasted for more than two minutes. It was helped by James who continued to lick at her clitoris until she had to clamp her legs together and use her knees and hands to push him away. At one stage she did actually think she was going to die.

'I'm so embarrassed,' she says a little while later as they sit against the headboard drinking their glasses of champagne. (Clara is not embarrassed at all.) 'That was so unladylike. What must you think of me? You'd hardly touched me.'

'It certainly was quick. You enjoyed it then?'

'That would be one word you could use. And now it must be your turn.'

'In a little while,' he says. 'Do you need some food?'

'I do actually. I'm absolutely *starving* after that.'

'Well, we must take care of the inner woman.'

'Later,' she says. 'Food first.'

Clara and James will end up spending thirteen hours together. Afterwards, it becomes known to both of them as 'The Thirteen Hours'. Clara thinks of it as thirteen hours of sex but it is not what we today, courtesy of a tabloid headline, would regard as 'thirteen hours of non-stop sex'. James orders some food and rather than eating it all at once they dip into it throughout the night. The room is warm and they spend the night naked. Clara has never done this before – never walked around naked as the day she was born. Not to mention that she is doing this with another person who is also naked – and a man at that.

After Clara's first orgasm and they've eaten something they make love again and James explodes inside her. They fall asleep for a little while after that but both are conscious of how little time they have together. Clara is dozing when she becomes aware that James is kissing her breasts and their lovemaking begins all over again. If the first time for both of them was gentle, this is more physical, more adventurous. Clara wonders if she will shock James if she engages in some dirty talk but she is confident enough of him to try.

'Put it into me,' she commands. 'Now!'

The feeling that he is being ordered seems to spur James on. He enters her and in a few urgent, driving strokes, he climaxes again. Clara feels as though his penis grew bigger inside her each time he pushed into her.

After this James lies in her arms, spent. But Clara is wide awake now. She waits a little while but then takes his hand and brings it down between her legs.

'Come on,' she says briskly. 'No slacking now, no going to sleep. There's work to be done.'

And so the night goes on. Clara will eventually only be able to remember it as a blur of pleasure – food, champagne, kissing, cuddling, stroking, exploring, the sensation of naked bodies holding each other and more orgasms than she has ever thought it was possible to experience over such a short period. Sometime during the night, James checks his watch.

'What time must you leave?'

'Six. The train's at seven.'

'What time is it now?'

'Only two. We have lots more time. And you'll be able to stay here. Sleep late. Have breakfast in bed. It's all paid for. You should pamper yourself. You never get to.'

To Clara it doesn't seem like any time at all. She lies in the crook of James' arm. The first he notices she is crying is when he feels the wetness on the skin of his arm. He takes her and enfolds her.

'Oh my darling, don't worry,' he says. 'It's all going to be fine.'

'I'm frightened,' she replies.

'We're all frightened, darling Clara.'

'Oh James, you must think me so selfish,' Clara snuffles. 'Here's you going off to war and me saying that *I'm* frightened.'

'It's not the war I'm frightened of.'

She turns to look up into his face.

'What? What is it then?'

'I'm frightened that you'll change your mind. That you won't have the courage to go through with all of this. Leave Henry. Marry me. That this –' he pauses – 'will be all we ever have.'

Chapter 2
The Group of Death – reprise

The Group of Death has been running for a few months now – since August. If anyone had told any of the managers – Grey, Poincaré, Der Kaiser, Berchtold and the Tsar – back in those impossibly distant, irretrievable, golden summer days, that after four months, the Group of Death would not only be in full swing but furthermore, would show no signs of ending, they would have been roundly ridiculed. The popular view at the time was that, worst case, it would be over by Christmas. In other words – now.

If these selfsame managers had read a prediction of how many people would have been killed or wounded or maimed so far, they would have said that the figures were incorrect – that they contained the wrong numbers of zeroes – one, two, even three zeroes too many.

Despite these miscalculations of biblical proportions, there have been no sackings amongst the managers. Sir Edward Grey is still Foreign Secretary. His aversion to foreign travel isn't really a problem now as with the German U-boat menace nobody is really travelling anywhere any more – not if they can avoid it. And his job has become considerably easier since pretty much everything is now constrained by military events quite outside his control. Or to put it in the footballing terminology which is perhaps more appropriate to a chapter with the title it has, Grey has become sidelined.

And it's not just Grey. Raymond Poincaré still holds the title *President de la Republique* but in a couple of year's time, Georges Clemenceau will become Prime Minister and Poincaré will find *himself* being sidelined. So too Der Kaiser, whose power is going in ever decreasing circles. These days he finds himself mainly involved in handing out medals and honorific duties. And the Tsar, while nominally presiding over an army of five million soldiers, is in reality in thrall to his generals who in turn are busily converting as many of these soldiers as they can into corpses.

While there have been no sackings, there *has* been one resignation. Count Berchtold is gone. He has retired to his magnificent country estate and there will live a long and contented life until dying in his bed at the age of seventy nine in 1942. One has to wonder if he slept well at night during those years. Or in the small hours when we lie fretfully awake, did the ghosts of some of the millions consumed in what was by then being known as the *First* World War, come to visit him?

Not only has the Group of Death gone on longer than anyone had expected; not only has it shattered far more lives than anyone could possibly have imagined, it has also widened so that many more managers and teams have become involved. In general, politicians have been replaced by generals. And it is the fortunes of two of these that we will follow throughout the rest of this book.

The generals. While they are all obviously different people, they look remarkably the same. On the British side, picture Stephen Fry in the final series of *Blackadder*. Unbelievably shiny, high brown leather riding boots, immaculately pressed uniform with cavalry breeches, plenty of red tabs on the uniform and a Sam Browne belt as luxuriantly polished as the boots. A red-banded officer's cap, the peak pulled down low over the eyes. Beneath the peak, the face. Get past the moustache that any walrus would envy and you see confidence, authority, and a how-dare-you-question-me sort of look. Think that same arrogance of some of the police officers involved in the Hillsborough Disaster cover-up.

All these generals have very long names. Here's one, for instance, Lieutenant-General Sir Aylmer Gould Hunter-Weston

KCB DSO GStJ. When you've added in their ranks, numerous names and decorations, they have names that, in most cases, seem to be longer than their penises.

But now these generals are going to do what generals do best. They are going to make plans.

Chapter 3
Thursday Christmas Eve 1914

Clara is in the kitchen doing the last of the cleaning up. The goose has been prepared and stuffed and is in a roasting tray in the pantry covered with a tea towel. She will do the potatoes and other vegetables in the morning. She has made a sherry trifle and it too sits on the table in the pantry with a plate on top of the bowl. Platoons of sausage rolls sit cooling on a wire tray, having just come out of the oven. Their fragrance fills the warm air.

Clara finds that she is singing a ditty that she heard Virginia singing before she went to bed. The child had had her bath and was in her pyjamas in front of the fire waiting for her hair to dry. She was playing with some bricks. The song went like this:

> *'Someone been dreaming of,*
> *Someone been scheming of,*
> *Someone been crying at your door.'*

Virginia just kept repeating it over and over again in her tiny voice. Clara asked her what she was singing and Virginia replied, 'Just a song.'

'Where did you learn it?' Clara asked.

'In a dream,' said Virginia, in that way children have which means that the conversation is over.

Virginia is only a year and nine months old so she can't even know the meaning of some of the words in this song. It reminds Clara again of her conviction that Virginia is an old soul and has been here before.

And the words of the song strike her as well. They could be describing Clara's relationship with James.

She squeezes out the dish cloth and puts it on the draining board. That's everything. Then she pours herself a generous glass of sherry, puts three warm sausage rolls on a plate and goes through to sit by the fire in the living room.

Like almost all children, Clara loved Christmas when she was a child. But in recent years she has found herself hating it. It reminds her of all she has lost. People who have died and gone from this world. Her grandparents and parents. Bits of herself that she lost in her marriage to Henry. Even the joy of the children and their reaction, can't seem to make up for the melancholy she feels when Christmas hoves into view. Once December the first comes round, she finds herself wishing the season would just come and go as quickly as possible. On the other hand, she likes those last dying days of the year that come after Christmas. She finds that for her they are mostly a time of hope when she starts to imagine what the New Year might possibly bring.

For the last few years though, that had not been so. She has had no illusions that the New Year would be any different from the old one. She had made her bed and she would have to lie in it, to use one of her mother's most oft-quoted sayings. And then, on the 29th of June, she had met James and everything had changed.

How she misses him now. How she feels like bursting into tears remembering the bliss of the night before last and the fear she now feels that something terrible will happen to him. He is on his way to France. Maybe he has already arrived there. What does the future hold for him? Why is it that just when she found him, he may be snatched away from her again? Because she knows that if that happens she will never get another chance at happiness again. Why is that fair?

And why should it have happened that James has gone to France but Henry is in Malta where there is no war? Henry's probably just putting it around over there just as he did with that woman.

And then Clara's mind takes her through the now familiar circles. It starts with picturing a future where James comes back and Henry doesn't. She can't help but feel that it is a joyous future. But then guilt throws its black cloak over her – what a terrible thing to be thinking. And from there she is pulled away by the thought of Henry coming home blind or in a wheelchair or an invalid in some way. And she imagines the long dark corridor of a lifetime spent caring for him. Feeding him, changing his soiled clothes, washing him, helping him to go to the toilet. She's not sure whether that fear isn't worse than the fear of what will happen to James.

How happy she was with him for those few hours, the Thirteen Hours. She felt no guilt about being unfaithful to Henry. After all, hadn't he done that long before her? No, she just felt pure, unadulterated happiness – that this was how life is really meant to be; that this was the bed of roses she had always thought existed. And exists for her too.

The children's stockings are hung up on either side of the fire. Clara remembers her childhood when it was her and her brother's stockings that would be hanging there. Her childhood ended too soon. When her mother took to her bed when Clara was nine, and she had to take over running the house – that was when she began to hate Christmas. And she's not sure how she feels about it now. She suspects that if she were spending it with James she would feel very differently. Will she ever get to spend a Christmas with him? Or will that be snatched from her by a random act of chance just like the one that brought him to her?

Henry spends Christmas Eve night in Malta where he has been since mid-September. He has rarely been happier. Before he left England he spent as many nights as he could with Mary. She was like putty in his hands – not wanting him to go and fretting about what might happen to him. At the same time he knew that she was fuming at her powerlessness. She couldn't push him to divorce. Whenever she drifted anywhere near the subject, Henry fobbed her off with any number of excuses. 'We only have a short time together – why waste it on that?' or

'I can't just take time off whenever I need it – I'm in the Army now' or (his favourite) 'Who knows what will happen – I may not be coming back.' (There were also no issues with Clara about the nights Henry spent away from home as – again – the Army provided a convenient excuse.)

Henry and Mary eventually had a final night together and a tearful farewell the next morning. Undoubtedly Henry was sad to leave her and was going to miss her. But he was also excited about his new life. And any apprehension he might have felt about being shipped to France was quickly dispelled. They weren't shipped to France at all but to Malta, arriving in Valetta on the 14th of September.

It was never really clear why they had been sent there, other than a vague notion that the Germans might launch some sort of operation to seize the island. Why they might do this wasn't that obvious either – maybe to disrupt Allied shipping in the Mediterranean – but to Henry and his fellow soldiers it mattered little. Malta was a paradise.

It was September so the weather was more glorious than the best English summer. There was very little rain. For someone who, up until a few months ago, had been anticipating another damp, foggy, smoky London winter, the place was a tonic. There wasn't much to do – guarding the Grand Harbour, the docks, various bridges and other installations, sentry duty at a number of lookout points – but that was about it. If this was soldiering then it was a very fine life indeed.

And there was plenty of time off. The wine was cheap. And there were women – plenty of women – who viewed the British as their protectors, if not their saviours. Henry was careful. After a lurid lecture from the medical officer on the dangers of venereal disease and having been introduced to the idea that there would be regular short arm inspections, Henry didn't go anywhere near the places frequented by the men. Instead, he discovered that many Maltese men had gone off to join the British forces especially the Royal Navy. This had left quite a number of very lonely (not to mention attractive) women behind.

In the end, Henry has ended up bedding two — one for just one night, but a second who has become something of a regular. Her name is Maria, strangely enough, not that Henry dwells on this when he is with her. And while all of this is going on, he writes regularly to Mary, to Clara and to the girls. The letters to Clara are something of a duty but Henry feels he can hardly write to his children and ignore his wife. Anyway, he finds he misses her a little — at least the old Clara, before she found out about his affair and began to behave the way she did. He hopes that when the war is over things can just go back to the way they were — Clara at home with the girls and Mary, or someone else, on the side.

But there is no need to worry about any of that now. The war, which everybody had said would be over by Christmas, certainly isn't going to be now — unless something rather miraculous occurs tomorrow. So best to just take things from day to day and see what happens.

But later that evening Henry's contented frame of mind is disturbed by a rumour that they will be leaving Malta. Unhappily, by midnight, it has been confirmed. They are due to ship out on January 2nd.

Mary spends Christmas Eve in her parent's house with her brother and sister. It is lovely to be with them all but Mary is heavy hearted and more than once, her mother has found her in the bedroom she shares with her sister, crying. This hasn't been helped by her father making supposedly joking references, from to time, as to why Mary, the eldest, doesn't 'have a man'.

She misses Henry — she really has fallen for him. And she would so much like to talk about him but of course, she can't. Her family would be scandalised to know that she was carrying on with a married man.

And Mary is now fearful of so many things. Fearful that he will be killed or maimed or crippled or blinded by the war. Fearful that, when he comes back, things will go back to the way they were — with no divorce and Henry just stringing her along. Fearful that when he comes back as a hero, he will just drop her. Fearful that even if he does get a divorce while the war is on, leave his wife and marry Mary – all of that – that he will come back an invalid from the war. What a punishment that would be – that what would have been his bitch of a wife's responsibility ends up being Mary's and she spends the rest of her days taking care of the village idiot. Mary believes in God though she isn't very religious. But there are times when she thinks this is exactly how God might punish her for the way she has broken the sixth commandment.

And the worst part of all is that Mary – practical, hard-nosed Mary – can't think of a single damn thing she can do to fix this situation. She lies awake at night, she racks her brains, but Henry seems to be holding all the cards. And it is while she is asleep on this Christmas Eve night that the decision comes to her or gets made or however these things happen while someone is sleeping.

Chapter 4
Friday Christmas Day 1914

Midnight has just sounded from the nearby church. It is Christmas Day. Clara pulls on her coat and goes outside into the back garden to look at the stars. The moon has set behind the houses and the sky is dark blue velvet with the stars like little jewels scattered across it. She has done this every Christmas ever since she was a child. Then, she was looking for Santa Claus. In her teens she used to do it as a sort of private joke – imagine if she saw him. Now she does it to recapture those times. It is a bitterly cold night and the grass under her feet is crunchy from the hard frost.

How her life was so uncomplicated when she was a child. At least until her mother's gradual disintegration began. How beautiful those times were. And that, of course, brings her to wondering if she could ever have such happy times again. A chill runs down her back causing her to shiver. She doesn't know whether it is from the cold or because of her fear of what might happen to James. She goes back inside.

Clara pours another glass of sherry and returns to the cosy living room. She lights a candle on the mantelpiece whispering a silent prayer for James. Then she puts some more coal on the fire, and settles into the armchair in the candlelight.

It is so funny. When Henry was here, she always felt alone. Now that she is by herself, she doesn't feel alone any more. How is *that* possible? She shakes her head and takes a drink. And if her life was uncomplicated when she was a child, it's unbelievably complicated now. Well, not *right* now, but it will be as soon as the war is over. Last Christmas Eve, she was here with Henry staring down along a weary procession of years with death at the end. Now, even though she sits in the same chair in the same house by the same fire, everything is altered. There are so many different lives waiting for her, so many different things that could happen.

The first one is a return to her old life. Supposing Henry was to come back from the war and James didn't. The thought causes her to shiver again. Things *couldn't* go back to the way they were, she tells herself. She would *have* to get a divorce from him. But then her other great fear surfaces – Henry comes back, James doesn't but Henry is an invalid or an idiot or both. She *couldn't* leave him then. So what would she do? Find another man to replace James – and then she would end up as the one having the affair? How ironic that would be.

But the world is like that. Fate – Clara doesn't really believe in God – is like that. The tricks it plays. You ask for something and sometimes it's as though you're never heard and just ignored. But other times you get what you asked for but not at all in the way you had been expecting. Her marriage to Henry is an example of that.

So those are two possible futures that lie ahead for her. A third is that neither man returns. Then, as Henry's explained, she would be reasonably comfortable financially. She would have two pensions – one from Henry's job and the other from the Army. What would she do then? Find another husband? She can't imagine ever meeting a man that would equal James and she wouldn't settle for something less. She wouldn't just marry for the sake of being married. Spend the rest of her life as a widow? It's not what she would want but it would be better than being Henry's nurse. Or wife, for that matter.

And then supposing they both came back? She would divorce Henry and marry James. Yes, but supposing Henry was invalided? Would she have the courage to leave him then? And she has always imagined James coming back whole, but supposing *he* came back as an invalid? Henry whole and philandering and James at home in a wheelchair. What would she do then? Become a sort of angel of mercy taking care of him while turning a blind eye to Henry's goings on? Or if they're both invalided become a permanent nurse?

How many possibilities is that now? Is that seven? Her head is starting to feel like it is going to explode just as it always does when she tries to think this through.

And there is not a lot of solace in the last possibility, the one she finds herself dwelling on most. This is where Henry is killed in the war and James comes home in one piece. He and Clara marry and they live happily ever after. Whenever Clara thinks about this she realises that this is basically wishing for Henry to die. And while she doesn't love him any more and while she has felt profound hatred for him sometimes, she doesn't actually hate him. And she certainly doesn't wish him to die. At least this is what she tells herself.

But increasingly, this is the outcome that she finds herself dwelling on. It solves all her problems. She has money from the two pensions; she and James are free to marry – after a decent interval, of course. The girls lose their actual father but they gain another one whom she thinks would be every bit as good as Henry and perhaps even more so. She knows she shouldn't think these thoughts but she can't help herself. Whenever she finds herself lost in the Maze-of-all-the-Other-Possibilities, this gives her a way out. It is as though she suddenly discovers a gap in the hedge of the maze and can just run out through it into the open.

What should she do? What should she hope for? What should she ask the stars and the Moon for when she stands outside at night?

She stares into the settling coals of the fading fire but no answer comes.

Clara, Henry and Mary will all sleep in their beds tonight. A man who will get no sleep nor see a bed until late on Christmas Day is James Walters, formerly of the Foreign Office, now a private in the King's Army and, as of two nights ago, Clara's lover. The ship carrying his battalion to France crosses under cover of darkness to avoid any marauding submarines. It is a rough crossing and James discovers that he is not a good sailor.

Previously, when he journeyed to France, it was in summer. Then, as he remembers fondly, he sat on deck in the sunshine reading a book and smoking his pipe. Tonight, due to the high seas, nobody is allowed out on deck and the interior of the ship is unbelievably hot and stuffy. James spends most of the crossing vomiting into a toilet bowl or − when those are all occupied − into a sink or − when these are unavailable as well − onto the floor of the toilet.

When he is not getting sick, James tries to fly from where he is to where he was two nights ago with Clara. He had never known himself to be so aroused. And that was even before he saw Clara naked − and much more beautiful than he had imagined her. Her small breasts, her petite but − to his eyes − perfect figure, her magnificent thighs, her pert bottom in his hands. His body can remember how it felt as he slowly entered her. She had been so wet. It was like going into a liquid tunnel. And when he was fully inside her, it was like he had always belonged there and was the only person who, from now on, ever would. When he exploded inside her, he thought he had actually exploded, that that bit of him had disintegrated. And she had held him afterwards like a baby and he had felt safer than in the womb.

One of the first things James decided after he enlisted was that the letters he would write to Clara would contain the unblemished truth about the Army and the war. (He was able to write to her now that her husband had also gone overseas.) He had a vague idea that when it was all over − and assuming he survived − his letters would constitute a history of this part of his life. If Clara did eventually become his wife and if they actually did have a child together, it was something he would be able to pass on to his children and step-children.

If that was one of his first thoughts, his next was probably that that was a very bad idea indeed. Because James finds the Army rather ghastly. He hates the lack of privacy and freedom, the bad food, the communal washing and bathing – James is rather fastidious – and the regimentation. He has always tried to see the best in everything – he is a hopeless optimist. He has always tried to consciously get the most out of each day – especially when he was going through a bad time like his divorce and its lonely aftermath. But he finds it a struggle to discover anything good in the situation that he is in now.

He has decided he doesn't want to communicate any of this to Clara. She is worried enough about him and he has come to see that she is a terrible worrier anyway. The first time this really struck home to James was when he wrote her a letter after his first experience of bayonet practice. They lined up and then attacked a series of sacks filled with straw. Every second sack lay on the ground or hung from what looked like a clothes line. The sergeant demonstrated first – particularly violently – and after that the men took their turns. It was when James put his foot on a sack to withdraw the bayonet that he pictured what that might be like doing it to a man. Would blood spurt out? Would there be a crunching of bone? What would the man's face look like? Would he try to grab the bayonet to stop it from going in? Who was this man anyway? Did he have a wife like Clara? Children?

James mentioned none of this to Clara. Instead, he wrote, 'I have never slapped a child and I can't remember ever having kicked a dog. I wonder how I will get on in a bayonet charge.' Clara's response had been so almost hysterically anxious – there were actually splotches on the paper which he assumed were caused by tears – that he thought he had better steer clear of things like that in future.

And so he does.

In the letters he writes now he tries to portray a jaunty view of army life. On the long marches that they have had to endure, James spends much of the time composing these letters to her, remembering amusing things that happened or that he can make up to include in his next missive. These thoughts are generally enough to take his mind off the pains in his back and legs that these long marches cause.

And it is these funny incidents that have become a key part of his coping with army life. These and trying to find happiness in simple things. A mug of army tea with rum − like nectar after a route march or a training exercise. Sunrises, of which he has seen more than his fair share. Birdsong while they are marching. The smells of England that he tried to capture during his final weeks there. And tonight there is the blast of icy, fresh air that greets him as he comes down the gangplank from the hellish, vomit-stinking interior of the ship.

They disembark under arc lights that stand along the quayside at regular intervals. Once on French soil, there seems to be no clear sense of what is to happen next and so the men mill around, smoking, mostly silent. Another inexplicable delay. James has come to think of these delays as standard operating procedure in the Army.

He hears the seagulls, wheeling and crying overhead in the darkness. James' command of French is good enough to know that they are called *mouettes rieuses* − laughing gulls. And indeed their shrill calls do sound like laughter. It is a shrieking, hysterical laughter with a sort of warble running through it. The laughter of a madwoman. You wouldn't want to be married to a woman with such a laugh, James thinks with a smile. The seagulls circle invisible overhead and laughing their insane cackle.

One *mouette* lands on the crosspiece of the stanchion of one of the arc lamps. He (James assumes it is a male) is big − probably the biggest gull James has ever seen. The bird cocks its bum and defecates, continuously moving its head in that way that all birds do; sometimes with curiosity, sometimes reacting to a sound or some other intimation of danger, sometimes reckoning it is safe enough for it to turn its head and plunge its beak into its feathers to look for crawling things or to groom itself. The bird tilts its head sideways slightly to look down on the assembled men. What must the creature make of all this, James wonders.

Then the bird does an extraordinary thing. Standing on one leg it pushes the other out behind it, at the same time unfolding its wings and stretching them in the same direction. It is for all the world like a ballet dancer's arabesque. The gull holds this pose, stretching for ten, fifteen, maybe twenty seconds before it returns its foot to the ground and draws its wings back into their resting position. It fluffs its feathers a few times before it finally seems to be happy with everything.

The bird is quite magnificent but at the same time James knows how incredibly fragile it is. Gulls don't have doctors – or at least he has to assume they don't – though it sounds like a subject he can get some fun out of when he next writes to Clara. So presumably if a wing or a leg gets damaged that's the end of the seagull. If anything goes wrong it all goes wrong. There is no second chance.

It is while he is thinking these thoughts that a second bird lands on the crosspiece. James expects the big male to chase the second one away but quite the opposite happens. The big male seems to make room for the other bird. James wonders if they are mates. But then he notices that one of the second bird's feet is missing. Its leg just ends without a foot so that it has to work hard to balance on its remaining foot.

James wonders what could have happened. The only thing he can think of is that the bird got its foot caught in a fisherman's net and had to eat through its own leg to release itself. The alternative was to die. The thought gives him a chill that has nothing to do with the piercing December cold and wind around him. And yet the bird is still alive. These beautiful, seemingly strong, yet so fragile creatures with no second chance, can survive. And he wonders whether the key to their survival is the constant curiosity and being on the lookout for danger. Because even though the pair of seagulls seems quite comfortable beside each other, both are now engaged in the never-ending surveying of their surroundings.

A sergeant bellows an order and the unfamiliar sound startles the birds. As one, they lift off and fly upwards, disappearing into the night.

James feels a pang of sadness. He is in France but, half a year ago, who could have imagined it would be under such circumstances?

Three hundred and sixty five kilometres away from where the chill of the French midwinter's night is starting to crawl down James' spine, British and German soldiers are standing in no-man's-land chatting and exchanging food, cigarettes, alcohol and souvenirs. This is what will become famous in years to come as the Christmas Truce. It started yesterday, Christmas Eve. It will be the first and last year that such a thing happens. When the generals find out about it they will issue orders strictly banning any fraternisation with the enemy.

Another man who doesn't approve, but who – at this time – can't do anything about it, is a young corporal in the 16th Bavarian Reserve Infantry. His name is Adolf Hitler.

Chapter 5
Wednesday 6 January 1915

The ship carrying Henry's battalion arrives in Marseille after its journey from Malta. It's a grey day, bitterly cold, with a raw wind and a weary drizzle. The port of Marseille – the cranes, the dirty ships, the dejected looking warehouses, the stinking water strewn with bits of wooden packing cases and rotting vegetables – looks particularly uninviting. But if the port is unwelcoming, the people are not. As the men march, singing, through the streets to the railway station, thousands turn out to greet and cheer them. Women give them flowers, food and bottles of wine to swig from. Both men and women hug the soldiers and plant kisses on their cheeks and mouths. Henry has never seen men kissing men before and finds the custom distinctly odd. There will soon come a time where the arrival of British soldiers in any French port will be the cause of no reaction whatsoever, but it is not that time yet. Though the participants don't know it, it's still very, very early in the Group of Death.

Henry would have liked to have stayed in Marseille. His assessment is that in fine weather, it wouldn't be such a bad place at all. But it is not to be. Instead, at the railway station, they find a long line of goods wagons waiting for them. Each wooden slatted car is marked on the outside '*8 chevaux, 40 hommes*'. A deep bed of straw is to be their only comfort during the long journey north. (These same cars will be used less than thirty years hence to transport French Jews from Drancy to Auschwitz where most of them – men, women, children – will be murdered. Then, the French police, who will supervise the loading of the cars, will force up to a hundred people into each car. It's a thought that doesn't bear thinking about.)

This January day in 1915, nobody seems too bothered about the wagons or the straw or the number of men in each one and the singing continues long after the train has begun its journey northwards.

Henry has come to the conclusion – he has been aware of this for several months now – that he really likes the company of men. Lest you're wondering, my modern-day reader, I don't mean by this that he has discovered he is gay. Rather it has dawned on Henry that his life before the Army consisted entirely of *women*. He lived in a house full of them – Clara, his two daughters, Mrs Parsons, if it came to that. He had a wife and there was Mary, his mistress. Outside of work, pretty much all of his time was spent in the company of women.

Yet up to the time he had married that had not been the case at all. At work Henry was part of a group of men that went drinking every Saturday at lunchtime. He was in an athletics club – a males only athletics club obviously – that had travelled the country to attend meets. Then, Henry very much thought of himself and would properly have been described as a 'man's man'.

He has rediscovered that side of himself in the Army. He has found, for example, the pleasure that comes from knowing that people find your jokes funny. And Henry has remembered that he has a rather large supply of them, ranging from the somewhat innocent to the downright obscene. He continues to be astonished at the number that he is dredging up out of his memory. But of course it's hardly *that* surprising. In the company of women there was very little opportunity to tell these jokes. And even the innocent ones, which he knew would have given Clara a laugh, he had stopped telling for that very reason. But here in the Army he has free rein and has become known as a 'very funny man', the life and soul of the party. It is a role that Henry relishes.

His own favourite jokes are the clever ones. There are three which he finds get a lot of laughs at the moment. The first one, while he wouldn't in any way agree with the sentiment, is very, very funny.

'What do you tell a woman with two black eyes?'

'Nothing – you already told the bitch twice.'

Henry would *never* hit a woman but he is clear that some of the men laughing at it wouldn't have the same scruple. The next one is also very clever.

Two men meet in a gentlemen's' club. The first says, 'I haven't seen you here in a while.'

'That's because I'm a country member,' the other replies.

'Ah yes,' says the first. 'I remember.'

It takes the listeners a hesitation and a moment or two to get that one.

And his personal favourite right now goes:

'How do you make your wife cry during lovemaking?'

'Telephone her.'

For people who haven't heard it before the joke has triggered gales of laughter. But Henry only has to think of it and he finds himself chuckling quietly to himself. It isn't just the joke. He pictures it actually *happening. To him*. He is busily rogering Mary and in the midst of it, he reaches across to a telephone on the bedside table. (It's obviously a top class hotel where they would have such a facility.) Henry lifts the receiver and while continuing to drive in and out of Mary, asks to be connected to Clara (who has somehow become the possessor of a telephone.) She answers and Henry lays the handset on the bedside table just as Mary climaxes and cries out. 'Oh my God – Henry! Oh Henry! Oh Henry!' in a long, sustained orgasm. There have been times, especially with some alcohol taken, where Henry had found himself laughing uncontrollably at this picture.

Henry's being the centre of attention hasn't gone unnoticed by the Army. But it has been interpreted, not as Henry being a very funny man but rather that Henry is a leader. As a result he has been promoted to Lance-Corporal, something of which Henry is inordinately proud.

Chapter 6
Friday 8 January 1915

Clara has an unpleasant duty to perform. It is so unpleasant that she wasn't even able to think about it over Christmas and New Year's. She had intended to carry it out last Monday, the first Monday of the New Year. (Clara has always felt that if there is a day when disagreeable things are best done, then Monday is that day.) But Monday came and she was unable to do it. So too with Tuesday and right on through to the end of last week. Now she can procrastinate no longer and so she sits at the kitchen table, hands curled around a cup of tea, waiting for Mrs Parsons.

To put it in modern terms, Clara needs to fire Mrs Parsons. Not that the dear old lady has done anything wrong. Quite the contrary. Despite slowing down somewhat in the years that Clara has known her, Mrs Parsons continues to do everything she is called upon to do – and always with great cheeriness. Clara can't remember that she has ever seen Mrs Parsons down. So the issue is nothing to do with Mrs Parsons' performance. No – it has to do with money. Clara is in a financial crisis.

When Henry was working at the insurance company, he gave Clara monthly housekeeping money. She had no idea what amount he actually earned but the money he gave her was just about enough to keep everything running along relatively smoothly. But now Henry no longer draws a salary from the insurance company. Instead he is paid two shillings a day – fourteen shillings a week. Clara also gets twenty one shillings separation allowance. While Henry's pay will increase a little now that he has been promoted, this thirty five or so shillings, all of which is paid into Clara's post office bank account, is nowhere near enough to pay for everything. A loaf of bread costs one and two pence. Tea is two shillings for a quarter pound. A pint of milk for the girls is eight pence. She has run up a bill at the grocer's – something she never did in the past and she knows that if she is to have any hope of clearing it, then Mrs Parsons has to go. So now Clara sits at the table rehearsing how she is going to say this and dreading what she believes will follow.

In the end, Clara is unable to do it. As the words she has prepared so carefully are coming out of her mouth, she is already adjusting them. Instead of firing Mrs Parsons, Clara explains that she will only be able to afford to pay her for half days – which she isn't of course. Mrs Parsons appears to take it all in her stride. She says she understands and she'll be happy to work the new arrangement until the war is over.

'We all have to make sacrifices,' says Mrs Parsons, and Clara knows the other woman is thinking about her son in the trenches.

As it turns out, the new arrangement works out even better than before. Clara saves a little money and Mrs Parsons stays well past lunchtime and often until the girls are home from school. It's the familiar story that she loves being with Ursula and Virginia. And, without saying anything, Mrs Parsons starts to bring over food. Rather than just cook for herself as she presumably did in the past, she'll now make a full meat pie and bring over the remainder for Clara and the girls. She'll appear with a bag of apples saying they came from friend who has an orchard and cost nothing. Or Mrs Parsons will appear with two of something saying they were on special offer somewhere so she got one for each of them.

Clara knows that most of this probably isn't true. But what can she say? She is sometimes overwhelmed at what good people there are in the world.

Chapter 7
Friday 29 January 1915

Henry is not the only person of our acquaintance who has been offered a promotion. On this Friday evening James finds himself in a large institutional building that has recently been used as a stable. Of all the appalling places James has been since he joined the Army this is by far the worst. There are mounds of horseshit everywhere, the floors are wet and reek of piss. What little straw there is, is soaking wet, filthy and has to be vermin infested. Rats can be heard scurrying through the straw.

James tries to take his mind off the problem of finding some place to sleep by returning to an issue that has been tormenting him a lot lately. Most of the men seem to be able to just go from day to day. They grumble or cheer depending on what is happening. If they can fill their bellies, not have too much to do and find a dry place to sleep for the night, they appear to be content. If they think about the future at all then they keep it to themselves.

But it is exactly about the future that James keeps wondering. They marched east today from near St Omer and the word is that they will continue going eastwards tomorrow. They are clearly heading towards the front so that James knows that sooner or later he will find himself doing 'real soldiering', as he thinks of it. He will be in battle or under battle conditions.

Up to this point, as far as James is concerned, everything they have done – route marches, firing on the rifle range, digging defensive systems, attack practices – all of these have been playing at soldiers. Not that James has treated them lightly. He has tried to learn everything there was to be learnt and to become good at the things he was taught to do. He has treated all the privations they have had – hunger, bad food, being soaking wet or freezing cold almost all the time, the lice that now inhabit his body and drive him almost insane with the urge to itch and tear his flesh – he has treated all of these as things that must be suffered and which will increase his ability to endure.

But a single question gnaws away at him. When the test comes – the only true test of a soldier – when he is in combat, how will he respond? Will he forget what he has learnt and make a mess of things? Will he freeze? Or make a mistake so that some of his fellow soldiers die? Will he turn out to be a coward? And will the other men see this? Or in some ways – what would be even worse – if nobody sees it and only James knows that he is yellow.

He fears these things more than he fears dying or being maimed or blinded or castrated or losing Clara or never seeing her again. So that when he is summoned in front of the CO and told that he is being promoted to Lance-Corporal, James says, 'I respectfully am going to have to decline, sir.'

There is astonishment on the CO's face and from the sergeant who accompanied James into the room and now stands behind him comes a reflex gasp of outrage which the sergeant instantly cuts off. The Army is such a silly place in so many ways, James feels. A silly place with many silly people. He finds his eyes being drawn to the CO's magnificent, sandy coloured moustache. James wonders how the CO keeps the moustache so perfect. Is it like that when he wakes up in the morning after a night's sleep or is it all tossed by being pressed against a pillow? Does the CO have to sleep on his back all night and keep ramrod still to avoid any damage to the perfectly groomed object beneath his nose?

'May I ask why?' inquires the CO. 'It means extra pay, you know.'

'I'm aware of that, sir. The pay isn't the issue. It's that I don't think I'm qualified to lead other men until I've been in battle, sir.'

'But you're well-educated, man. You're intelligent. Weren't you some kind of manager in Civvy Street?'

'More a civil servant than a manager, sir.'

'Well, whatever,' says the CO. 'I'm sure you'd make a damn fine leader.'

This just confirms something that James has already seen happening in the battalion. Promotions seem to have very little to do with skill at soldiering and everything to do with class. It is the middle or upper class people, those with the good educations or better accents who have been promoted. Maybe it makes sense, maybe it is what the men expect, but for James he feels it would only increase the pressure on him if he were now responsible not only for his own conduct but that of other men.

'I'd very much like to be considered at some time in the future, sir,' James says. 'But only after I've seen action.'

The result is that the CO finds himself quite speechless and James is dismissed.

James finds an evil-smelling spot in a corridor and puts down his groundsheet. Then, with his head on his pack, he lies back and smokes a cigarette, staring at the ruined plaster of the ceiling.

His first idea about when he would go into battle had been the idea that he came to call 'the grey land'. The grey land meant that, when he went into battle, he would regard himself as already dead. This was what the grey land was – the land of the dead. If he was already dead, he reasoned, then he wouldn't be frightened. There would be nothing to fear because there would be nothing to lose.

But he quickly gave up on this idea. He reckoned it would make him too blasé or even careless. He wanted to be a good soldier but he didn't want to be reckless or win a posthumous Victoria Cross. He just wanted to do his duty and go home and make a life with Clara. He doesn't want to inhabit the grey land. Since he fell in love, he is more alive now than he has ever been.

Another theory of James' had been that if he remembered everything the Army taught him, then that would be his best chance of surviving. But he had given up on that even before he had given up on the grey land. He had quickly come to understand that much of what the Army concerned itself with was unbelievably stupid, pointless and downright wrong.

Now, as he lies in this building in France, in circumstances he could not have possibly imagined, James finds that – bizarrely – he is thinking again about the seagulls. He remembers the way they were constantly looking around – curious, yes but also on the lookout for danger. Learning – and quickly – especially in new and unfamiliar situations. The British sergeant bellowing an order startled them because they had never come across anything like that before. But now it was part of their scheme of things. They would not be surprised by it again but rather would know what to do.

And for the seagulls the stakes are very high. They get one chance. There is no second chance. Maybe this then is how to deal with the ordeal that lies ahead. Look around, notice things, be curious, learn quickly, and anticipate things.

It isn't much, but it is all he can think of right now.

Chapter 8
Sunday 7 February 1915

I t is evening and Mary is at home ironing her skirt for work tomorrow. The smell of the hot fabric just serves to remind her of the miserable loneliness and domesticity of her life. She knows things are about to change, but the change cannot come soon enough for her. On Christmas Day, Mary decided that she would volunteer to become a nurse. Like all of the decisions Mary makes, her rationale was carefully thought out. The starting point was that she couldn't be sure of Henry. Who knew what the war might do to him physically or how it might alter the way he felt about her? She had to have a back-up plan. And she also had to take matters into her own hands.

Her thinking is this. There is nobody she knows of, either in the office or of her acquaintance, married or single, that she would class as eligible or want to pursue. So she needs to widen her circle and meet more men. What better place to meet them than in the Army? She imagines meeting a lightly wounded officer who falls in love with her. By 'lightly wounded' she decides that she could settle for an arm missing but no more than that. Legs definitely not. Maybe a scar or two provided they weren't too ugly – and preferably not on the face. Apart from that though, everything else would have to be undamaged and in working order. She still wants to have a child and so that would all have to be a hundred percent.

If she becomes a nurse in a Voluntary Aid Detachment, she reckons that Henry will take a lot more notice of her than if she is just a drone in an office. Her making a move like this should also serve to unsettle him a bit – to not take her for granted.

And she feels good about the idea that she will be doing her bit for the war. She has also heard of women becoming drivers. Maybe she could get a job driving officers around. Then she mightn't even have to deal with the wounded. And these might be more senior – and more well-heeled, which couldn't hurt. Finally, she might get to go to France and she has suddenly found that the notion of travelling appeals greatly to her. She had never really thought about it before. It had never seemed like something that would ever be a possibility for her. But now it appears as though the war is opening up new possibilities and horizons. Mary is excited and can't wait for these changes to happen.

But she has heard that lots of women are thinking similar thoughts and that the rejection rate for women wanting to join the VADs is very high. So Mary has decided she needs to make herself as proficient as possible before she goes to enlist. As a result she has enrolled in a three month First Aid and Nursing course to give her the basics. She is also doing elocution classes.

This may seem like a strange thing for Mary to be engaging in but, as usual, her logic is faultless. She doesn't have a common accent but neither is it posh. She feels that with a few classes her voice will come to sound somewhat more sophisticated and upper class. This can only be a good thing, she imagines, when she goes to enlist and certainly when she meets the man of her imagining. While she tells everybody she knows, about her nursing class, she tells nobody about *these* classes.

Chapter 9
Monday 8 February 1915

James is marching with his battalion on the road that runs from Oudredom to Ypres. He is in Belgium. He has never been to Belgium before. As a man who hopes one day to return to the Foreign Office, he likes the idea of chalking up another country.

Ordinarily, the men have no idea where they are going or how long they will be on the march. Instead they will just be turned out in full marching order and told to go in a particular direction. What will follow will be fifty minutes marching followed by ten minutes rest, repeated seemingly endlessly. When James first started doing this, what he used to find utterly exhausting was not knowing how many hours they would be marching. Had he known in advance – five or fifteen – there wouldn't have been a problem. It was the not knowing that he found wearing.

So James has adopted a simple stratagem for dealing with this. The most they have ever done is to march for twelve hours straight. So he now assumes that any march that begins will last twelve hours. As a result he is almost always pleasantly surprised. It is such a silly thing, he knows, but he finds that the effect is really quite wonderful.

It is an important discovery for him. James is starting to comprehend what a lot of men before him have discovered – that the Army often makes bad mistakes and that much of what it requires its men to do is unbelievably stupid. You could argue, he thinks, that this whole war is unbelievably stupid. The country has gone to the expense of shipping vast numbers of men to France to fight with an equally vast number of people with whom James personally has no quarrel. He thinks of all the sensible things he could be doing. Sheltering from the cold, for example. It might be quite bracing to be out in weather like this but really, it would make far more sense – for both them and the so-called enemy – to be indoors in front of a roaring fire eating a hearty breakfast or sharing a drink and finding out about each other.

Today there is no mystery about how far they have to march. Given where they have been for the last week and the direction they are now travelling, there can be only one destination – Ypres or 'Wipers', as the troops call it. It is a short six mile march. Probably not even enough time to get hungry again after the fine breakfast of bacon, eggs, fried bread and strong tea that they had before setting out. It is a piercingly cold day with a stiff north-easterly wind. But at least it's dry. There is a washed out blue sky with some high clouds reflected in the puddles on the roadway.

James listens to the rhythmic tramp of the boots on the *pavé* as they march. He looks down at his own boots and pictures the hundreds of thousands, perhaps even millions, of soldiers' boots that have tramped across the roads in this part of Europe in the last two thousand years. He has now become one of their number.

James has become fit since he came to France. He could never have been described as fat but he has shed whatever spare pounds he did have. His belly is dead flat, his thighs as solid as oak trees and the muscles of his arms are hard in a way they never were when he was in civilian life. When he marches with his chest forward, he imagines it being like a shield. He feels strong, physically strong – almost a different man from the soft creature who worked day after day behind a desk in the Foreign Office.

Of course he knows that this shield won't stop a bullet, but he feels that the physical strength and endurance he has built up will all help when the great test comes. He is a soldier. There are times when he thinks it's bizarre that this is where he has ended up. But he has always tried to excel at what he does and he intends to do the same here.

Up ahead, he can hear the rumble of artillery. It is significantly louder compared to when they first noticed it many miles back. Some dark, ominous clouds have formed in the north-east and now, these drive in on the wind. Beyond them the sky is still blue and the land sunlit but suddenly overhead there is a blanket of grey cloud from which cold, heavy raindrops start to fall. The rain transforms into small pellets of hail and the initial spattering becomes a torrent. The men keep marching as the wind drives the stinging particles like buckshot into their faces. James narrows his eyes and finds himself leaning into the wind. Glancing around him, he sees that all the men are doing it.

The hail lasts just long enough to completely drench them. Then it passes and the sun returns. The men, who had stopped singing during the hail shower, resume with 'Tipperary'.

The singing fizzles out as they enter Ypres. Much of the city has been reduced to rubble. If this is what can be done to buildings, James tries not to think of what can be done to men's bodies. They pass the shell of the Cloth Hall, cross the moat and are billeted in the Cavalry Barracks.

James had hoped that this short march and relatively comfortable billets would mark the beginning of an easy day. He should have known better than that in the Army.

That evening they go up to the trenches for the first time.

Chapter 10
Saturday 20 February 1915

James tries to write to Clara every day. He has explained to her that while he will try to do this, it won't always be possible. And even if he could write every day, if he's in the front line, it may not be possible to have letters sent to the rear to be posted. He's explained this to her so that, if she doesn't receive a letter from him for a few days, she is not to worry.

He is writing to her now. He is in billets in a barn near Poperinghe, about a dozen miles from the front line. They left Ypres around midnight and arrived here soon after dawn. Most of the men are sleeping and James too is exhausted. But he hasn't managed to get a letter off to Clara for a few days so he is anxious to write – even if it is only a brief note – to reassure her that he is well. It is a little under two weeks since he had his introduction to trench warfare. It is far, far worse than anything he could have conceivably imagined.

My darling Clara,
We are safely back in billets after having spent several days in the front line. It wasn't too bad. The trenches were somewhat damp.

James pictures one of the trenches that he occupied during the last twelve days. It would actually be wrong to describe it as a trench. It was really a stagnant stream or a deep drain. The water came up to their waists and any attempts to pump out the water had long ago been given up. Conditions weren't helped by a terrific thunderstorm with torrential rain that lasted most of the night. There was no place to lie down so the men spent the entire twenty four hour tour standing. Several men fell asleep and slipped into the water. One drowned. James saw a rat swimming along on top of the water like a bather at a municipal swimming pool. The weather was bitingly cold so that by dawn a thin layer of ice formed on the surface of the water.

… but we were not in much danger.

In the last twelve days James' company suffered a large number of casualties mainly due to random shelling. But the picture he remembers most vividly is that first night when they weren't actually manning the trenches. They were just providing (the oh-so appropriately named) fatigue parties to take food, water and ammunition up to the front. They had arrived in the front line trench – a relatively dry one on this occasion – and were standing waiting to deposit their stores. Jeffers, the man ahead of James had deposited his load onto the fire step and stepped aside so that James could deposit his. James was friendly with Jeffers. His wife had just had a new baby that Jeffers had not yet seen.

Suddenly and without a sound, Jeffers fell to the ground as though he had fainted. James thought first that he *had* fainted – that it was just weakness caused by lack of food or weariness. (They had eaten nothing since breakfast the previous day and it was now 3 AM) James dropped his load and squatted down beside the fallen man. It was probably this that stopped James becoming the second victim of the sniper that had shot Jeffers clean through the side of his head.

We are back in rest now away from the front line and hope to be here for a few days. So far I'm sure you'll be pleased to know that I think I'm coping pretty well with this soldiering business and being in the front line. I think I'm making not a bad fist of it.

This much at least is true. After the initial shock of the trenches, James made the decision that there would be nothing he might encounter that he would be unable to deal with. There would be no conditions, no matter how terrible, that he wouldn't just take in his stride. That was what he did when he stood all night up to his waist in ice-cold water. He had simply decided that he would be able to cope with this so that each time some other man crumbled, James felt that tiny bit stronger.

Admittedly, the sniping took him completely by surprise and it was only luck that stopped him joining Jeffers in the mud at the bottom of the trench. But he has learnt. He will hone his skills so that he can anticipate danger. He will be as observant as a hunted animal. The sniper was nearly his death sentence. He has been given a reprieve and a second chance.

Chapter 11
Saturday 27 February 1915

Henry has also had his baptism of fire in the trenches and has found them to be every bit as ghastly as James did. But there is a part of Henry that has blossomed. Even though he is only a Lance-Corporal, in charge (and only if the Corporal is killed or wounded) of twelve men, Henry has taken to leadership like a duck to water. Henry's corporal, Corporal Smith, is younger than Henry, a fact that Henry resents. Smith is better educated than Henry, bookish, gentle and shy. Henry takes all of this to be weakness.

Not that Henry has been anything other than congenial to Smith. Henry likes to think he treats everybody the same. He has learned that Smith lived with his parents before joining up. He sang in a choir. He is very religious and never swears. Privately, Henry wonders if Smith is a poof.

And so Henry has pretty much become the real leader of the section. The men like him. He shares a joke with them – or to be more precise he is the centre of attention when it comes to jokes. He drinks with them, he marches and swears and sings with them. Smith does very little of any of these things. For the first time Henry wonders about trying to become an officer.

Clara hasn't had an orgasm since the night of the Thirteen Hours. The fact is she has become superstitious about it. If she can have an orgasm without James, her thinking goes, she can have a life without James. And this is something she cannot countenance.

She lives in a state of permanent anxiety that makes the worries of her old life seem very mild indeed. Of course, she still has those worries. There are the routine ones about running the house and the terrible ones of the possibility of something happening to the children. But now added to these are the severe money worries. And on top of all this is the heart-clutching fear she feels every day whenever the door bell rings and she wonders, as she hurries out to answer it, whether she is going to be greeted by a telegram boy. And only slightly less frightening is the sound of the postman. The metallic clang of the spring loaded letter box cover being pushed in and the soft flop of letters falling on the wooden floor.

Since James writes and sends letters to Clara, she always makes it a point to intercept the post. If there is one from Henry, she will read it to the girls. James' she keeps for later when she can get some time alone.

When Henry first went overseas he used to write to all three of them separately but now, there is just one letter every few days to which Clara always dutifully replies. Her letters are all the same, filled with the minutiae of domestic life, Mrs Parsons, the girls and any rumours that do the rounds. The girls each include a letter of their own with drawings and pictures. Clara often wonders what kind of letters Henry writes to that other woman.

James' letters are a different matter. If there isn't one from him she feels terror rising within her that she finds difficult to control. Her heart races and her whole body becomes hot. Several times, when this happened first, Clara felt so ill she had to take to her bed, claiming a headache and leave Mrs Parsons to take care of the children.

She has had to develop some way of dealing with this. She tells herself that there is no point in worrying about it; that all the worrying in the world can't change or control what is going to happen to James. And she has managed to get to a point now where, at least during the day, her rational mind can keep a lid on her irrational feelings.

But in the small hours of the night, should she wake, images of what could happen to him play in her mind like a devilish picture show.

When there *is* a letter from James it is all different – at least for a few hours. When she reads his words, he is there with her. They are back in the park or in each other's arms during the Thirteen Hours. She will keep the letter in her apron pocket and read and re-read it. She will touch the words on the paper and, as she does so, she is touching his face. For these few hours she is at peace. Until the thought re-surfaces that he could already have been killed or wounded since this letter was written and then the whole process begins again.

Today, Clara doesn't manage to be first to the mail. Ursula is coming downstairs and is passing the front door when a single letter flops onto the floor. Clara is in the kitchen and hears it. She is too late.

'Is it from Daddy?' asks Ursula, excitedly, bringing it into the kitchen and handing it to Clara.

'No, it's not,' says Clara.

'It's not a bill,' says Ursula and Clara regrets having ever talked about bills and how you could recognise them from their window envelopes.

'So who's it from?' persists Ursula.

'Some of the men fighting in France have no friends or relations to write to them,' Clara is forced to invent. 'So the Queen made an appeal that these men are written to. So I do that.'

'What's the name of the man you write to?'

Dear God, will the child not stop!

'Er, Walter. His name is Walter.'

This seems to satisfy Ursula and she does stop. Clara wonders if she should have made up a different story – if the lie would hold if it was tested. But then there is a knock on the door, it is Mrs Parsons and as Ursula runs out to answer it, Clara slips the envelope into her apron.

Later, in her bedroom, she reads it. There is only one page and it is spattered with spots of mud.

My darling Clara,

We are safely back in billets after having spent several days in the front line. It wasn't too bad. The trenches were somewhat damp but we were not in much danger. We are back in rest now away from the front line and hope to be here for a few days.

So far I'm sure you'll be pleased to know that I think I'm coping pretty well with this soldiering business and being in the front line. I think I'm making not a bad fist of it.

I miss you, my beautiful darling and am aching to see you and hold you.

All my love

James

The letter is nothing like the lengthy and cheery descriptions of trench life that Clara has been receiving up until now. She knows that there is something wrong. James is in great danger or undergoing terrible suffering. Clara finds that her hand that holds the letter is shaking.

Chapter 12
Saturday 10 March 1915

Perhaps you have been wondering, my inquisitive reader, whether you were going to hear something – or indeed anything at all – of the generals I spoke about in an earlier chapter. Well, wonder no more. The hour is at hand, as is the man.

He is General Henry Seymour Rawlinson and today Rawlinson has a simple problem he hopes to solve. I say 'simple' in the sense that it's simply phrased; it doesn't necessarily have a simple solution.

The Allied (British and French) and German armies face each other from two roughly parallel lines of trenches that run from the Swiss border to the Belgian coast. Between these two lines of trenches is a devastated strip of ground known as no-man's-land and indeed it is. When the war began there were plenty of troop movements. You may remember, for example, that whole mobilisation thing – the Von Schlieffen plan and all the rest of it. Those days however, are long gone. These days nobody is going anywhere. Technology – massed artillery, machine guns and the devastatingly simple but fearsomely effective barbed wire – means that anybody who ventures out into no-man's-land is unlikely to come back.

Since neither side can make any headway against the other then clearly, as long as this situation persists, the Group of Death can never end. So one side has to break through the other's lines. If you are reading the original, English language version of this book, one can most likely assume you're rooting for the British to do this.

In order to make this happen, the simple problem facing Rawlinson is that he must get his men (or at least as many of his men as possible) safely across to the German trenches. The problem, of course, is that the Germans can sweep no-man's-land with rifle, machine gun and artillery fire, making transiting that stretch of ground a deadly undertaking for any group of flesh and blood men that would try to do it.

So Rawlinson is going to give this a shot today and after some considerable foot dragging which has annoyed his boss, Douglas Haig no end, Rawlinson has come up with a plan.

Rawlinson's mission is to capture the ruined village of Neuve Chapelle which is currently behind the German line. The reason for this is not a particularly inspiring one. This is no D-Day to begin the liberation of the continent of Europe from Nazi enslavement and tyranny; no Gettysburg to free the millions of black slaves in the South; no Trafalgar to decide who will have mastery of the seas. No. Rather it is this. The German line juts out into the British line in a sort of bulge. Military men like to call this a 'salient'. So the purpose of Rawlinson's attack is to remove the bulge.

Great, I hear you say, my about-to-be-sadly-disappointed reader – and then what?

Well, er nothing.

Nothing?

No. That's it.

That's it?

That's it.

Anyway, come on – don't you want to know about the plan?

Okay, if you must. What's the plan?

The plan is to lay down a thirty five minute, so-called 'hurricane' bombardment on the German trenches. Then, at the end of this, Rawlinson will move the bombardment to behind the village of Neuve Chapelle thus sort of sealing off the front line so that the Germans can't send up reinforcements. At the same time his infantry will advance and capture the village, thus removing the bulge.

Well look, I'm excited – even if you're not.

Chapter 13
Saturday 10 March 1915

It's the end of the first day of the Battle of Neuve Chapelle. Rawlinson writes in his diary, 'We have had a grand day – our plans succeeded admirably … Douglas Haig is certainly pleased … Altogether things have gone quite as well as I expected.'

Chapter 14
Monday 12 March 1915

Travel to Neuve Chapelle these days and you'll find it a somewhat dreary, unattractive place located in equally dreary, flat, poorly drained countryside. The ninetieth anniversary of the battle passed in March 2005 with little or no comment or notice. On a cold and grey 12th of March 2005 there were few, if any battlefield visitors there. It is not the kind of place one would want to have given one's life for.

The Battle of Neuve Chapelle is over. The British have suffered, over the three days of the battle, 11,652 men killed, wounded or missing. If you want a comparison, at the Battle of Waterloo British casualties were about 17,000. Waterloo ended the military career of Napoleon Bonaparte and brought peace to Europe for more than fifty years.

If this was 'a grand day', one can only wonder what Rawlinson would have regarded as a bad day. And in fact, later in the book, dear reader, we shall find out.

And the bulge?

Sorry?

The bulge. What happened with the bulge? You know. On the map.

Oh, the bulge. Sorry, didn't I say?

No, you didn't.

It was straightened.

Chapter 15
Saturday 3 April 1915

James' battalion marches south from Dranoutre to new billets but just after arriving they are paraded again. They march back the way they have just come, then marching a total of eight miles further north to Locre. This is all because the Bishop of London has come to conduct a service. The Bishop turns out to be an hour late during which time the men stand in stinging cold and full marching order.

Eventually the Bishop appears. He wears a white surplice that looks like it has numerous layers underneath it and a large cross on a chain. The man has thin lips, a hawkish nose and a healthy complexion that looks like it's never had to endure a lot of hardship.

'As you could not come to the Church,' the Bishop intones. 'I have brought the Church to you.'

A voice somewhere behind James mutters, 'Pity you didn't bring it a little nearer.'

Chapter 16
Friday 7 May 1915

O n an afternoon of pale blue sky, warm breeze, spring sunshine, sparkling water and the promise of summer, the Group of Death takes a horrifying turn.

Just as in a regular group of death, there are rules, so too there are rules in our Group of Death. One set of rules, governing when the Group of Death is played at sea, is known as the Cruiser Rules. Amongst other things these state:

1. In their action with regard to merchant ships, submarines must conform to the rules of international law to which surface vessels are subject.
2. In particular, except in the case of persistent refusal to stop on being duly summoned, or of active resistance to visit or search, a warship, whether surface vessel or submarine, may not sink or render incapable of navigation a merchant vessel without having first placed passengers, crew and ship's papers in a place of safety. For this purpose the ship's boats are not regarded as a place of safety unless the safety of the passengers and crew is assured, in the existing sea and weather conditions, by the proximity of land, or the presence of another vessel which is in a position to take them on board.

Eleven miles off the Old Head of Kinsale on the south coast of Ireland, a German submarine, the U-20, commanded by Captain Walther Schwieger, breaks the Cruiser Rules. Instead of placing the 'passengers, crew and ship's papers in a place of safety', at 2:09 in the afternoon and without warning, he fires a single torpedo at the luxury liner *Lusitania*.

Unlike *Titanic* three years earlier, the *Lusitania* is carrying more than enough lifeboats for all of the nearly two thousand passengers and crew on board. And the ship doesn't begin to founder in the middle of the night as *Titanic* did. Rather it is in broad daylight. Nor does this all happen in the middle of the ocean, far from land. Instead, the fate of the *Lusitania* is witnessed from the shore. It is seen from the lighthouse and coastguard station at the Old Head of Kinsale. A family from nearby Bandon, picnicking high up on the Old Head of Kinsale where the grassy slope is gentle, watch powerlessly as the horror unfolds.

The explosion of the impacting torpedo is followed by a second, far more powerful explosion. Almost immediately, the ship takes on a heavy list to starboard meaning that it is unable to launch the lifeboats on the port side of the ship. And the list also makes it difficult to fill or launch the lifeboats on the starboard side. As a result only six of the forty eight lifeboats are launched successfully. And while there is not, as there was on *Titanic* the sense that the ship is 'unsinkable', there is the thing, repeated from *Titanic*, that people feel safer on the ship and are reluctant – at least for a short time – to get into the boats.

But all of this is somewhat irrelevant anyway since unlike *Titanic*, which took over two hours to sink, the *Lusitania* goes down in just eighteen minutes. The picnicking family sitting amidst the daisies on the grassy slope watch in horror as the huge ship is swallowed by the sea. It leaves behind a great cloud of steam and when this clears, what looks – from this distance – like a large brown stain on the water. The stain, of course, is the nearly one thousand people thrown into the sea, along with all of the flotsam of the dead ship.

Eleven hundred and ninety eight of the souls onboard die ghastly deaths in the bowels of the ship or trying to escape the sinking monster or in the cold waters amidst the scum of wreckage afterwards. The death toll is not that far short of *Titanic's* fifteen hundred and two.

Only two hundred and eighty nine bodies are ever recovered, sixty five of which are never identified. A hundred and sixty nine bodies are buried in mass graves in the Old Church Cemetery, a mile north of what is now Cobh, Co. Cork.

In September, one body — that of First Class passenger Mrs Frances Washington Stephens — will be embalmed, casketed and embarked on the ship *Hesperian* to be shipped back to her family in Canada. Eighty miles southwest of the Old Head of Kinsale, the *Hesperian* will be torpedoed by Captain Schwieger and the U-20. In one of the many ironies of the Group of Death, this means that Mrs Stephens is torpedoed *twice* by Captain Schwieger. The *Hesperian* goes to the bottom along with Mrs Stephens' metal casket, where presumably it still lies.

Captain Schwieger will also eventually find a watery grave when in September 1917, his subsequent command, the U-88 is chased by a British ship and hits a mine, sinking and entombing all hands.

Chapter 17
The Group of Death again

Obviously it's impossible to say exactly how many artillery rounds were fired by all participants during the Group of Death. However, some sources have estimated the figure at around a billion – 1,000,000,000 give or take several hundred million.

If we assume that for each artillery piece there were thirty machine guns and that an artillery piece could fire four rounds a minute while a machine gun could fire 600 and, if we further assume that the machine guns and artillery pieces fired for roughly the same amounts of time, then it would appear that the number of machine gun bullets fired during the Group of Death would appear to be 30 x 150 x 1 billion. In other words 4,500 billion.

If we also assume that the same number of bullets was fired from small arms – rifles and pistols, then we get a figure of 9,000 billion.

And finally, let's round it up a little to make the arithmetic easier, we get 10,000 billion.

Estimates put the number of people killed during the Group of Death at around ten million. If we assume that seventy five percent of these were killed by shellfire and if our numbers are anyway accurate it would appear that it took an average of three million bullets to kill one person. It sounds like a ridiculously inefficient way to kill people. (The Nazis of course, realised that mistake after World War One and so devised far more cost-effective ways of doing it.)

Chapter 18
Saturday 8 May 1915

It may come as a surprise for you to learn, my common sense reader, that General Henry Rawlinson – or 'Rawly' as he is affectionately known – proclaimed the Battle of Neuve Chapelle a victory. (I feel we can call him 'Rawly' ourselves now as we are coming to know him more and more with each passing game.) An assiduous correspondent, he wrote to the Adjutant-General, the Minister for War, Lord Kitchener, and even the King (via his aide-de-camp) trumpeting his success.

And you may be even more surprised when you hear that his boss, Douglas Haig, was pleased enough with Rawly's performance that he has decided to give him another outing. Rawly's going to play another match in the Game of Death. And this time – happily – there's actually a sensible objective. Well, slightly more sensible, anyway.

Behind Neuve Chapelle is a piece of marginally higher ground known as the Aubers Ridge. Rawly's job is going to be to capture it. While this objective could hardly be described as crusade-inducing, at least it has the value of being a piece of ground. And while the whole idea smacks somewhat of Edmund Blackadder's pithy summing up of the entire Great War – 'Haig is about to make yet another gargantuan effort to move his drinks cabinet six inches closer to Berlin' – at least it isn't about straightening out a coloured squiggle on a map.

After Neuve Chapelle, Rawly tries to divine what lessons can be learnt from the experience. The most obvious thing is that with a sufficiently heavy and accurate artillery barrage, the German front line can actually be broken. The problems happened after that when, with insufficient artillery bombardment, the British tried to press on. It was then that they sustained most of their casualties.

So Rawly comes up with a philosophy that he calls 'bite and hold'. The way to get his men safely across to the German line is a devastating artillery bombardment after which they will capture a piece of the enemy's trench system. The artillery then moves forward and the process is repeated.

So now Rawly is itching to give his theory another shot. He writes about his men that they 'have their tails right over their backs now & are spoiling to get at the Germans again.' Even the wounded are 'dying' to return to the line, he writes in a particularly unhappy turn of phrase.

And so what does he do with all these lessons he has so carefully extracted from Neuve Chapelle?

Why, he ignores them, of course.

So in May, Rawly and his team line out for the Battle of Aubers Ridge. Now when I say line out it is just as in regular football where the players are on the field and the manager is in the dugout. In this case the manager's dugout is a chateau several miles to the rear of where the team will be attempting to play on the Aubers Ridge.

On the eve of the battle Rawly writes, 'I think things look hopeful for our breaking the line ... The guns are well registered and we have enough.'

The British soldiers standing in the front line trenches at 5 AM on the morning of the 8th of May and preparing to go over the top might not have agreed with him. They will say afterwards – those that survived, of course – that the bombardment was rather ragged. The 'noise nothing like as bad as one had been led to expect, and general opinion seemed to be that the bombardment was not so intense as at Neuve Chapelle.'

And if the bombardment wasn't heavy, neither was it accurate. The British artillery was firing short, so that shells were dropping on the selfsame men in the trenches. The Battle of Aubers Ridge turns out to be a catastrophe. The British get nowhere near Aubers Ridge. In fact they gain no ground whatsoever – the drinks cabinet doesn't get moved at all. And the British team sustains over 11,600 people killed, wounded or missing – almost exactly the same as at Neuve Chapelle.

A particularly unpleasant aspect of Rawly's character and something we haven't really mentioned up until now was that after Neuve Chapelle he tried to blame the failure on one of his divisional commanders, Joey Davies. Rawly tries something similar now, recording in his diary, 'I fear that the E. Lancs and some Battalions of the 25 Brigade got cold feet and did not advance with the dash they ought to have done in the first instance … The E. Lancs did not gain the enemy's trenches – it is doubtful if they tried very hard.'

Presumably these are the same East Lancs that suffered four hundred and fifty four casualties out of a total of about a thousand men that day.

On the same day, thirty or so miles to the north, James has his first taste of actual combat.

Two weeks earlier the Germans used poison gas for the first time, releasing one hundred and sixty eight tons of chlorine not too far from where James now stands. While James' battalion was not on the receiving end of it, they were later in trenches upon which the gas had been released. Apart from the lingering chlorine smell and the constant feeling of drowsiness due to the gas, James found it hard to suppress his terror at the thought of this terrible weapon being used on him. If the air itself became unbreathable, what chance did anyone have? However, no gas attack came. James has yet to experience that particular horror.

Just after midnight, his company, in trenches on the Frezenburg Ridge for the last six days, is relieved. They retire to dugouts behind the front line arriving there about 4 AM. But these dugouts are not very far behind the front line and the Germans know where they are. Around 6 AM the German artillery opens up and the company takes many casualties even though it is not in the front line.

Later that morning they are ordered to advance back towards the Frezenburg Ridge. They have a few minutes to ready themselves in the trench and then the whistles are blown. After that, everything just seems to happen very quickly, like a frantically speeded up newsreel.

When a machine gun is being traversed and fired, and as each bullet leaves the gun it follows a slightly different trajectory. This is due to the vibration of the gun, atmospheric conditions and the traversing action. As a result it is possible for the target (if he or she is lucky enough) to end up 'between' two adjacent bullets. On the morning of the 8th of May, James Walters isn't quite that lucky.

He climbs up the trench ladder, holding on with one hand while he carries his rifle in the other. The rough timber of the ladder seems incredibly well-defined – he can see tiny splinters in it. It is as though James is viewing it through a magnifying glass. He has a memory from when he was a child of holding a ladder while his father climbed up it. Climbing a ladder. It seems such an incredibly harmless thing to do – something a painter or window cleaner might do. It is anything but harmless today. As he reaches the top and stands for an instant on the parapet he feels utterly naked. He is *in* no-man's-land. Not furtively, at night, under the cover of darkness but in broad daylight. In broad fucking daylight. (James has come to swear an awful lot more since he joined the Army.)

In front are the thick belts of British wire like malevolent iron thorn bushes. These obscure anything else from view. But a gap has been cut in the wire to let the advancing soldiers through and the men in front of him are channelling towards it. Each side's artillery is firing and explosions are occurring both in the ground and in the air above no-man's-land. Men are shouting but it is the heavy-industrial sound of machine guns that slices through the clamour. James has another memory from his childhood – when his father took him to see a steam threshing. The sound of the machine guns is the same sound.

James starts to run towards the gap in the wire. But even as he does so, his mind is putting a terrible two and two together. A gap in the wire and machine guns. This is where they will meet.

The machine gun bullet that hits his right upper arm and shatters his humerus is something of a fluke. The German machine gunner was traversing his machine gun at about a metre off the ground – essentially at groin height. However, towards the end of the bullet's trajectory and just before striking its target, a tiny updraft of warm air caught the bullet and lifted it about a foot higher. Though James will never know it, this insignificant atmospheric event has had huge significance for him. It has stopped him from being castrated.

And he has a further stroke of luck. The next bullet from the machine gun, also caught on the warm air, misses James' heart by a couple of inches. (It goes on to punch directly into the chest of the man to the left of James, killing him instantly.)

The bullet that strikes his upper arm has about the same force as a well-directed sledge hammer blow swung by a strong man. He feels the bone shatter. This in turn causes the fingers in his hand to go limp so that he is unable to hold his rifle. His left hand by itself isn't sufficient to hold the weight of the weapon so it falls to the ground.

James bends to pick it up but as he does so the shock of the bullet causes his body to break out in an instant sweat. At the same time, he becomes dizzy and blacks out, falling to the ground.

He is not there for very long. In fact he lies there just enough time for the machine gun that shot him to make several more traverses back and forth above his prone body. When he comes to, there is a fearful pain in his arm but he is soon aware that he is alive and not actually badly wounded. By this time the attacking British troops – at least those that are still standing – have made some progress towards the Frezenburg Ridge. As a result, the German machine gunner is now firing forward of James' position.

James works all this out as he lies there. He knows what he has to do next. He is not badly wounded. He has to pick up his rifle and carry on.

This turns out to be easier said than done. With some difficulty he uses his good left arm to lift himself into a kneeling position. Then, catching his rifle in his left hand, he stands up.

But he cannot do anything with the rifle. He can hardly hold it in one hand, never mind aim it or use the bayonet. He tries again to make his right arm move but it fails to respond.

'You're out of it for today, lad.'

James realises he has been looking down at his hands – the one that still works and the useless one. Now he glances up. Two stretcher bearers are lifting a groaning man whose belly is a pulp of blood and dark pink where his intestines are showing. It is one of the stretcher bearers that has spoken.

'Best go to the rear, lad. There's not much more you can do today.'

James is glad to have the decision made for him. He slings his rifle onto his left shoulder and then, cradling his right wrist in his left hand, he trudges the few yards back to the trench where he began. He wonders what time it is and gingerly checks his watch. He had checked it just before climbing up the ladder. It was 11:35 then. He is shocked to see that it is not even 11:50 now.

Chapter 19
Tuesday 11 May 1915

Clara receives a letter in the morning post in an unfamiliar and what she determines to be female hand. She wonders if it is from the woman who told her about Henry. As soon as she can, she takes it to her bedroom and tears it open anxiously. It reads:

Dearest Clara,
Am wounded in my right arm & can't write so this very kind nurse is writing this for me. Being returned to England arriving Tuesday (11th). Will be in our usual spot at our usual time tomorrow (12th).
Love
James

Clara totters to the bed and sits down, staring at the words on the paper. She reads them again to make sure she hasn't misunderstood them. She finds that she is crying.

At almost exactly the same time that Clara is reading his letter, James steps off a train at Charing Cross, his right arm in a sling. He has spent a lot of time brooding since he was wounded. None of his questions about how he will react in combat have been resolved. He keeps replaying what happened trying to understand how he felt. When he first stood at the top of the ladder, in plain view, he remembered a momentary rush of surprise and terror at being there, unconcealed in no-man's-land. But then, as he began to go forward, he recalls that he didn't really feel afraid. He just wanted to get on with it. It felt almost business-like. And then had come that stupid wound in his arm. Incapacitating enough not to be able to go on but hardly a serious wound given some of the wounds he was to see during the rest of that day. He had *wanted* to go on. But there was no point. He wouldn't have been able to do any fighting – he would only have gotten himself a more serious wound or been killed.

And so all the doubts he has about himself remain unresolved. He knows he is incredibly lucky and he aches to see Clara. But somehow, he wishes it had been otherwise.

Chapter 20
Wednesday 12 May 1915

It's a day of Virgin Mary blue sky and warm, except when the sun goes behind the cotton wool clouds. Though Clara is early, James is earlier still. While she is still a long way off, she sees him, the bright swan-white of the sling in striking contrast to the khaki of his uniform. He is pacing up and down and smoking, the cigarette looking awkward in his left hand. As she approaches and he catches sight of her, his face breaks into a smile that she can only describe as weary. He throws away the cigarette and hurries to her. He is thinner than when they were last together – bony, almost. His face is very thin and tired looking. There are great bags under his eyes.

Clara embraces him carefully, conscious of the sling. For a while they just hold each other. He is indeed thinner, much thinner. The way he feels in her arms is not what she remembers. They kiss, the longest, slowest, eyes-closed, damn-whoever's-watching kiss Clara can remember.

'I made sandwiches,' he says, indicating the bench where a brown paper packet sits, along with two bottles of lemonade.

'I've missed you so much,' says Clara. 'I've been so afraid. I can't believe you're here. That it's not a dream. It's like a miracle.'

'You can't kill a bad thing,' James says.

Clara says nothing but just looks at him. She is not fooled by any of this. To fill the silence, James says, 'It's not too bad. We haven't been in much danger.'

Clara looks into his eyes. There's something in them that wasn't there before. A fear maybe. Or is it a secret – something he's not telling her?

''It's terrible, isn't it?' she says.

After a long pause, he replies, 'It's truly terrible.'

'Oh, James,' she says. 'My poor, poor, James.'

She takes him again and holds him, like a mother embracing a child.

Apart from the time when he will depart again for the front, this is the only time that Clara sees James show any sign of weakness. By the time he pulls apart from her, he is (or appears to be) his old self again.

'The good news,' he says. 'Is that this will take three to four months to heal. That means I should be in England for most of the summer.'

'Maybe the war will have ended by then.'

'I doubt that very much. But I thought could we ... maybe ... we might go away for a few days. Could you? Would it be possible?'

'I'll have to find a way, won't I?' she says.

They arrange to meet again on Friday. She knows it is very soon and somebody – one of the girls or Mrs Parsons – is bound to remark on it but Clara just can't bear the thought of James being in London and not seeing him.

That part she can deal with. It is the going away with him that is going to be problematic. The first thing she needs is an excuse. Then she needs to involve Mrs Parsons who will have to mind the children while she is gone. And finally – and most difficult of all – is that she needs to work out a way that Henry never hears about this.

The germ of an answer comes to her late that afternoon as she is walking up Horn Lane from the omnibus stop. She perfects the story that night in bed.

Clara has an aunt and uncle and cousins on her father's side who live in Axminster. The last time Clara saw them was her father's funeral. It is not that they are estranged or anything of that sort but just that, apart from funerals and Christmas cards, they have very little reason to be in touch. But it is the funeral thought that is the key. Clara will announce that her uncle or aunt is very ill and she wants to go and visit them. With a day travelling there and a day to get back and two days down there, Clara reckons she can have four blissful days with James.

She daren't go away for any longer than that. While she trusts Mrs Parsons completely, what if something *were* to happen to the girls? Or the house burned down? And Clara was away on a trip that turned out to be made up?

Chapter 21
Thursday 13 May 1915

The very next morning Clara puts her plan in motion. After Ursula has gone to school and while Virginia is having her nap, Clara writes a letter to herself purporting to come from her aunt. Clara disguises her handwriting and writes simply that her uncle is grievously ill and that if Clara would like to see him, she should come at once. Later, on her way to pick up Ursula, Clara posts the letter.

Chapter 22
Friday 14 May 1915

Clara's letter duly arrives. She is tearing it open just as Mrs Parsons bustles into the kitchen.

'Oh no,' Clara says.

She says 'oh no' rather than the more calamitous-sounding 'oh my God' so that she won't alarm Mrs Parsons too much and make her think that something has happened to Henry.

Mrs Parsons looks frightened anyway but Clara quickly calms her and explains the situation. Clara wants to travel down to Axminster. Would Mrs Parsons mind coming to stay for three or four days while Clara does that? The older woman seems delighted at this change of routine and asks if she can bring her cat. Quickly, it's all arranged. And happily Clara now has an excuse to go into London to meet James. She must get some things for her trip.

When she meets James they arrange that they will go on Sunday. And while they aren't going to go to Axminster, they will not be too far away, by the sea at Teignmouth.

Chapter 23
Saturday 15 May 1915

How her life would have been so different, Clara reflects as she rushes around trying to get everything ready for her trip, if she had met James rather than Henry. (Yesterday, she bought new underwear and a nightdress. Now she packs it all into one of the suitcases that was part of her father's wedding present.) If she had met James what a totally different course her life would have taken. It's as she's always said – the gods play cruel tricks.

And Clara has also discovered that there is one weak point in her plan. It dawned on her yesterday when she was explaining to Mrs Parsons what she would be doing and Mrs Parsons said, 'Don't you worry, my dear, I'll take care of everything. And just in case, I shall write down the address where you're staying – in case I need to send a telegram or something.'

Clara knows what Mrs Parsons is referring to. It is the thing they probably have most in common. They both have somebody at the front – she has both Henry and James, Mrs Parsons has her son, Alfie. Clara will give Mrs Parsons her aunt's address alright but supposing something *does* happen and she *does* need to get in touch. Clara spends the whole day racking her brains but can find no solution. She will just have to leave it be and hope that nothing goes wrong. And with this thought a dart of terror strikes her heart. What if something was to happen to the girls and she couldn't be contacted for four days? If it were something truly bad, like an illness or something, then she would never forgive herself, the guilt would never leave her. And Henry would blame her for the rest of his life.

She wrestles with this problem for most of Saturday but finally she forces it out of her mind. Her thinking goes like this. It is far more likely that something will happen to James when he returns to the front than will ever happen to either of the girls. If it did, and she never got to spend at least these precious few days with him, she really isn't sure how she would be able to go on. And so she's going to take a chance that the gods will smile on her; that nothing will happen to the girls or the house and that her tryst with James will go unnoticed by everybody except the two of them.

Chapter 24
Sunday 16 May 1915

Clara steps out of her front door trying to appear downcast – after all, she is meant to be going to see a dying relative. She hugs the girls and kisses them goodbye. She thanks Mrs Parsons again and the old lady tells her for the umpteenth time not to worry and that everything will be fine.

By the time Clara reaches the Tube station, her sense of guilt and the worry she feels have faded dramatically. All she can think about is James and the four long days they are to have together.

Clara feels like a girl again and thinks how wonderful it would be to always feel this way. It is like she has passed into a world parallel to this one but separated from it by a pane of glass. Behind the glass, the ordinary workaday world goes about its business but here on this side there is only happiness. When she has to engage with people from that other world, like the ticket seller in the Tube station, she feels the joy flowing out from her like a physical force.

James is waiting for her at Paddington with first class tickets. And so their journey begins. The day is summery, a perfect day for watching the world, and especially England, from a train. They eat a beautiful lunch on the train, are in Teignmouth by evening and have a gorgeous candlelit dinner in their seafront hotel, James having signed them in as 'Mr and Mrs James Walters'.

Chapter 25
Monday 17 May 1915

The postman brings a letter and Mrs Parsons sees that it is from Mr Kenton. (She never thinks of him as Henry.) She imagines that it will be a nice surprise for Mrs Kenton when she returns home.

James and Clara are walking along the seafront in Teignmouth, arm in arm. Seagulls are wheeling and crying overhead. One or two children are playing on the beach and one hardy soul wades into the water before diving in and swimming strongly away from the shore.

'I love you so much, Clara,' James says. 'Every time I see you I just want to tell you. When this stupid war is over, I want to come back and marry you as quickly as possible.'

'Oh yes please,' she replies. 'There's nothing I want more. Why didn't we meet before we both got married? Or when we were children?'

'It would have been nice, wouldn't it?'

'Do you think we might have a child?' he asks.

They stop and she turns to look at him.

'I hadn't thought I would any more,' she says. 'But I would love to have a baby with you, James. I think it would be an extraordinary child.'

'Oh, my darling,' James takes her in his arms.

While they are embracing they notice that a seagull has landed on the railing only a few feet away from them and is staring at them with an angry eye.

'Did I tell you about the seagulls in Le Havre?' he asks.

'You wrote about them in one of your letters.'

'But I don't think I *really* told you,' he says.

That night Clara lies naked in the crook of her lover's arm listening to the gentle exhaling of the waves as they settle onto the beach. The curtains are open as is the window. Clara thinks she would like to live by the sea. Just then James says, 'What would you think of living by the sea?'

'I was just thinking that,' she says. 'How strange.'

'It's not strange at all,' he replies. 'We were made to be together. It just took us all these years to find each other.'

'Could we? Live by the sea, I mean?'

'We can do whatever we want once the war is over.'

She turns onto her side and snuggles closer to him, her breasts pressed against him and an arm across his chest. Her groin is still wet where he climaxed inside her. After a while she says, 'You know what we were saying today about having a child?'

'Yes.'

'I'm thirty three now. If we're going to do it, you'll have to hurry up and win this war.'

Chapter 26
Tuesday 18 May 1915

By late afternoon Clara is starting to get that feeling she used to get as a child when it was Sunday evening and she knew she would be heading back to school on Monday. How she hated it as those last hours of freedom ticked away. If her mother hadn't taken to her bed she would fuss over Clara. Did she have clean clothes? Did she have all her books? Had she done her homework?

Clara, of course, would have taken care of all these things. She had started to do this as soon as she realised that her mother couldn't be relied on. And so she preferred it when she was left to herself, her mother's intervention being doubly irritating for both its random occurrence and its pointlessness.

They are seated in the lounge of the hotel, having had afternoon tea, scones with beautiful strawberry jam and clotted cream. James is reading the paper and Clara had been reading her book – Thomas Hardy's *Under The Greenwood Tree*, a story that she loves. But now it lies in her lap as her mind goes back to her school days. She remembers an argument she had with the teacher about something or other and how it turned out Clara was right. How spirited she had been then.

'What are you thinking?' James asks with a smile, looking up from his paper and lowering it.

'I was just thinking about school. Sunday nights.'

'Sunday nights?'

'You know, school on Monday.'

'Ah. I went to a boarding school, remember? It was like every day was a school day.'

'This great doom used to descend on me on Sunday evenings at the thought of going back to school on Monday. I'm starting to feel like that now.'

The letter from Henry that arrived for Clara yesterday now sits on the little hall table awaiting her return. It is a quick note telling her that he has been granted five days leave and will be arriving home on Tuesday. In fact, Henry has been in London since Monday. When he discovered he was getting what is actually seven days leave, he wrote two letters – one to Clara, the other to Mary. To Mary he told the truth namely that he would be arriving on Sunday around lunchtime, that he would book a hotel and they could spend the next two days there. Then on Tuesday he would have to leave to 'spend some time with the family.' This gave him two nights with Mary.

They were less than satisfactory, he reflects now as he travels home on the Tube and walks up Horn Lane. He had thought Mary would be creaming herself to see him. He had visions of returning the conquering hero to her adoring arms. In reality she seemed somewhat withdrawn and distant. Yes, she ate the food and drank the wine in that damned expensive hotel which he had saved so carefully for. And yes, she did everything he expected her to do in bed. But for the first time Henry suspected that she may have been pretending to orgasm – that all that moaning and whimpering and head rolling on the pillow and grabbing his hand to interlace her fingers with his and the final scream accompanied by a theatrical clamping of her hand over her mouth – that all of that was the lady protesting too much (a phrase that Henry remembers from his schooldays as being something out of Shakespeare).

They parted and are going to meet again, as arranged, to spend Wednesday night in the hotel before Henry has to leave on Thursday morning. But Henry is not longing for it like he expected he would be and it is the cost of another night at that place that is foremost in his mind.

The gate doesn't make its familiar squeak as he opens it. Clara must have oiled it. He remembers that long ago she stopped asking him to do this and similar jobs around the place. A good thing too, he reflects. He is somewhat surprised not to see faces at the front window. He thought they would be looking out for him. He also remembers that his front door key is somewhere in his pack with a number of other personal things. Irritated, he knocks on the door and is again surprised when it is some time before it is opened. When it is, it is Mrs Parsons, wiping her hands on a towel and not Clara who stands there.

'Mr Kenton,' she exclaims. 'What a lovely surprise. Girls! It's your father.'

Ursula and Virginia come thundering downstairs and leap into his arms. Henry takes one on each arm and carries them towards the kitchen. He has become strong in the Army – there was a time when he couldn't do this. Clearly Clara is being more of a bitch than usual and didn't even have the common decency to come and meet him at the door. Instead she chose to send Mrs Parsons who is rabbitting on about making him a nice cup of tea and something about Devon, while the girls too, chatter on excitedly.

When he reaches the kitchen and finds that Clara is not there, Henry asks in an icy voice, 'Where is Mrs Kenton?'

Mrs Parsons, who was carrying the kettle towards the sink, stops and says, 'Well this is what I've been telling you, Mr Kenton. You know her uncle and aunt in Axminster in Devon. Well, apparently her uncle is near to death's door and so Mrs Kenton has gone down to see him. One last time, I suppose, sir.'

'But they were never that close,' says Henry. The statement is made more to himself than to anyone else in the room.

Mrs Parsons continues with her kettle filling.

'But family is family, Mr Kenton. And Mrs Kenton is such a big-hearted soul.'

Henry is irritated by this remark but he lets it pass. Instead he takes some tea but he is really quite in shock that his wife is not here but off gallivanting somewhere. He gives the girls the presents he bought for them and they hurry off to play. There are one or two items of post to look through but no big backlog – before he left, Henry arranged that Clara would deal with all of that. As Mrs Parsons goes off to do whatever the hell she does, Henry begins to get angry. Very, very angry indeed.

Henry dwells on Clara's absence for the rest of the day. He met those relatives of hers once at Clara's father's funeral. They were invited to the wedding but never came. It wasn't a snub, Clara maintained at the time – just that they weren't particularly well off. A fact that was confirmed by whatever pathetic wedding present they sent. Henry can't even remember now what it was. So why should she go off there for four days, leaving that irritating woman sleeping in the house to mind his children?

Henry's humour isn't helped by the dinner that Mrs Parsons serves up. She is nowhere near as good a cook as Clara and while the children seem to lap it up, Henry eats very little. He is actually very hungry but he sees his not eating as a protest against Mrs Parson's very presence. Henry is seething with anger. He's been off in France risking his life while Clara has been here letting everything go to pot. Christ, but he'll have some words with her when she returns.

Mrs Parsons brings the children in to say good night. They have had baths and are in their nightdresses.

'Mrs Parsons is going to read me a story,' says Virginia.

'I read my own story,' Ursula announces.

Henry kisses them goodnight and he hears the three of them going upstairs. Some time later Mrs Parsons makes her way slowly down the stairs and into the kitchen. Henry follows her in. If that woman thinks she's spending one more night here she's got another think coming.

The kettle is steaming and three biscuits sit on a plate on the kitchen table. The woman's cheek is astounding. Here she is in his house, eating his food and drinking his tea. Is there no end to the impertinence?

'I won't need to take up any more of your time tonight,' Henry says, deliberately not saying her name. He is delighted to see a look of surprise cross the woman's face.

'Oh it's no trouble, sir,' she tells him. 'Anyway I arranged with Mrs Kenton that I would be here until she came back tomorrow.'

'Yes, but now that I'm here, we don't need that arrangement any longer, do we?'

'No, I suppose we don't, sir.'

'So you can just run along and we'll see you again in the morning. In fact, you know, why don't you take the day off tomorrow? The last few days must have been hard on you and I'm sure you could do with a bit of a rest.'

'Oh no, sir, it's no trouble at all. I'll be here bright and early just as usual.'

Henry feels like screaming at her, reminding her who the employer is here. Instead, he says, 'The fact is – Mrs Kenton and I would like some time to ourselves when she returns tomorrow. I have to leave again tomorrow evening so our time is precious. I'm sure you understand.'

'Of course I do, sir – and so I can take the children for you so that you can have the day to yourselves.'

Henry explodes.

'Good God, woman – have I not made myself clear enough? Do not come here tomorrow under any circumstances. Mrs Kenton will see you again on Thursday.'

With that, Henry turns and storms out of the kitchen, leaving Mrs Parsons blabbering on about just packing her things and how she'll be gone in five minutes.

Henry feels immensely satisfied.

A few minutes later, Mrs Parsons in hat, coat and carrying her small suitcase, looks in and wishes him goodnight.

'Good night,' says Henry, without meeting her eyes. Moments later he hears the door close. The next time he sees Clara, Henry is going to tell her to get rid of that woman.

Henry pours himself a large whisky and downs it in one gulp before refilling his glass. Jesus Christ, he thinks. He comes back to spend a little bit of his precious leave with his wife and children and this is what greets him. My God, he's going to give Clara what for when he sees her. He should have stayed with Mary. But there was something not quite right about that bitch too. And these people – he's risking his *fucking* life for them.

Henry fumes for the next couple of hours, going over these thoughts endlessly, unable to think about anything else. They gnaw at him as he rehearses things he will say to Clara when he sees her. In the process he consumes half a bottle of whisky so that by the time he totters up the stairs he is quite drunk.

Unable to find his way out of his trousers and bone weary after the nights with Mary and the events of the day, Henry just pulls back the covers and climbs into bed. He falls into a dead sleep and dreams strange dreams that he will not remember in the morning. But somewhere in those crazy, tortured, mixed-up scenes of his life before the war and life in the trenches, a thought, an idea, a fact comes to him. So that later, when he is woken by his bulging bladder and pounding headache, and as he swims up from down deep, he knows it.

He knows the signs.

Why of course he does.

Clara is having an affair.

Chapter 27
Wednesday 19 May 1915

While visiting the toilet Henry wakes up enough to think that the idea is preposterous. Women don't do that. Well, alright they do sometimes. But Clara wouldn't do that. For one thing, how would she have ever had the opportunity? The only time she goes out of the house is with him. And those occasional forays into town, of course. But during the day? Clara with another man? The notion is ridiculous.

But now that he is back in bed, Henry is unable to sleep. He still feels some residual anger about what happened earlier – Clara off somewhere and that appalling woman in the house. But now this idea that Clara is having an affair, having pushed its way into his mind, refuses to leave. It takes hold of him. Henry feels he has a good nose for these things. And now he thinks back to Clara's behaviour around the time he joined the Army – when almost overnight, she changed from being a dutiful wife to an insolent bitch. If she stopped caring what he felt about her or how she treated him, then there is only one explanation for all these facts. She obviously has another iron in the fire. A man who would take care of her so that she no longer needed to depend on Henry. It's an outrage. And now, he decides, he must find proof.

But what? Henry thinks about his own affair with Mary. He has been very careful to hide his tracks. It could have stayed hidden from Clara for years if that stupid cow Mary hadn't written that letter. So he has always destroyed any receipts from hotels or restaurants. Once Mary got lipstick on his shirt so that he went out at lunchtime, bought a new shirt, changed into it in the men's toilet at work and went out and dumped the stained one in a bin. Mary occasionally wrote him little love notes on office stationery but having read these, Henry always burned them. No point in being sentimental about things like that when their existence could bring down such problems on his head.

But Clara *is* sentimental, he reminds himself. She keeps everything – old Christmas cards, things that belonged to her parents, all of the children's drawings. And if Clara has taken up with some fellow there's a good chance that he's the writing kind. That would be the sort of cove that Clara would go for. So there must be letters or cards or even poems. (Henry is appalled at this last thought.) Here in the house. Here in this very room.

Henry jumps out of bed.

James first began writing to Clara after Henry went off to the Army. Only then did Clara think it was safe to have James' letters come to the house. And as Henry rightly believes, Clara has kept all these letters. When they first started to come, she would read them – usually numerous times during the day – but then at night, when Mrs Parsons was gone and the girls were asleep, Clara would climb up to the attic and store the letters in an old trunk of her father's to which only Clara has a key.

But it had been such a chore doing this every night. She had to fetch the ladder from the cupboard under the stairs, carry it upstairs, climb up to deposit the letter and then bring the ladder back downstairs again. And there was always the danger that tired after a long day, the ladder would topple over or she would fall off and hurt herself.

So after a few weeks of this, Clara began to put the letters in a locked suitcase on top of the wardrobe. The suitcase also contains old papers, letters and drawings from her childhood and all of the things the girls have done since they first started to play with crayons and pencils and paints. Amidst these she hid James' letters.

Now, on average, James writes Clara one letter every day and this has been going on since early September of last year. As a result, Clara has a couple of hundred letters. Since these won't all fit in the suitcase, what she does is that one night a week she transfers any letters from the suitcase to the trunk in the attic. Thus, at any given time, there are at most only a handful of letters from James in the suitcase.

Now, of course, if Henry were to climb up into the attic and find the trunk and open it, all would be lost. But Henry has never once gone into the attic in all the time they have lived in the house so she reckons the letters are as safe as they can be there. And as for the suitcase, her thinking is that if someone – that someone being Henry – did actually ever end up opening it, all he would see would be old papers and children's drawings.

Henry begins with the drawers where Clara keeps her things. He gets a momentary dart of excitement when he opens her underwear drawer but rifling around there, finds nothing of interest. He looks in the wardrobe where she keeps her dresses, coats, jackets, blouses. There is a vague smell of her there but no letters. Her shoes stand neatly in pairs along the floor of the wardrobe and he knocks over most of these as he probes the dark at the back of the wardrobe but finds nothing. He looks under the bed but apart from the chamber pot, which only Henry uses, he again draws a blank.

The more fruitless Henry's search is, the more agitated he is becoming. He drags the stool from Clara's dressing table over to the wardrobe. Standing on the stool, he feels on top of the wardrobe with his hands and finds a suitcase. He lifts it down and places it on the bed. It is locked. 'Damned bitch,' Henry curses. But he feels sure now that he is on the right track.

He goes down to the cupboard under the stairs where Clara keeps a small bag of tools. Henry finds a screwdriver and a claw hammer and he brings these back up to the room. He breaks open the left hand lock with no great difficulty. He goes to repeat the same thing on the right hand one but the screwdriver slips and stabs him in the back of the hand, making a deep wound. 'Damn and blast it,' Henry exclaims, as blood splashes over the quilt. He takes the handkerchief from his trousers and wraps it around the wounded hand before continuing. Under the combined assaults of the screwdriver and the hammer's claw, the right hand lock eventually gives way.

His initial reaction is that there is nothing there. The bloody thing is full of kids' drawings. But the suitcase is big and it is packed very full. Henry reasons that the kids can't have done that much scribbling in their short lives. So with both hands he reaches down into the depths of the case like a man drinking water from a river. The topmost layers spill out onto the bed and floor. But there seems to be nothing here either – just things from Clara's childhood – old, curling, flimsy papers and yellowing envelopes opened who knows how long ago.

Henry is just about to start putting the spilled papers back into the suitcase when he notices a patch of new white paper that stands out from the rest of the dusty yellowy-brown mass. Reaching in and pushing away what surrounds it, he discovers it to be an envelope addressed to Clara. The postmark is the 10th of May of this year – little more than a week ago. Henry opens it, unfolds the paper and reads. The first handful of words tells him that he has found what he is looking for.

On the train up from Devon, in her last couple of hours with James, Clara already feels that he has left her. They occupy the compartment with three other people so they can't really talk even if they wanted to. Instead she and James sit side by side and stare out the window. But mentally Clara has left James as she tries to focus on her return to Horn Lane. There is the story of the miraculous recovery of her aunt to be rehearsed. Clara can already hear Mrs Parson's interjections of wonder and delight that will inevitably accompany the story and the thought depresses Clara. And she has also begun making the mental lists of the things that she will have to do to catch up on when she returns. And all her worries about something having happened to the children while she was away have also returned like a conquering army.

It is early afternoon when they arrive into London. James offers to send her home in a cab but they agree it's better if she returns as she left – just in case anybody sees her. They part at the Tube station. Clara would so love to see him again tomorrow – Thursday, their regular day – but she knows she needs to spend some time with the children to make up for her having been away. James says he understands and so they agree to meet again a week from tomorrow – the 27th. As Clara sits on the train while it rackets along, she feels a physical pain in her stomach as though her insides have been torn out. She is desolate as she walks along Horn Lane and home.

She opens the gate and closes it carefully behind her, walks up the path and opens the front door with her key.

There is Henry standing in the hallway.

Clara is literally speechless as she stands in the open doorway looking at her husband. It is he who speaks first.

'Afternoon dear, been out for a little jaunt, have we?'

'Darling,' Clara recovers. 'You're home! How wonderful to see you.'

She goes to Henry and embraces him but it is like embracing a statue. Henry shakes her off, turning away from her and into the sitting room. She follows him in. Henry steps past her to shut the door. Clara is puzzled to see that there is a fire burning in the grate. It is too early for it to be lit and the weather is warm enough that it should not have been lit at all.

'Presumably Mrs Parsons told you where I was – ' Clara gushes, trying desperately to restore some sort of equilibrium.

'She didn't need to,' says Henry brightly. 'These did.'

He holds up a handful of letters.

'These told me all I needed to know.'

Clara is beyond outraged. The pent-up anger of the last few years explodes out of her now. To begin with, she is angry at herself. Angry for all that kowtowing to Henry, trying to make sure that his life ran smoothly and, in the process, becoming nothing more than a meek little housekeeper that he fucked once a week. How stupid she has been. How she has wasted all those years.

And then she is *biblically* angry at him. That he is already having an affair and then takes her to task because she pays him back in kind. It really is too much.

And finally, Clara reminds herself that James' letters are not very explicit. Given that he is a private, everything he writes is censored by his commanding officer, so that James has had to severely restrict the things he would like to say. There is a code that has evolved between them. When James makes any reference to 'thirteen hours' Clara knows he is talking about making love to her. 'That place where you live' is her body and this in turn, has given James the opportunity, which he has relished, to make lots of references to front and back doors, upstairs and so on. But there are also references to Claridge's and St James Park, Clara remembers. There is enough in the letters to be totally incriminating so there is no point in denying anything.

All of these thoughts flash through Clara's mind in a fraction of a second.

'How dare you read my private letters,' she says.

'Your *private* letters. Your *private* letters about your sordid little affair. You're off with your fancy man while my children are left in the hands of a senile old bat.'

'The children were perfectly safe with Mrs Parsons.'

'How do you know?' says Henry, with a smile. 'You haven't seen them. You don't even know if they're alive.'

For a horrible moment, Clara wonders if something *has* happened. Has Henry gone mad and done away with them to get his revenge on her? She notices for the first time that a rifle stands in the corner of the room. She has heard stories before of men whose wives have thrown them out and who have killed their children. But then – mercifully – a voice from out in the hall calls, 'Mummy, are you back?'

It is Virginia.

'Yes, my darling, I'll be out in a few minutes. Daddy and I just have something to talk about. Are you and Ursy alright?'

'We're playing.'

'That's good. You keep playing and I'll see you in a few minutes. And I've got presents for you.'

Virginia squeals with delight and runs off into the back of the house, presumably to tell her sister.

The interruption plus the reassurance that the children are safe has given Clara time to get fully back in control. This is a moment she has known would always come and, in some ways, she has been waiting for it, anticipating it, even looking forward to it. Now she savours it. Reaching into her handbag, she extracts the letter she received on the 20th of July last year, the one that told her that Henry was having an affair.

'I have a letter too,' she says, holding it up. 'You talk to me about carrying on with somebody. You were carrying on nearly a year ago.'

For a few moments Henry is speechless as the dart strikes home.

'I'm going to destroy you,' he declares. 'And I have the power to do it. By the time I'm finished with you, you won't have a house, you won't have children, you'll be on the streets like the filthy whore that you are.'

The words actually terrify Clara. Maybe Henry does have this power. She doesn't know. Can he take the house? Her house – which she inherited and brought to this marriage. Can he take away her children if she's guilty of adultery which she is? She knows she should have found all this out before now. But instead she just let herself be swept along with James.

She tries not to let the fear show on her face. Her response is defiant.

'I'm not afraid of you, you pathetic little man. And all I have to do is tell your Mr Faber that he has an adulterer working for him and that'll be your precious job gone. What will you come back to then?'

Clara has hoped that this barb would hit home but Henry ignores it. Instead he holds out the letters towards her.

'Give those back to me,' she demands. 'They're addressed to me. They're my property.'

A sly smile takes hold of Henry's face.

'Oh no, not now, they're not. They're mine and soon they'll be in the hands of my solicitor.'

'You were an adulterer long before I was,' blurts out Clara and then regrets it.

'Ah, but it's different for us men,' says Henry. 'As you'll find out.'

Clara wonders if this is all true or is Henry just making this up. She is very frightened.

'And I'm not going to keep all your precious letters. Just the juicier ones. The rest? Well, there's only one place this kind of filth belongs.'

And with that Henry throws the letters into the fire. Then picking up the poker he harpoons them in amongst the coals. The papers begin to curl, blacken and catch fire.

Clara's first reaction is to run to try to save the letters. But she doesn't want to give him the satisfaction of engaging in some kind of tussle for them or trying to rescue them from the fire. Anyway she can see they are already pretty much lost. And now Henry is holding a poker and she is starting to feel afraid that he might actually do some physical harm to her. He has never hit her before but she has never seen him angry like this. It's an anger that doesn't seem quite rational.

'Do you know the worst thing of all?' asks Henry, as he continues to poke at the burning papers causing a few blackened fragments to float up the chimney. His voice has gone a little quieter. To Clara it sounds theatrical and self-pitying.

'At the front all we talk about is home. Our wives, sweethearts, children. How we're fighting to save them from the clutches of the Hun. And this –' he points the poker at her ' – this, is what I'm risking my life for.'

'And why not,' Clara can't help but say. 'You have a wife *and* a sweetheart to fight for.'

She is pleased to see from the expression on Henry's face that this one struck home. A part – a tiny, tiny part of her – thinks what a good joke it was and how funny James will find it when he tells her.

'Get out of my house,' commands Clara. 'Get out now.'

Henry turns to face her. The unpleasant smile has returned to his face.

'Oh, you'd like that, wouldn't you? I'd just clear off and make room for your fancy man.'

'And you could go off and live with your slut,' Clara interrupts.

If she had hoped Henry would rise to the insult, he doesn't. He just continues.

'Make it nice and easy for you, that's what you'd like, isn't it? But I can tell you now, my darling, it's not going to be easy for you at all. Oh yes, you've had it easy up until now while I worked night and day to keep you in your big house. Meals out, nice clothes. Oh yes, you've had it nice and easy but from on, it's not going to be *easy*. From now on, it's going to be nasty. Very, very nasty indeed.'

Chapter 28
Wednesday 19 May 1915

Henry just wants to leave. He wants to go off, be with Mary and fuck her. But he will not give Clara the satisfaction of giving up the house to her. As a result, he spends another couple of hours very deliberately playing with the children. That is, once he can tear them away from their newly returned mother and the little presents she has brought for them – something which just serves to fuel Henry's rage.

His fury is directed at the war, which has turned out to be nothing like he expected. Like many others, he assumed there would be a lot of parading and marching, perhaps a little bit of shooting which he had actually quite looked forward to and then everybody would go home. He would be back in his job, a hero, before Christmas. The Germans, instead of being sausage-eating clowns in short trousers, have turned out to be fierce and tenacious enemies. He is furious at them.

He is furious at Mary whom he fears is going lukewarm on their relationship. When he thinks of all he has given that bitch, all he has given up and all he has risked and this is the thanks he gets.

But mostly, Henry feels a visceral anger towards Clara. He really would like to hurt her. As he gathers up his pack and rifle to depart, it occurs to him that he could shoot her and he would have done so except that it would have ended up hurting himself more than her. And he wouldn't have wanted the bitch to have had that satisfaction. As he walks away from the house in Horn Lane to his rendezvous with Mary, he feels like he is about to explode, such are the feelings that are seething inside him.

It should all have been so neat that even something like the war shouldn't have changed things that much. Mary as his mistress, Clara at home with the children, a good job and Henry living the kind of full life that a good man deserved to live. The war should only have enhanced that. It should have been just about some rich experiences of comradeship and then back to the fixed points – the women in his life.

Now, thanks to Clara, it's all gone to hell. Who knows what kind of world he will return to – even if he survives the war, which is showing no signs of ending. Even if he comes through unscathed, Clara will be off with her man. In addition, Henry isn't sure – he needs to check this – but he thinks the house would revert to Clara. Henry couldn't afford to buy a house – at least not like the one in Horn Lane – so then he would have to go back to living in lodgings, just as he did before he met her. And as for Mary, she has nothing. So if she goes, Henry would have nobody and if she stays, she is going to want Henry to marry her and support her. Dear god, it would be like starting married life again from scratch, but with none of the advantages – notably the house – that he had when he married Clara.

That stupid bitch. What the hell was she thinking of, going off and having an affair like that? She's gone and ruined everything. He's going to cut her money. Jesus, he's going to do that first thing in the morning.

Henry stops in a pub and has several whiskies in quick succession but these only serve to make his anger worse and his thinking muddier. When he meets Mary, she seems genuinely delighted to see him and he can almost smell that she is eager for sex, but Henry is unable to put his anger aside. Since she is the first person he meets, his fury boils over at her. The result is that, seeing the way the land lies, she storms off and Henry is left to spend the night in an expensive hotel room by himself, where he drinks himself to sleep. Next morning, nursing a brutal hangover, he entrains for France.

He is sick on the train and again on the troopship and it is only when there is nothing more in his stomach, he has slept fitfully and his headache has faded to a dull throb that he knows he must start to think, if his whole world is not to fall apart.

Clara only stops shaking when the door slams and Henry leaves the house. She is afraid. Very afraid. She doesn't know what Henry can do under the law. But it is what he might do outside the law that worries her most. She has to wait for Mrs Parsons to go and the children to be in bed before she has time to consider all this. By then she has calmed down a little and her thinking is clearer.

Henry is either back in France or on his way. He personally can do little to harm her from there. But he can initiate divorce proceedings. He could do that by writing.

But then Clara has to almost slap herself. Isn't this what she wants? If Henry would initiate divorce proceedings, many of her problems would be over. There's just the children and – to a lesser extent – the house. What would happen to each of those? She needs to find out. She needs to be on firm ground. She will ask James tomorrow. She has delayed going to a solicitor long enough.

Chapter 29
Thursday 20 May 1915

Henry knows he has immediate concerns. He is on a troopship that is taking him back to France. By tomorrow he will probably be back in a front line trench. He has come to learn, just as James has, that survival in the trenches, while it has much to do with chance, is also about focus. Focus on the tiny details that can make a difference between life and death. The sound of an incoming shell and the ability to estimate where it might land. A seemingly insignificant dip in a sandbag wall that provides a passage way for a sniper's bullet. A second spent here or not spent there that marks the difference between continuing to stay alive and suffering some ghastly maiming.

He knows he should be trying to re-focus on these things; to get his mind back to the tight concentration it was capable of, just before he went on leave. He is only too aware that if he doesn't come back in one piece then everything else doesn't matter.

He knows he should – right now – be composing a letter to Mary to try to mend the rift between them. He knows he should be trying to work out if there is anything he can do to try to sort out the shambles that his life has become. He knows he should be trying to work out what future he wants so that he can start to see how he can salvage that. But the only thing he can think about – it elbows its way back into his mind at every turn – is how he can hurt Clara.

He has a fantasy which he knows will never come about. But this doesn't stop him from indulging in it. In it, he has made Clara undress in front of him. Then he has thrown her on the bed and used her stockings to tie her wrists and ankles to the four legs of the bed. She lies X-shaped, writhing to try and pull herself free. But of course, it is impossible – the stocking bindings are virtually unbreakable. Sometimes she lies face down, her face buried in a pillow to muffle her sobs and screams. He uses a cane, as his teacher did in school, and lays it across the cheeks of her bottom. He remembers she has a pert little bottom, ripe for caning. When she is face down and can't see him, he swishes the cane through the air before starting on her. The whistling sound and the anticipation of that on her skin cause her to struggle even more and squeal in terror.

Sometimes, in his fantasy, Clara is tied to the bed but is on her back. Henry has stuffed her underwear into her mouth to stifle her screams. He canes her cunt and tits. (He doesn't think of her as a woman having a vagina and breasts. Instead – now – she is a slut with a cunt and tits.) The cane leaves red weals across her body.

But of course, he will never get to do this to her, except in his head. Instead he racks his brains as to how he could best hurt her. He could, he supposes, find somebody to physically hurt her – to beat her up or even rape her. And he is strongly tempted to do that. There are one or two men in his company that he is sure would know somebody who would know somebody. But supposing she was hurt so badly that she couldn't mind the children? Or even killed? Would he be allowed to come back to take care of them? The idea takes hold of him for a few moments. He thinks of all the problems it would solve. He would have his revenge on her and he would be out of the firing line and back home safely in the house. If she was dead, the house would be his and he'd be free to marry Mary. And then take a mistress, he thinks to himself cheerfully. Marry the mistress and create a vacancy.

But that particular light flares and then goes out. It is too fraught with danger and uncertainty. Suppose Clara dies and then he isn't allowed back to mind the girls? They'd end up in an orphanage. And supposing whoever he did get to kill Clara then blackmailed Henry or the police found out that he was behind it? Then he'd hang. No, that's all too risky. With great reluctance, Henry decides that this plan isn't going to work.

He needs to find a way to hurt Clara that will stay with her for the rest of her life. Henry had a small taste of this when he burned Clara's letters from her fancy man. Henry kept some of the more lengthy ones back, on the basis that at some stage he'd need to show them to a solicitor but it gave him a small dart of pleasure to know how much their loss had hurt her. Clara was a woman who treasured such things and she would have seen their loss as being irreplaceable. He needs to find other ways like that.

And they have to be ways that don't affect the children. Clara needs to be there to mind them but somehow Henry has to find a way to break her heart. In theory, the way is obvious. If Henry can cause her to split with her fancy man, then Clara's heart will indeed be broken. The bitch is sentimental enough to spend the rest of her life in mourning for what she would have lost. But how is he to do this?

And then Henry has an idea.

Chapter 30
Friday 21 May 1915

Henry has arrived back in France and caught up with his battalion. They are in billets. Tomorrow they will be going back up the line but tonight they have a few hours to forget about all of that. Most of the lads are going down to an *estaminet* where they will have *omelette frites* and raw *vin rouge*. Ordinarily Henry would go with them but tonight he has a letter to write.

The answer, when it came to him, was so obvious that he found it incredible that it had taken him so long to think of it. In reality all he had to do was remember what Mary had done – the action she had taken last year that had so messed up Henry's neat little world. Because now Henry is certain that exactly the same thing will work for him.

However it takes him a long time before any words come. He doesn't know whom he is writing to and for Henry – never a great writer – that makes the task very difficult. He tries to imagine Clara's fancy man receiving the letter. What is he like, this bastard? For a long time nothing comes. Then Henry has an idea. It strikes him that Clara's fancy man is like Corporal Smith, the man who commands the section of which Henry is Lance Corporal. Smith is bookish, soft, almost girlish. A ponce. Henry imagines that Clara's man is like this. That is the kind of man she would like. Somebody she could control and order around. So now with this picture in his head, the words come relatively easily.

Taking James' address in the Army from one of Clara's letters, Henry writes:

I know you are having an affair with my wife. I strongly urge you to stop it forthwith. If you don't, then very bad things could happen to you both. If you care for her and if you value both her safety and yours, then leave her alone and never see her again.

DON'T TEST ME ON THIS.

Henry is strongly tempted to put a bullet in with the letter but he isn't sure whether this is a crime or not. He wouldn't want the whole thing to backfire on him with this fucker James going to the police and Henry subsequently being arrested. In the end he decides against the bullet.

Chapter 31
Saturday 22 May 1915

In a rare occurrence for the Army, Henry is allowed to sleep late. When he does eventually wake, he discovers that there has been a change of plan. They will not be going up the line until tomorrow. While he is all too conscious that this could change again, he utters a silent prayer of thanks. Ordinarily, he would start to think about how he might spend this reprieve, these blessed empty hours, but today there is something else on his mind. That letter he wrote. Henry realises it's not going to work.

Clara's fancy man may be a pathetic little poof but supposing he is not? The man is in the Army – not that this proves anything. Corporal Smith is in the Army and look at him. But Henry thinks of the three men that have been part of Clara's life – her father, her brother and himself. These are (or were) all manly men – the father and brother cut from the same cloth. Supposing this James fucker is exactly the same. Supposing he is a lot like Henry but with more of the bookish and sentimental things that Clara seems to set so much store by?

If Henry were to receive such a letter how would he react? Well, he certainly wouldn't feel intimidated. Instead, he would try to meet the threat head on. In fact now that Henry thinks about it, he would be angry – angry at the threat to someone he loved, if nothing else. And he would marshal all the forces at his disposal to deal with the threat. He would go to the police. He would go to a solicitor. He would try to track down the author of the letter and scare the living daylights out of him.

So Henry believes he has gotten it all wrong. But he also estimates that the situation can be saved. There is another letter he can write.

Chapter 32
Monday 24 May 1915

Henry's letter, forwarded by the Army, reaches James at his London home on Monday. He reads and rereads it several times.

I know you are having an affair with my wife. I strongly urge you to stop it forthwith. If you don't, then very bad things could happen to you both. If you care for her and if you value both her safety and yours, then leave her alone and never see her again.

DON'T TEST ME ON THIS.

In terms of fears for himself, the letter has no effect whatsoever on James. He has spent most of this year in mortal danger – what would he have to fear from an unsigned letter written by a bully boy? But the threat against Clara worries him. There are a range of things that he pictures Henry could do to Clara and none of them are good. James wonders briefly if he should go to the police but is sure there would be little point in that. What would they do? Give Clara police protection? Give Henry a warning? Most likely they would tell James to stop seeing a married woman. And now his relationship with Clara would be a matter of police record. No telling where that could lead.

James is consoled by the fact that at least he is in London for the next few months. He can do something about trying to keep Clara safe. He is at hand if something should happen. But it is small consolation. He wonders if he should show her the letter but knows that, being the worrier she is, this will probably have a dreadful effect on her.

He knows that the best thing now is to get her to a solicitor and begin the divorce proceedings. They are due to meet this Thursday. He will broach it with her then. In fact, he may even write to her beforehand to prepare the ground.

Chapter 33
Tuesday 25 May 1915

Henry's second letter arrives in the morning post. This is what James reads:

Dear Mr Walters,

I must apologise profoundly for the previous letter I wrote to you & which you should now have received.

<u>I should never have written or sent such a letter.</u>

All I can say by way of excuse is that I am under great strain. I am in the Army, at the front, as you are. So I don't need to explain to you how that wears a man down over time. And then there is my marriage which – entirely through my own fault – is in great distress. I am frantic with worry as to the effect this is having on my wife and my two young girls.

It was all of this that led me to write the previous letter. I hope you will forgive me.

And then I must ask you for something else, Mr Walters. You owe me nothing I know, but I shall ask it anyway.

I want and oh so desperately hope that my wife and I can repair our relationship. I want her and my two children to be happy – especially if it is the will of fate that my time with them will not be long.

Therefore I ask you not to see my wife again. Please give us the time and space to see if we can mend our marriage. If you cannot do it for my sake, then at least do it for hers and the sake of our children.

I know I have no right to ask this but I do so anyway, Mr Walters – in the hope that as a gentleman, you will see that it is the best for all of us.

Your obedient servant

Henry Kenton

Chapter 34
Thursday 27 May 1915

James has spent the last two days in turmoil. He has been unable to sleep as he wrestled with this problem and tried to find the best thing to do. By Thursday, as he goes to meet Clara, he thinks he has found the answer.

She is already there when he arrives, sitting on their bench beside the water. She stands up and is taken aback when the slow kiss she offers is returned with little more than James brushing her lips.

'What's wrong, darling?' she asks.

James has spent a lot of time thinking back over the events of last summer that began with the assassination of the Archduke and led up to the outbreak of war. If there is one thing that's become clear to him it's that people weren't straight and truthful. Everybody was either playing games – as in the case of the Germans – or else they weren't prepared to call a spade a spade – the most obvious example being Sir Edward Grey.

The lesson James has taken from all of this is that people have to be truthful. Only then can problems be solved. If people hold back on what they are really thinking, then it is impossible to understand what is really going on and as a result of that, what the best course of action is. He has decided that he needs to be perfectly, one hundred percent honest with Clara. If he is, he believes, they will find the best solution to the predicament in which they find themselves.

'What is it?' Clara asks again.

James motions to the bench and Clara sits down. He starts with Henry's first letter. Clara reads it in astonishment. When she looks up, James says, 'I'm frightened for you, Clara – what he might do to you.'

'But he's back in France now.'

'It doesn't matter,' says James. 'There are ways. And even though I'm in London now, once I go back to France, I have no way of protecting you. Not that I can protect you much now – unless I come to live with you.'

James laughs an empty laugh.

'So what do you think we should do?' asks Clara.

James ignores the question.

'And then there's this second letter,' he continues, handing it to Clara.

Her head moves as she reads quickly. Then she looks up at James. Uncertain about what she sees in his face, she replies, 'You know this isn't true, don't you?'

'Yes, I know.'

'So what do you think we should do?' Clara asks again.

'Begin the divorce process with a solicitor,' says James. 'And in the meantime, in order to keep you safe, you and I pretend that we have given up our relationship.'

'Pretend?' asks Clara. 'Give up? What does that mean?'

Up to this moment and ever since his declaration of love for her, Clara has had no doubts about how James felt about her. But suddenly she feels herself on unsteady ground.

'Just that. I write back to him agreeing to what he says. You initiate the divorce proceedings.'

'And?'

'And what?'

'And you and I. What happens to you and I?'

'We stop seeing each other until your divorce comes through. We stop writing when I'm back in France. That way he won't harm you.'

'So you won't help me? With my divorce I mean?'

Clara isn't stupid. She understands very clearly what James is saying and rationally, she can see no fault in it. But a tiny fear has entered her head; a fear that grows as each moment passes. Instead of voicing it, she says, 'But supposing he's killed? Then there'd be no need for a divorce.'

'Supposing he's not,' James suggests.

'And anyway, do you think he wouldn't be capable of harming me once he knew I was looking for a divorce?'

It is the one flaw that James knew was in his argument.

'So what do you propose?' he says and he is unable to keep the note of irritation out of his voice.

'Just carry on as we are and see what happens. Enjoy the time we have together.'

'And these?' James asks, holding out the two letters.

'Just ignore them,' Clara says with a bravado she doesn't really feel.

Last year, at the height of the July Crisis, when Austria had delivered its ultimatum to Serbia, the Russian Tsar had wondered what to do in response. Eventually he had mobilised his army with the cascade of results that we have seen. The Tsar must often wonder these days what if he had done nothing? Just left the Austrians guessing as to his intentions. Would they have backed down? A part of him tells him that they would and this whole terrible unceasing bloodletting would have been avoided.

But the hardest thing in a crisis is to do nothing; a fact that James is discovering for himself.

'And you seem to have forgotten my children,' Clara states and she can't help but sound angry.

'No, I haven't forgotten your children. I'm just trying to find a solution that works, that keeps you and your children safe.'

James is aware of how weak his statement sounds.

'You're dropping me,' says Clara. 'Aren't you?'

There – she's said it. And now that she has, she sees how it is all part of a picture. The picture of her life. Just as when she married Henry and she thought that her being alone had come to an end, it's exactly the same now. She has been foolish enough to think that James was a new beginning, that now she would have a companion on life's journey. But once again, she's been a fool.

'Now that it's become complicated you just want to get out, don't you?' she asks.

James goes to speak but Clara is in full flow.

'And you know, maybe you're right. Maybe I have asked too much of you. I don't know what horrors you have to face out there. My life and its complications must seem so pathetically trivial by comparison.'

'Clara – please … stop,' James implores.

He reaches for her hands but she pulls them away.

'Look, we'll do as you say,' he says. 'We'll just carry on and see what happens.'

He smiles for the first time since they have been together.

'I need to go,' replies Clara. 'I'm sorry to have been such a burden to you. That was never my intention.'

'Clara – you're not –'

But Clara has stood up and is already turning. James is saying something but she doesn't know what it is. With tears in her eyes, she walks away.

It is night and the children are in bed before Clara has a chance to think clearly about what has happened. Henry has won. The little chance she had for happiness is gone. In the end the obstacles in her way were too great.

Of course it is not James' fault. Nor Henry's either, if it comes to it. It is as her mother often said. Clara has made her bed. Now she'll just have to lie in it.

All this talk of divorce. She couldn't have put her children though all of that. Tearing them away from their father. It was that really that she understood today. Today wasn't about James or Henry. It was about her and the life she will lead after today.

Chapter 35
Friday 28 May 1915

Next day, Clara writes two letters. To Henry, it is just one line: *We have done as you asked.*

She tells James that she is sorry for having led him along, that she should never have become involved with him. She writes that no fault attaches to him for what happened yesterday, that it is her and her realisation that she is married and that it must continue that way, for the sake of her children if nothing else.

She says that she will pray for him. (Clara wonders how this will strike him since they have often talked about how both of them don't believe in formal religion.) She hopes that he will come through the war unscathed. She tells him that he must not contact her any more; that each of them must now get on with their lives.

She finishes by saying that she hopes he will meet somebody some time in the future and that he will find great love and happiness. (At this point she is in tears.) She wonders for a long time how to end the letter but finally – and this decision takes longer than the letter itself – she finally just signs it 'Clara Jordan'. Bitterly she thinks how the use of her maiden name is just a tiny flicker of the struggle she has been through that is now ending.

Later that day, she posts both letters.

And now, my possibly theatre-going reader, we shall leave our characters – Henry and James and Clara and Mary – for a while. Had this book been a play, we could imagine them leaving the stage and going back to their dressing rooms. There they might shrug off the heaviest and hottest pieces of their costumes and wigs. And while consuming some water or tea with lemon and honey or coffee or even something stronger, they might have reflected on how the play has gone so far.

Henry would be mighty happy with his performance. Everything has gone just as he might have hoped. Now, if he can survive the second act, he will come home to the life he had hoped for. He is unsure if Mary will be in that world but he sees this as being of little importance. There will be plenty of other Marys. In fact, it has occurred to Henry – it must be part of working in insurance – that, if the Game of Death continues as it is, with men dying at the rate they are dying, then after the war, there will indeed be lots of Marys. Daughters without fathers, wives without husbands, single women looking to marry. The pickings should be very rich indeed. All he needs is to survive.

For James on the other hand, things are very different. He will not attempt to change Clara's mind. In that, he feels the playwright has got James' character just right. James thinks of himself as an honourable gentleman. In truth, it had sometimes troubled him that he was carrying on with someone else's wife. So now that she has been the one to call a halt to all of that, he will not go against her wishes.

But James is devastated. He feels, or rather, he felt that in Clara he had found someone truly special. He had loved every moment he spent with her. She made life in the trenches bearable. The Thirteen Hours and the weekend he spent with her in Teignmouth were probably the happiest moments of his life. And provided he survived the war, he had pictured that they would have a life together that would be as perfect as those few stolen hours and days. He had pictured them so often in France – he, she and a little ready-made family. But that is all destroyed now just as part of the France he loves so much is being destroyed.

Now, all James wants to do is to return to the Army. He can't wait for this interlude to be over so that he can get back on stage.

And finally, Clara. Clara has seen her courage grow, swell and then wither. Now she feels tiny, defeated. She has no passion for anything any more. Yes, she will go on in the next act, but now it will be just a weary repetition of what has gone on before she met James. Now she will indeed slide down slowly (or maybe not so slowly) to death. She pictures the future big events in her girls' lives – because Clara sees there will be none in hers. Their weddings, the births of their children. These will now be the things that Clara lives for. And she sees herself as a middle aged matron, a mother-in-law and grandmother. This now is what the rest of her life will consist of.

Sitting in front of her dressing room mirror, we can picture her weeping.

Chapter 36
Tuesday 1 June 1915

Clara receives a letter from Henry. She knows that his letters are censored by his commanding officer. It reads:

My dear Clara,

Thank you for your most recent letter and the good news that it contained.

I look forward to being in the bosom of my family when I next return on leave and when this war is eventually over.

Yours always

Henry

The word 'always' is underlined twice.

Chapter 37
Thursday 17 June 1915

Rawly has just finished another battle, this time at Givenchy. It's one he would class as a small-scale engagement, dear reader. He presumably measures this in terms of the 3,500 casualties his men sustained.

One supposes it says something for Rawly's military skills that he never thought this attack was going to work in the first place. In his diary he calls his plan 'a pious aspiration rather than anything that is likely to be carried into effect.' But if he felt this, Rawly failed to pass on any of it to his boss, Douglas Haig.

In addition, in the fashion that has now become quite familiar to us, Rawly blames the troops for the failure. This time it is the Canadians who took part in the operation. 'I don't think they meant business,' Rawly comments.

This, about a unit that suffered 600 casualties trying to carry out Rawlinson's 'pious aspiration'.

James' arm continues to heal. On an impulse, he goes to the Foreign Office to see old friends. The older ones are still there but anyone of his age or younger that he used to know are long gone into the Army. He leaves the building more depressed than when he came in.

He sees a couple of women handing out white feathers. They approach him but he is in uniform. They tell him how much they admire him and how grateful they are for what he is doing.

Later he thinks he sees Clara on Oxford Street. He sees her from the back – the blonde hair, the familiar clothes, the hat. The woman appears to be Clara's height. He hurries to catch up with her but when he overtakes her and looks at her from the side, he sees that it is not her at all. The woman smiles questioningly at him. She is much older than Clara and nowhere near as pretty.

That night, Clara, alone in her bed, does two things. One is something she has never done before and the second, something she has not done in goodness knows how long.

It is a warm night, so after she has undressed and is about to put on her nightdress, she pauses. She folds the nightdress again and puts it back in the drawer. She is going to sleep naked. And later that night she wakes and treats herself to an orgasm. It is the one small part of her life where she can be free, where the world with all its possibilities can still open up to her.

But afterwards, she still goes to sleep crying, as she has done so many nights since she last saw James.

Chapter 38
Thursday 1 July 1915

The first day of July. Clara has always thought of it as the real beginning of summer. The beginning of that endless procession of sunny days that she remembers from her childhood. Days spent in the very same garden she spends them in now. Days of books and the sun on her back and legs. The early morning singing of birds and sleepy drone of bees in afternoons as golden as the honey they were busily making. Days of emptiness to be filled up or not as she chose. Days when being alone was a happy thing. In fact – weirdly – it never even occurred to her then that she *was* alone. Was it that the characters in the books and the birds and butterflies were all the company she needed?

Why can she not feel that now? When did that change? For her? And when does it change for all people? And why does it? Why, she wonders, do we develop the need to be not just with other people, but to find one special person that we will want to be with always? Where does that dependency come from? Why can we not just stay happy and alone since that's the way we start out?

All these questions and no answers. All she knows is that she feels no pleasure at the prospect of the summer that lies ahead.

Chapter 39
Saturday 3 July 1915

Rawly's boss, Douglas Haig, has been asked by *his* boss, Sir John French who in turn has been asked by the French to carry out a combined attack with them. The attack is to take place on the French left in the area around Loos.

Haig calls a meeting of his corps commanders, one of whom is Rawly. However, since the 1st of July, Rawly has been on leave in London. He's been to the dentist, played tennis and – he notes in his diary – went to 'Buck House', where he was made a Knight Commander of the Order of St Michael and St George. Presumably this is for services rendered thus far. One really has to wonder what reward he would have been given had he had any successes up until now. He returns to France on the 8th.

Clara has found herself thinking a lot lately how she would have loved to have had a baby with James. A little boy. How the girls would have adored that. A little brother of their own for them to take care of and love.

And what an amazing child it would have been, Clara feels. Part James, with all his qualities and then part Clara. Along with that unique part that comes with every baby that makes parents wonder – where did *that* come from?

But it's the 'part Clara' bit that she dwells on particularly. What would that have been? Loving? Definitely. Generous. Funny – a great sense of humour. And not just funny but fun-loving. The phrase comes into Clara's head like an actor stepping out of the wings onto the stage. No, not fun-loving. If Clara was fun-loving, she would have chosen something very different.

Chapter 40
Wednesday 1 September 1915

James arrives back in France, his arm fully healed. The same day, to make up for casualties that the battalion has suffered, he is offered a commission as a second lieutenant. He accepts.

Chapter 41
Saturday 25 September 1915

Rawly has his next outing at the Battle of Loos. We should also have perhaps mentioned before now that while Rawly may have developed his theory of 'bite and hold', he isn't exactly fully committed to it. Whenever his boss, Duggy Haig, proposes a new battle, Rawly always proposes a bite and hold. Haig, by comparison, can be guaranteed to put forward a much grander scheme involving breaking through several lines of the German defences and then sending cavalry through the gap –

Cavalry?

Yes, you heard right – cavalry.

Cavalry? Men on horses?

That's right.

Against machine guns.

Yep.

Invariably when Haig proposes something like this, Rawly backs down on his bite and hold. This despite the fact that all the evidence up to now seems to show that bite and hold is the best that can be achieved – and this only with a sufficiently heavy and accurate artillery bombardment.

Of course, we shouldn't be surprised by this. The fact that Rawly owes his position to Haig means that he will want to continue to seek Haig's approval. This means that he is never likely to question his boss.

Back to the Battle of Loos. Once again, Rawly is going into it with nothing like the weight of artillery he had at Neuve Chapelle. To make up for this, to find a new way to get his men safely across no-man's-land, he decides to use the latest weapon that has become available to teams on the Western Front: poison gas.

And so the battle at Loos kicks off with the release of poison gas from 2,550 cylinders.

Rawly is safe, six miles behind the front at Vaudricourt. Apart from the gas, which is being used by the British for the first time, the plan has another new element in it. This is the first time that the new so-called 'Kitchener' divisions are being deployed on a large scale for an assault. The Kitchener divisions, in case you're wondering, dear reader, are the divisions formed from volunteers like James and Henry who enlisted at the start of the war.

Rawly's planning has followed a pattern which we have just noted and with which we are becoming depressingly familiar. He started out with some modest objectives. Meanwhile Haig had a madly ambitious plan. Rawly sees no reality in Haig's plan but rather than voice any objections, goes along with it anyway.

Also – and here's something for you to remember for later in our story – the attacks are to be made at a fast pace in the hope that the momentum of the attack will smash through the German lines.

Rawly himself will sum up the first day's action in a letter he will write to the King's adviser Stamfordham, a few days later. 'From what I can ascertain, some of the divisions did actually reach the enemy's trenches, for their bodies can now be seen on the barbed wire.'

And there's really not a lot that one can say about that.

In the first four hours of the battle, the twelve attacking battalions suffer 8,000 casualties out of 10,000 men.

Another person who has a plan – you will recall, my dear reader – and who has, in fact been working steadily on it, is Henry's mistress, Mary. Back in February, Mary had resolved to become a nurse. To this end, she had begun taking classes in both nursing and elocution, and while, on the face of it, this had seemed like an odd combination, in fact – as we saw – it made perfect sense. And unlike Rawly's plan for the Battle of Loos and the shambles that has resulted, Mary's plan is about to bear real fruit.

Clara wonders if she had lived in a different time whether it would have all been different. After all, look at Nelson's mistress Emma Hamilton, a hundred years ago. Why couldn't Clara have been like her?

She returns to her Atkinson Grimshaw dream of last year. But now she no longer finds any pleasure in it. She enters the side gate and walks through the withered garden to enter the house. But now the house is empty. There are no signs of life or of recent habitation. And she cannot find the warm upstairs room where the great bed and the hot bath were. Doors creak when she opens them. There are cobwebs everywhere. Nobody has been here for a long time.

Chapter 42
Thursday 14 October 1915

The battle at Loos finally comes to a halt. There have been about 25,000 casualties on the German side and double that number on the British. Nothing has been achieved.

And the gas? That didn't help?

'Fraid not. There were 2,632 British gas casualties (from the British gas, that is) – although only seven actually died.

To the relief of the troops and all concerned – and I'm sure yourself, dear reader, Rawly will not be having another outing in 1915.

Oh no, he's saving himself for something far, far bigger.

Mary, however, has had a major success. Instead of ending up as a nurse, she has ended up as a driver for officers. And in fact, she is far, far happier about this. The more she had continued with her nursing training, the less attracted she had been to what the work would actually involve. A visit to a ward of a hospital for wounded officers had eventually made up her mind. It was all far too horrific, so much so that she had to leave the place and go out and sit on a park bench in the sunshine to calm herself.

After that, with typical Mary resourcefulness and drive, she set off to find out about becoming a driver. By September she was and it was when going to pick up a wounded officer to take him to a hospital appointment that she met Captain Frank Richards.

Richards is everything Mary could possibly have wanted. He's six years older than her, not ugly by any means, hasn't been badly wounded – just a broken leg that is busily mending – doesn't appear to have been too shaken up by the war – at least not so far – and while not wealthy by any means, does have an income (from stocks or bonds or something – Mary is not quite sure what) for which he doesn't have to work.

Frank Richards is very taken with Mary and soon they are seeing each other. It is just perfect, Mary reflects, because his leg wound will keep him in England until at least the end of the year.

Now Mary has to confess that Frank isn't as good company as Henry. In fact, to be honest, he can be rather dull. Mary saw this when they went to have their first meal out together. Frank didn't talk. It was as though meals were for eating not speaking. And Mary found this quite alarming given the easy and entertaining and often very funny conversations she had with Henry over food.

But she shrugged. There were lots to be grateful for with Frank Richards. And maybe after he got to know her better he would talk more.

Chapter 43
Monday 13 December 1915

The same day that Frank Richards' plaster comes off his leg, he and Mary make love for the first time. They are in Frank's comfortable house in Kingston. Frank is a competent if unadventurous lover and Mary is well acquainted with faking the things that have to be faked. There is the same problem that occurred during their first meal together. Mary likes to talk during lovemaking. Sometimes – and Henry particularly liked this – she used to say dirty things. But Frank says nothing other than answering Mary's questions. Things like, 'Am I hurting you?' 'Is that nice?' 'I'm not pressing on your leg, am I?'

After Frank has climaxed and fallen asleep, Mary wonders what has attracted him to her. But of course, there is much. She is young – younger than him, anyway – vivacious, fun loving, and now, he has discovered, she is good in bed. Mary imagines that it will be easy enough to keep him faithful. She can imagine having his child. On balance, while she would have preferred Henry because he was more fun, there is not too much to complain about here. And there was always the fear that Henry would stray – even if he had left his wife, which she doubts he ever would have anyway.

No, overall, Mary is happy with the way things have turned out.

Chapter 44
Monday 15 February 1916

General Sir Douglas Haig KCB KCVO KCIE ADC, Commander in-Chief of all the British Armies in France and Flanders, has gone to the place where – as the Jews of Eastern Europe will put it until they are silenced forever three decades from now – 'even the Kaiser himself has to go on foot.' In other words, he is on the toilet. He is on the toilet and thinking about golf.

Specifically, he is thinking about the Royal and Ancient Golf Club of St Andrews. How he wishes he were there now, on the first tee in a soft, salt-scented summer breeze, getting ready to tee off. Instead he is engaging in a different form of teeing off. He *is* teed off.

Sir Douglas or 'Duggy', as the troops like to call him, carries a responsibility that few men will ever carry. He is responsible for the largest army Britain has ever (or will ever) put into the field. Literally millions of lives are affected by the decisions he makes. For some reason that he's not at all clear about, this morning more than most, that responsibility weighs heavily on his shoulders. And not just on his shoulders. He is spending a long time on the toilet and he doesn't think it's just the good beef he had for dinner last night which always has this effect upon him to an extent.

It has been customary in many quarters to regard Duggy Haig as an idiot general. 'The Butcher of the Somme' or 'Butcher Haig' are two of his soubriquets. And perhaps you had been expecting, somewhat complacent reader, that I would follow that line of thought here. So I hope I will not surprise or upset you too much if I don't. At least not one hundred percent.

Haig bears a heavy responsibility and he is a product of his times. We have to wonder how we would have coped had we had to shoulder that burden. Imagine it. Imagine it now. Imagine that you woke tomorrow morning and that somehow, magically, it was 1916 and somehow, even more magically, you were in charge of this vast army.

Would you have made mistakes? Of course you would – even if you'd had the best military training available or were the finest military mind of the age. Would men have died as a result of your decisions? You know they would. When generals decide, men die. Would you have learnt from your mistakes? You'd like to think you would. But the mistakes were complicated ones involving many factors. And so the learning from them was complicated – not necessarily always clear or obvious.

Maybe we should just be grateful that we *didn't* find ourselves in that water closet on that chilly February morning – and I'm not talking about the problem caused by the beef.

However, being the Commander-in-Chief is not without its perks. There is good food and wine, cooked and served up to you, the beef being the most recent example. There is no having to do the washing up if you're Duggy Haig. There's a comfortable bed at night, someone to drive you around, your own horse if you want to go riding, as Duggy likes to do. Essentially, there are people catering to your every whim and need. You have the ability to go home and see your family pretty much whenever you like. The responsibility is heavy for sure but the perks offer some consolation.

And perhaps the biggest perk of all is that there is very little likelihood that Duggy Haig will die a violent death on the battlefield. He is unlikely to end up gassed, maimed, eviscerated by a shell fragment, blown to spots by a mine, blinded, dismembered, crippled, shot by a sniper's bullet, machine gunned, entombed underground or killed in any of the other ways that death can come on the Western Front. Prior to 1914, the last significant land battle fought by a British army in Europe was at Waterloo. Here, the Commander-in-Chief was on the battlefield sharing the dangers with his men. But those days are long gone. Now Commanders-in-Chief are most likely to die in bed.

Haig finally gives up, pulls up his trousers and adjusts his tunic. Outside the cubicle, as he washes his hands, he checks his appearance in the mirror.

He is tall, broad shouldered with fair hair, steely blue eyes and − naturally − an impressive moustache. His hair is impeccably groomed, parted in the middle and combed back with just a hint of brilliantine. You'd have to say that he is a handsome man. His khaki tunic carries rows of Service and Order ribbons. His boots are highly polished, this having been done by a valet overnight and he wears spurs. (He will go riding later.) He tucks his red banded cap under his arm and exits the bathroom. Like all cavalrymen he walks with a rangy, swinging stride as he returns to his desk.

In case you've been wondering, curious reader, where this has all been happening, we are in a house called Beaurepaire, a few miles from Montrieul in France. It is what the English would call a country house and the French a chateau. Here in one of the front rooms is where Duggy has his office. The original furnishings of the room have all been kept and a fire blazes cheerily in the hearth. This scene of well off country living has been augmented by Haig's desk and a map table behind it. While there is a telephone on his desk, Duggy dislikes using it and so generally leaves that to his staff, unless it is unavoidable.

Duggy Haig is not a man noted for being garrulous. He is taciturn and this gives a sense of him being cold and aloof. He can be hard work for others. (If Mary had found herself dining or making love with him − a most unlikely occurrence, of course − she would have found much the same problem that she finds with Frank Richards, namely the lack of conversation.) So it is with Duggy. The thundering silences at mealtimes can be particularly difficult. He is deeply religious and was quite sickly as a child. The result of the latter is he likes things to be just so.

After getting up and bathing, he likes to take a walk in the grounds of the chateau, returning for breakfast at exactly 8:30. After breakfast and the visit which he has just completed, he will work at his desk for the morning, alternating paperwork and meetings with his staff or other visitors – politicians, journalists, foreign generals and so on – who come to GHQ. A lot of the paperwork involves correcting or commenting on papers submitted by his staff. Anyone who works in a senior management position in a large, modern-day business would recognise much of Duggy's working day as their own.

If he has visitors, he will give them lunch but this rarely lasts more than half an hour. In summer especially, Duggy likes to take a picnic lunch when he and his entourage head off in a convoy of motor cars to visit some headquarters or unit. Most of his afternoons are spent in this way. It makes him feel he is keeping in touch with his army.

Returning after such a visit, he will often rendezvous with his horses because he likes to ride for exercise. Otherwise, he will perhaps walk back to GHQ. Dinner will be at 8 PM where often again, he will have guests. After about an hour, Duggy will excuse himself and return to his desk for more work and to write up his diary. He is usually in bed by 10:45.

And so, as the new week begins, Duggy enters his office and pauses at the map table. On it rests a huge relief map of the Somme area. This is where the British will play their next big match in the Group of Death.

The idea of playing a game on the Somme has its roots in an agreement made between the British and French Prime Ministers in Paris the previous year. On December 17th, these two gentlemen met and agreed that there should be a permanent committee to coordinate action between the two teams.

Soon after the Prime Ministers' meeting, the French general Joffre circulated a memorandum: *The Plan of Action Proposed by France to the Coalition*. In this document he proposed simultaneous large-scale attacks with maximum forces by the French, British, and Russian sides as soon as conditions were favourable in 1916. These proposals were accepted by all concerned. By the 14th of February 1916 it was settled that in the West, a combined Franco-British offensive should be carried out across the River Somme round about the 1st of July 1916.

Chapter 45
Friday 16 June 1916

James loves music. All kinds of music. Popular songs, classical music, opera and – most of all – Gilbert & Sullivan. He loves their entrancing tunes and sharp, witty lyrics. One of his many regrets is that he never got to take Clara to a concert or an opera. It was one of the things he had pictured them enjoying together. And indeed 'regret' is far too inadequate a word to describe the sense of loss he still feels.

His battalion is billeted in a place called Souastre and is in 'rest'. Let's be clear, dear reader, what this means. Every morning at 7:30 AM they march out with picks and shovels to dig the divisional cable line that will be used for communication in the forthcoming offensive. So it's not exactly what you or I might call 'rest' but it's rest in the sense that they are far enough away from the front line that the chances of being blown apart by a shell are pretty remote. They finish at 4:30 PM every day and return to Souastre for tea. Then, while there is no Gilbert & Sullivan on the Western Front, there *is* music. Obviously there is the constant singing that the men do while on the march but there are also occasional shows put on by the men themselves.

There is one running in a barn in Souastre entitled 'Bow Bells'. The title alone, with its memories of a London that is so very far away, is enough to reduce some men to tears. But it is the song 'My Old Kentucky Home' that has that effect on James. The singer – one Mark Leslie, according to the 1-page programme – sings the song while clog dancing, so it could hardly be described as a sensitive rendition. But the response of the audience is the noisiest and most enthusiastic of any of the turns that evening.

James assumes it's the mention of 'home' that so resonates with the audience. And it is what resonates with James too as the song is encored for the third time. Looking around at the laughing faces under a thick cover of cigarette and pipe smoke, James imagines the homes they are thinking of, the wives, the children. And it is this image that comes to James too – the wife he will now never have, the children whose father he might have become, the child he might have fathered himself.

In the end, it is too much. He has to get up and go outside into the warm night air. Artillery rumbles away to the east. The sky is cloudless and not yet dark enough for the lightshow to have started. A machine gun hammers away, startlingly near.

There are tears in James' eyes as he walks back to the barn where he sleeps.

Clara wakes during the night. She is thinking about her next door neighbour. Clara lives next to a family called the Fridays. There used to be the parents and a son, Lewis. She saw him from the window only the other day when dusting the front upstairs bedroom. He was returning from the direction of the shops and was eating an ice cream. She isn't sure exactly how old Lewis is but reckons he will probably have to be going into the Army soon.

But it is not Lewis that Clara is thinking about. Rather, it is his mother, who died about ten years ago when Lewis was only a boy. Now that she thinks about it, it was the year that Clara got married. Yes, that's right. That was the sequence of events. Clara got married, then *her* mother died, then Lewis' mother died. The great happiness of the wedding quickly got eclipsed by these two sorrows that followed. Grimly, Clara thinks that these double deaths were like an omen. In fact, really – in many ways – there were three deaths that year.

But at least Clara was twenty five when her mother went. The thought of losing your mother when you were a child seems too unbearable. Her children are eight and six now. Ursula is almost exactly the same age that Lewis was. What would happen to the children if Clara died? Would Henry install that woman here in the house? He probably would and life would just go on.

But it is not even her own children that Clara is thinking about now. Rather it is Lewis' mother, Mrs Friday. Susan was her first name and she must have been in her mid-thirties – pretty much the same age that Clara is now – when she died. Ever since that time, Clara had thought that life – in the way that it seems to – had just served the Fridays, especially Susan Friday, a particularly unlucky and tragic blow.

But now Clara finds herself wondering if Susan Friday was happy in her marriage. On the face of it she seemed to be. There were no sounds of screaming or arguments or wife beating from next door. But who can tell about such things? She's sure people look enviously at her marriage to Henry. A good man in a good job. Two beautiful children.

But what if Susan Friday was unhappy? She would have faced the same choices that Clara was facing. What Clara finds herself thinking about now is the way Susan Friday may have chosen to leave her marriage. The only way she may have seen open to her.

But what's most terrifying of all is that Clara finds she not only understands what Susan Friday's decision might have been. She now finds that she is thinking along these lines herself.

Chapter 46
Tuesday 27 June 1916

It is evening and James' section is moving up into billets behind the line. They pass fields on either side of the road where corn is ripening, golden in the westering sun. The patches of poppies that mix with the corn are blood red in the same light. It is such a beautiful country. Clara would have loved it here.

In the last week they have been through battalion, brigade and divisional practice attacks over replicas of the trenches they will be attacking in a few days time. The final one of these was referred to by the brass hats who addressed them afterwards as a 'dress rehearsal' for what is to come.

The men sing as always and there is a quiet confidence in the air. There appears to have been so much thought and care and preparation this time. The soldiers feel that somebody has actually thought about them for a change. And it looks as though the Army has at last learned the lessons of 1915. And that bombardment that thunders away to the east – it makes the original one at Neuve Chapelle (for those few survivors who can remember that far back) seem like very small fry indeed.

James keeps a diary where he notes all of this. He writes it up every evening as religiously as he can. It is what he does now instead of writing letters to Clara.

Chapter 47
Saturday 24 June 1916

It's nearly halfway through a new year and the Group of Death shows no signs of ending any time soon. In fact, the Group of Death shows no sign of going anywhere.

One big game is being played between the French and the Germans at Verdun but this is stalled. Meanwhile the British and Germans face each other across pretty much the same strip of no-man's-land that they faced each other across a year ago.

But as you know, well-informed reader, Duggy Haig is on the case. Since early in the year he has been planning a great new game. And by coincidence, he is planning it in exactly the area where James had intended to go on his walking holiday in that long-ago summer of 1914, before he met Clara.

The Somme.

The River Somme rises in Fonsommes north east of Saint Quentin in Picardy. With a gentle gradient and a steady flow, it eventually empties – two hundred and forty five kilometres later – into the English Channel. Much of it is a river that a movie of *The Wind in the Willows* could be shot on – not that anyone could imagine anything so sacrilegious, that English classic being shot in France.

James loves England but he finds it too crowded. France has lots of empty space. His intention had been to walk the Somme for at least some of its length, starting at Fonsommes. Every day he would walk somewhere between ten and a dozen miles, eat a packed lunch and then find some small hotel or inn at which to spend the night. A nice dinner, some good French wine.

It had seemed like the perfect thing to do along such a beautiful natural feature as this river.

The team that Duggy has assembled to play on the Somme is known as the Fourth Army. And the man chosen to manage the team on the Somme? Well yes, you've guessed it, suddenly depressed reader. It's Sir Henry Rawlinson. Our old friend Rawly.

Now, as you know, Rawly's record so far hasn't been that great. In footballing parlance, you could put it like this. Played: 3; Won: 0; Drawn: 0; Lost: 3. There are some teams that would be considering changing their manager after a run like that. But nothing like that is going to happen to Rawly. Indeed, I don't think it's giving too much away if I tell you that he will be a manager throughout the Group of Death, right up to when it finally ends.

Still his record doesn't give much hope for optimism – and you've got to imagine that it's downright depressing for his players, these people that he's spent so much time trying to ensure a safe passage for across no-man's-land. He has had more than a year now, since Neuve Chapelle to think about the problem and come up with a solution. So let's see what ideas he has now – one year later – for getting his men safely to a destination other than eternity.

Once again Rawly proposes a bite and hold. Facing him are three lines of German defences. His idea is to bombard the first line, attack, capture it and beat off any counter attacks. Having succeeded in all of that, he will then move up his guns, along with fresh troops and supplies and then do the same with the German second line. And so on. He proposes this to Duggy.

A couple of days later Duggy responds. As usual, he wants Rawlinson to push beyond the first German line at the first bound. Duggy's analysis (from the Battle of Loos) is that there is a period after the first assault when the enemy is disorganised and demoralised and before they have had a chance to bring up any reserves. If sufficient British troops are moving up at that time, Duggy's thinking goes, then there is a possibility of exploiting the initial success. The infantry should push on, capturing the German guns if they can. On the 12th of April Duggy orders Rawly to do exactly this.

As we know too well by now, Rawly will always change his plans based on Duggy's criticisms and this indeed is what he does. So first he writes, 'It still seems to me that an attempt to attain more distant objectives, that is to say the enemy's second line system … involves considerable risks.' And then he capitulates utterly: 'I, however, fully realise that it may be necessary to incur these risks in view of the importance of the objective to be attained. This will, no doubt, be decided by the Commander-in-Chief, and definite instructions sent to me in due course.'

(Sound of arse being licked.)

And so finally, the plan that is agreed is a five day bombardment to kill Germans and destroy German defences. This will enable the infantry to easily cross no-man's-land and take the German defences. Ideally the infantry attack will open up a gap in the German line through which the British cavalry will then charge.

There are a number of problems with this plan. And again the words of Edmund Blackadder hover perilously close in our consciousness. To begin with is the location that has been chosen for the attack. It is undoubtedly scenic – as James would have attested to, had he had a chance to make his trip there. But unfortunately, apart from its beauty, if Duggy had been trying to find a place on his front *least* suited to this kind of offensive, he probably couldn't have chosen a better one.

In the Group of Death, the primary method of transporting men, equipment and supplies is via railway. The Fourth Army, for example, needs *seventy* complete supply trains *per day*. Only two railway lines come into the Somme front, both running into the town of Albert. In particular, rail communication behind the battlefront and across it is very poor. This means that switching troops quickly from one part of the battlefield to another is very slow. The lines that run behind the battlefront are already very busy taking coal from Artois to Paris and the south of France. A line that runs to Albert from Arras and which would have been perfect for such cross-battlefield transportation is no good because it runs across no-man's-land and for part of its route is in German hands. Bummer.

Being a quiet agricultural area, the roads of the Somme are in no way suitable for sustained heavy mechanical loads. As there is no local stone suitable for road building, every ton has to be brought from other areas of France and even from Cornwall and Jersey. The supply of manpower and road stone barely keeps up, and the condition of the roads even before the offensive begins is giving great cause for concern. The plan to create forward dumps of stone will never be implemented due to shortages. Once the weather turns wet, the roads will became almost impassable bogs.

As an example, in just one twenty four hour period, the traffic passing one point on a road at Fricourt includes 26,500 men on foot, 3,756 horse drawn wagons, 5,400 horses being ridden, 813 trucks, 95 buses, 330 motor ambulances and 63 artillery guns.

Men and horses need a supply of clean water. Other than the Rivers Somme and Ancre, and a small stream between Vadencourt and Contay, there is no surface water near or on the battlefield, and none within the range planned for an advance. Many bore-holes have to be sunk and miles of pipeline and pumps laid. Water refilling points are established at various places, from which the water tank wagons of each division will supply the forward troops. This in turn means more transport on the roads. Water for washing is at a bare minimum.

In short then, the choice of the Somme as a battlefield places an enormous and unnecessary burden on the Army. Not only that, all of this activity and construction is impossible to hide from the Germans who note it with more than a passing interest.

But all of these things are not the real problem with Duggy's and Rawly's plan. Nor is it even that the plan doesn't really have an objective. Sure, they want to take the first and second German lines. But then what? Push the cavalry through the gap opened up. Okay, but then what?

No. The *real* problem with the Duggy/Rawly plan, the central, overwhelming, problem with what they are proposing is as follows.

The plan calls for a pulverising bombardment on the German lines followed by an infantry advance. The Somme battle will primarily use soldiers of the so-called New Army – volunteers who answered Kitchener's 1914 call of 'Your King And Country Need You'. While most of these soldiers, like Henry and James have been in the trenches, very few of them have ever been tested in battle. Because of this Duggy and Rawly and their planners feel that the less that is left to these men's initiative the better. The infantry will advance in a series of carefully timed waves. Given that they need to push beyond the German first lines, they will also have to carry a vast amount of supplies with them. Rolls of barbed wire, posts, carrier pigeons, telephonic equipment, extra ammunition and so on. This will all have to be carried by the men so that, including their own personal equipment, they may end up carrying sixty pounds or more. This load means that the men will not be able to move quickly. But that's alright, Duggy and Rawly conclude, because the five-day bombardment will have taken care of the German defenders.

And what of the element of surprise – a key aspect of military planning? Well, this is what the great military strategist Sun Tzu has to say on the subject of surprise: 'Engage people with what they expect; it is what they are able to discern and confirms their projections. It settles them into predictable patterns of response, occupying their minds while you wait for the extraordinary moment — that which they cannot anticipate.'

Rawly is going to have an extraordinary moment alright – but perhaps not in the way he had anticipated. And really – I mean, really – we have to say the following.

There is something in the modern-day discipline of project management called risk analysis. It is about trying to anticipate what might go wrong on a project and then trying to do something about it before it becomes a problem. It works like this.

First you try to predict what things might mess up your project. Then you gauge how likely each of these things is to happen. Then you rate how serious an impact the thing will have if it does happen.

Had Duggy and Rawly used this technique on *their* project, they might have said something like the following. Risk. The Germans survive the bombardment in significant numbers. Likelihood. Did they really gauge this as low? Impact. Clearly, if it happened, it would cause a calamity.

Rawly has chosen as his headquarters a chateau at a place called Quierrieu, outside Amiens. Set in rolling parkland, the chateau still stands today. It is a fine, three storey building of grey stone with numerous tall windows facing to the front. There is a photograph of Rawly standing on the front steps. He looks directly at the camera, carrying his swagger stick in gloved hands. His face has a kindly look about it, like a favourite uncle who always brings presents or leaves money. Here the business of war − because it is a business with all the civilities that this implies − is carried on. Close your eyes and you could be at any modern or high-tech company on a business park in Surrey.

The day begins with breakfast − bacon, eggs, freshly baked bread and rolls, good strong coffee. Then it is down to the business of the day. Motorcycle couriers begin to arrive into the airy hallway with its marble staircase and decorative wrought iron banister. They wait, perhaps feeling somewhat shabby in their mud-spattered clothes, while immaculately turned out staff officers hurry to and fro. Then the couriers depart again bearing important messages or documents. Men hurry up and down stairs or along corridors carrying pieces of paper and looking purposeful. Meetings are held and minutes issued. Documents are written and circulated and commented upon. Letters are written and dispatched confirming delivery of supplies or other war material. Phone calls can be heard coming from behind closed doors, attempting to sort out this or that problem. In rooms that have been designated conference rooms, planning sessions are held. Visitors arrive and are given lunch, for there is round the clock catering here as one would expect to find in a good, modern hotel.

But happily, all of that eases off about five or six in the evening. After another long day, the men (and there are some women) at Rawly's HQ can relax and take a break from the rigours of war. A drink before dinner, time for a chat about the events of the day, talk about plans for a trip back to England.

Then dinner, cooked by professional and talented chefs – a handful of courses, washed down with some decent wine. Brandy and cigars or a liqueur to follow. Belts let out a notch. And then perhaps a quick stroll around the park and a look at the stars. But one can always hear the rumble of artillery and see the play of the light of explosions on the underside of the clouds or in the sky off to the east. Then a last cigarette smoked on the terrace and finally to bed. A deep, comfortable bed with clean linen and plenty of pillows and a deep, safe sleep.

The chateau at Querrieu is out of range of the German artillery. And in the incredibly unlikely event of a mass German breakthrough, there would probably be very little shooting at Querrieu. If Germans were suddenly to show up at the front door, the scenes enacted would be more redolent of the Napoleonic age with swords being handed over and prisoners driven away in comfortable carriages.

It really is a world away – indeed, it might as well be a different planet – from the place eleven miles up the road where men sleep in rat-infested, sodden holes; where their clothes crawl with lice; where poor and inadequate food leave them in a permanent state of weakness and tiredness; where sleep is fitful and life can be ended at any moment by a German shell or a trench raid; where men are being shot, stabbed, shelled, maimed, blinded, drowned and gassed. Yes, it really is another world entirely.

So now, at last, we're ready to start. On what is forecast to be a dull day of low cloud and heavy rain, following thunderstorms yesterday, a new game in the Group of Death is about to kick off. Just after dawn, as the grey, sulky day under lowering clouds gradually brightens, a British gunner of the

Royal Field Artillery pushes a shrapnel shell into the breech of an 18 pounder gun. The breech block is closed and the trigger lever pulled. With a detonation like an explosive smack, the shell leaves the gun through a billowing cloud of white smoke and heads for the German lines. The Battle of the Somme has begun.

Chapter 48
Tuesday 27 June 1916

The British bombardment has been going for four days now. The British artillery is firing about 150,000 shells during the day and there is no rest for the Germans at night when another 50,000 or so, shells are fired.

On an overcast and cloudy day, Duggy Haig motors over to Rawly's headquarters at Querrieu to see how things are going. There is a piece of high ground about two hundred yards from the main road from which it is possible to look out over much of where the upcoming battle will be fought. With a jaunty sporting analogy, Rawly has christened this spot 'The Grandstand'. He takes Duggy there now and the two immaculately dressed generals, accompanied by their staffs, observe the bombardment through field glasses.

The ground trembles underfoot. The sounds of the different calibre guns carry to them, ranging from the crack of field guns to the thunder and roar of the large calibre weapons. They look out over a pale green landscape being tormented by explosions. They erupt from the ground, they blossom in the air. Black and dirty grey smoke rolls across the land. Occasionally there is a bright flash of orange or red or crimson. It all looks terribly impressive.

Of course the Grandstand is a good fifteen miles behind the British front line, so how the two great minds might interpret what they are seeing is anybody's guess.

Chapter 49
Friday 30 June 1916

The attack, which is meant to take place on the 29th of June, is postponed for two days because of bad weather. It will now happen tomorrow, the 1st of July. So this evening, James' battalion leaves Bayencourt to begin its journey up to the front. The British artillery bombardment, which has been pounding away for nearly a week now, continues its thunderous work. They go along what's known as the 'Blue Track' from its marking on their maps. They go from Bayencourt, descending into the valley behind Sailly-au-Bois and then climbing out the far side through an artillery encampment. Despite himself, James is impressed by the vast amount of men, equipment and material that has been put in place for this offensive. Maybe, he thinks. Maybe this time. Maybe nothing could stand in the way of what has been assembled here for this offensive. They turn east onto flat ground that lies between Sailly and Hebuterne. They pass many concealed artillery positions.

James finds himself daydreaming. What if this push does actually end the war? He could probably be back in London before Christmas. He is conscious of that hoary old 'over by Christmas' phrase popping up again but it seems like this time it could be. He would return to the Foreign Office of course. And Clara? Find her? Try to get her to change her mind? No. He actually shakes his head. That is all over now and gone. Whatever vistas that opened up are firmly closed down now.

His mind drifts and he wonders about staying in France. Presumably there will be all sorts of rebuilding work to be done after the war. In fact, never mind rebuilding, there will be all these dead to be found and buried and catalogued. Would there be something for him here? He loves this country and would like to do something more fruitful with the rest of his life. Indeed, given how badly the Foreign Office failed the nation and its people, maybe it's the last place on earth he should be thinking of returning to. Maybe he should be really trying to get as far away from it as possible.

They reach Hebuterne and James' mind returns to the task in hand. Tomorrow, his platoon is going to be 'consolidators'. This means that they won't be in the first wave of men that goes over but rather in a subsequent wave. Their task will be to strengthen and enhance the sections of trench captured by the attackers in the previous waves. To enable them to do this they draw all manner of entrenching material including stakes and rolls of barbed wire from a supply dump near the ruined church.

'I'm like Christ on his fucking way to fucking Calvary,' James hears one man say, as he takes up one end of a post that carries a roll of barbed wire. The man and his colleague, bowing slightly under the weight, form up for the journey into the trench system. Those first waves better have done their job properly tomorrow, James thinks. Otherwise the journey across no-man's-land will be a catastrophe.

They enter the trench system and pass a sign that reads 'If you don't want to become a landowner in France, keep well down whilst crossing the sunken road.' They make slow progress. There are some desultory shrapnel bursts and at one stage a brief minenwerfer bombardment, but it is the width of trenches that is the main problem. They really haven't been dug wide enough – particularly for the loads the men are carrying. Again and again they are brought to a halt as a sheaf of stakes or a roll of barbed wire snags on some overhead telephone wire or some protrusion in the trench. Runners making their way down the trenches to the rear add to the delays as they try to work their way past the endless files of soldiers moving up.

James had hoped they would be in position by midnight. But in the end, midnight, one, two and three o'clock all go by. It is 3:40 by the time they time they reach their allotted position.

Henry's battalion also has a long night. The communication trenches up to the front are packed with soldiers searching for their allotted jumping off positions. All over this part of France, men take wrong turnings and end up in places they were not meant to be. When this is discovered they are sent back down the lines again, colliding with the endless stream of others who are moving up. There is much cursing and shouting and all the while, a steady German bombardment causes early casualties. Officers with lists and flashlights stand at trench junctions trying to sort out confusion. Others hurry past importantly. 'Let me through. I must get through.' All the while, the heavily burdened soldiers push forward, sometimes at little more than a shuffle, moving a few paces at a time.

In London, just after tea, Clara finds she has developed a headache. She used to get a lot of headaches in her childhood, when things were difficult between her parents. Then the headaches disappeared for a while after her marriage but she started to have them in the years leading up to the discovery of Henry's affair. Since she last saw James, they have been a regular feature of her life.

Ordinarily, Clara takes nothing for it and the headache passes. Or if one is particularly bad she will take aspirin. Very occasionally – it's happened once or twice a year – the headache is so bad that it will make her vomit and she has to take to her bed. There, generally, a night's sleep and aspirin every few hours will see it gone. After that, all that will remain will be a sort of drowsy numbness which will take a day or so to clear.

Tonight's headache rapidly becomes worse than normal. It is all she can do to get the children to bed and then she goes to bed herself. Mercifully, sleep quickly enfolds her. She dreams that she and James are together. He is in civilian clothes and they are in London. She wears a beautiful dress and a hat and they walk arm in arm. It is as though they are married. In the dream she has no sense of the existence of Henry. And the dream is incredibly vivid. Clara can hear the gentle murmur of James' voice. She can smell him. She can touch his hand or his face and when she does, the sensation of skin on skin is electric, sparkling, like the bubbles in champagne. She speaks and he smiles or laughs his warm laugh. Clara is happy, blissfully, unbelievably happy.

The dream is so real, so vivid that it catapults Clara into instant waking. And as she does so, she collides with the headache so that it feels as if she has been hit with a club.

Chapter 50
Saturday 1 July 1916

As midnight passes and the new day begins, the bodies of the men standing in the twenty five miles of front line trenches from which the assault will be launched begin to undergo a series of automatic physical changes triggered by the fear that they are feeling.

Blood diverts to the large muscles of their bodies, particularly their legs. This is to aid what is known as the flight response – their desire to escape. More simply, it is so that they can run away. The draining of the blood away from the skin means that faces go a corpse-like white. As the hour for jumping off gets closer, adrenaline pours into their bloodstreams and muscles.

Clara is still awake. Try as she does, sleep won't return. After six aspirin tablets her headache is as bad as ever. She wonders if she is dying. Has something terrible happened in her brain so that the end has come? She finds that the thought doesn't frighten her nearly as much as she would have imagined. She would miss the children, of course. And while there was a time when she would have worried what would happen to them, she finds she is strangely calm about that now. It's not that she knows, but rather that it doesn't really seem to matter to her any more. And the notion that this makes her a terrible mother doesn't really impact on her either.

If she died and James did too, then they would be together. And she finds the notion of a life together with him in that strange and far-distant other country very soothing. In fact, it doesn't seem so far distant any more. If she is dying, as she believes she is, maybe she is very close to it.

On the Somme, the moon has set and the cloud is starting to break up. James' men are exhausted and the trenches are jammed. The four platoons of the company are due to go over the top at seventy yard intervals. So the first platoon occupies the front line trench, the second the communication trench and the remaining two are crowded into the support line.

The commanders of the front line platoons have sent out patrols into no-man's-land. These have returned to report that a considerable portion of the German wire has been cut. This welcome news filters back to the consolidators. But it is the only good news in a grim few hours. German artillery is busy and between overhead shrapnel bursts and occasional high explosive shells landing on the crowded trenches, the battalion takes a number of casualties. A rum ration is given out along with hot pea soup.

At 6:25, the sound of the German artillery fire is obliterated as the final British bombardment opens up.

Over the next hour, as watches tick down to zero, the men experience a dramatic sharpening of perception and a heightening of their senses. The effect is quite unreal. They seem to be able to see things in much more vivid and minute, almost microscopic detail. A splinter on a trench ladder, crumbs of earth vibrating due to the bombardment, the coarse surface of the metal of the bolt of their rifle.

Time seems to slow down, so much so that without looking at a watch they can no longer judge it. The images they see and hear and smell – the men around them, the extraordinary blue of the sky, the smell of explosives – are imprinting themselves on their brains like a series of photographs taken in rapid succession. The men feel a knot in their stomachs as their digestive juices shut off. Their bodies are closing down any non-essential systems in preparation for escape.

The hands of Henry's watch are past 7:00 now. He makes his way along the crowded trench, amongst his men, checking on them. Doing it takes his mind off what is soon to come. One man is writing a letter with a pencil on a folded piece of paper.

Several are praying. Most are smoking, the cigarettes shaky in their hands. One man, King, is staring off into space. His eyes are wide and the pupils appear larger than normal. His face is so white he looks dead.

'All right, King?' shouts Henry, above the noise of the bombardment.

There is no reply, even when Henry repeats and almost screams, the question. Henry shakes King by the arm. This seems to have some effect.

'Twenty minutes, King. You all right?'

King looks at Henry as though he was a stranger and then seems to look through him.

Henry turns to the man beside him.

'Make sure he goes over, Peters, won't you? He has to go over.'

'Right-ho, sir. I'll push him up ahead of me.'

'Good man.'

When Henry has spoken to everybody, he takes his place at the foot of the trench ladder. He is *very* afraid.

Henry has been in the Army for nearly two years now. In that time he hasn't suffered a scratch. No wounds, no illness, no disease, nothing. During that time so many men have come and gone. The ones from 1914 – the men who joined up with him – there are hardly any in the battalion now. He is hard put to think of even a single one and that time, those first few happy, optimistic months, are like they were from another age – or happened to a different person. So many men have appeared and then disappeared again – taken by death or wounding. Henry has come though all of this unscathed. He wonders how much longer his luck can hold.

In fact he knows his luck cannot hold. And so he wonders if today will be the day.

At 7:30, the whistles blow and Henry, James and thousands of other British soldiers go over the top.

Henry is already out of the trench and standing on its lip, waiting for his platoon to get up the ladder and form up, when Peters, the man whom Henry had assigned to make sure King got out of the trench, tries to do exactly that. But King's flight response has gone awry. Too much blood has rushed from his brain to his large muscles. The result is that when Peters tries to push him towards the ladder, King faints, falling onto his knees. He is unable to fall any further due to the overcrowding in the trench.

'Fucking coward,' screams Peters, stepping over him – actually – standing *on* him, onto King's shoulder and then from there onto the second rung of the ladder. As the other men follow, King is left behind.

In the normal course of events, this is what would have happened. Military police working for the division's Assistant Provost Marshal would have found King behind in the trench with the rest of his unit gone over. They would have taken him away and within days he would have been in front of a court martial. The charge would have been 'misbehaving before the enemy in such a manner as to show cowardice', an offence which carries the death penalty.

In all, a little over three hundred thousand British soldiers are court martialled during the Group of Death. Since nearly ninety percent of these courts martial resulted in convictions, it is almost certain that King would have been convicted. The result of this would have been that shortly thereafter, he would have found himself standing in front of a British firing squad in the chill, watery light of dawn, smoking a last cigarette.

However, that is not what happens. A short while after he faints, a minenwerfer shell crashes onto the part of the trench where King now lies, having fallen face down. Mercifully he is still unconscious when this happens. When the smoke clears and the dust settles, there is no evidence that a man was ever there.

Clara has slept again but wakes a little after 6:30 AM – what would be a little after 7:30 AM in France. If anything, her headache is worse.

She knows she should think about the girls but all she can focus on right now is what is going on in her body. She needs to go to the toilet and slowly, gingerly gets out of bed. Because she has been sleeping naked, she has to put on the nightdress, which she still keeps on a chair beside the bed. The effort of doing this is almost too much. And it is so painful to be upright that she goes down on all fours and this is how she makes her way across the bedroom floor. Like a dog begging, she opens the door and then continues on her hands and knees to the bathroom. Here, kneeling at the toilet, she throws up what she last had to eat and continues to retch until there is nothing more.

Having gone to the toilet, it is all she can do to get back to bed where merciful sleep eventually overtakes her again.

Another man who goes over the top on this blue and green summer's morning is Captain Frank Richards, Mary's beau. Some officers have chosen to go over dressed as enlisted men. It is a well known tactic on both sides to shoot at officers leading an assault since the result can often lead to confusion and chaos amongst the attacking troops. But Frank, with an almost childish belief in what he has been told by his superior officers – namely, that the attack is going to be a walkover – decides not to do that.

In the end, it doesn't actually matter that much. The machine gun that rakes the line of men walking through the tall grass as though out for a country stroll, is completely undiscriminating when it comes to where it places its bullets. The weapon is well operated by an experienced gunner with plenty of ammunition. The man has spent a week underground with very little food or water and in terror of being buried alive. Now he is only too happy to be out in the air and getting a chance to retaliate. With the sun warm on his back, in shirtsleeves, like a machine operator on a hot factory floor, the gunner traverses his gun from left to right in relaxed, unhurried movements.

The result is like something seen at a fairground. The long row of men that stretches off endlessly in both directions falls as the machine gun tracks along them. The effect is quite literally like that of a scythe on high grass. Occasionally, a man is left standing where the gun has passed and the gunner tut-tuts to himself. But there is no problem. The gunner's colleagues, who line the parapet, take care of the remaining ones with their rifles. Indeed there is so little for the riflemen to do that they end up taking pot shots at any prone bodies that they see moving.

The machine gunner reaches the right hand end of his traverse, the belt of bullets is replaced and then he starts back again in the opposite direction. The first traverse put a bullet in Frank Richard's leg, the same leg that had been broken when he first met Mary. This drops him to the ground where he crawls trying to find some shelter. But the land is quite even here and there are no shell holes nearby. On its way back, the machine gun puts four more bullets into Frank Richard's head and shoulders. The result is that from the neck up he is unrecognisable – not just as having once been Frank Richards but as having been a man.

Rawly's plan doesn't just go badly wrong. It goes *catastrophically* wrong. Each of the key elements in turn goes wrong and these then combine to deliver a disaster of epic proportions. Even Edmund Blackadder, normally a man equal to the task of describing such a cock-up, would have found himself hard put to find words for this occasion.

The disaster begins with the barbed wire. The British decide to use shrapnel shells to cut the barbed wire. Shrapnel – many tiny steel balls inside a shell which is exploded in the air and then sprays out its lethal cargo in a cone shape underneath it – is an anti-infantry weapon. It is the modern day equivalent of the canister used by the gunners at Waterloo and in the battles of the American Civil War. Used against living men, shrapnel is a terrifying and deadly weapon. But against barbed wire, it has little effect.

High explosive, on the other hand, had it been used, would have essentially vaporised the German barbed wire. At worst it would have created paths through the German wire through which the British would have been able to pass. But the shrapnel merely succeeds in rearranging the German wire so that in some ways, it becomes an even greater obstacle than when the Germans first deployed it.

There are indeed some parts of the British front where the wire cutting by the artillery has been partially successful. It was one of these that was reported on by the men of James' battalion last night. But many patrols that were sent out during the night reported the wire as being uncut. As this unwelcome message was fed up the chain of command, the message that was passed back down was that the men in the front line – primarily men of the untried Kitchener battalions – were 'windy'. In other words, nervous, jumpy, nervy, panicky.

The second element of Rawly's plan that goes as wrong as it could possibly go is the seven day bombardment of the German trenches. As well as cutting the German wire, the other intention of the bombardment was to pulverise the German trenches to ruins and to either kill their occupants or reduce them to whimpering wrecks.

In reality this is not what happens. The Germans have had a good year and a half to prepare their defences on the Somme. They have put that time to good effect. The defensive systems they have created are truly terrifying – from the attacker's point of view. And just to make sure that they will get a chance to use these defences, the Germans have created protective shelters for their men. These shelters – dugouts which in some cases are more than forty feet below ground – can survive whatever the British artillery can throw at them. While the last seven days have not been a picnic for the Germans taking refuge in their dugouts, they are still alive and in full possession of their faculties. In fact they are raring to go and to have the chance to strike back at their tormentors.

And finally, just to make sure that no cock-up is left undone, there is Rawly's idea that the new Kitchener troops are not resourceful or inventive or capable of innovative action. As a result he has determined that they should make their way across no-man's-land in waves, walking – yes, it's not a typo, appalled reader – *walking* towards the enemy.

And so the disaster unfolds in the first hour or two of this perfect summer morning. The wire isn't cut in many places. This delays the troops who are already moving slowly anyway. Where the wire is cut, channels have been created through the wire. Where else are the Germans going to aim their machine guns?

Once the British bombardment stops, the Germans have ample time to hurry up their ladders from their dugouts and deploy their machine guns. And they needn't have hurried particularly anyway because between the wire and the slow pace of the British advance, they are in plenty of time when the long lines of soldiers in khaki, stretching off endlessly to either side, start to appear in their gun sights.

The walking to the enemy front line completes the catastrophe for the British. They lose almost sixty thousand men, killed, wounded, missing or captured. Nearly twenty thousand are killed.

This is the Group of Death alright, but a group of death on a scale few could have imagined.

For B Company, the company of which James' platoon is a part, it also all goes as wrong as it possibly could. The first waves have difficulty getting through their own wire. When they do, they find that a large proportion of the German wire is uncut. A few men eventually find a gap and go through but by the time James' men arrive carrying their loads, a German machine gun has taped the gap, resulting in quite literally a heap of dead, dying and wounded men piling up in front of it. James sees and hears this all happening in slow motion. A man goes down and James thinks he has stumbled under his load. There are numerous bright red sprays of blood and grunts and screams as two or three more men fall. There is a smell of a too warm butcher's shop – hot blood. But then men start falling like ninepins, piling up one on top of the other and the crazy racket of the several machine guns becomes loud. James thinks of a factory – the machines turning out falling men.

Once again, James is only in action for a short while. He is untouched by machine gun or rifle bullets. Instead, a shell, bursting about ten yards away from him, sends a jagged piece of red-hot casing flying through the air. The piece of shell is about the same size as a domestic coal shovel but made of far heavier material. Created by the detonation of the shell it has ghastly sharp edges. It flies through the air, spinning as it goes. The effect is as if a propeller had come off an aeroplane.

Of course all of this happens in a fraction of a second and the whirling piece of metal still has most of its momentum when it collides with the right side of James' body. His right arm is the first thing it connects with, instantly reducing it to a pulp of blood and tissue and skin and bone held together – well, sort of, anyway – inside his sleeve. The impact winds him and knocks him to the ground. But his arm also absorbs most of the force of the shell fragment so that it doesn't go much further or do any more damage to his ribs or internal organs. Instead it thuds to the ground. But by then James has already fallen and lies unconscious just on the British side of a pile of machine gunned men in khaki.

Henry finds himself in a German trench. He is struck by how well built it is and how the British bombardment, while it has certainly done some damage, hasn't done anything like what he would have expected. Either the bombardment missed most of the trench or else the Germans built it in such a way that it could withstand everything the British could throw at it. Neither thought gives Henry much comfort.

He thinks at first that the trench is unoccupied – that the Germans have either fled or are all dead. But there are no bodies and his first impression is quickly dispelled when a potato masher grenade appears in the air, falls and lands on the duckboards about two yards in front of him.

'Grenade!' he shrieks and without even thinking, ducks into the entrance to a dugout on his left. In the sudden gloom he can see a series of nicely carpentered wooden steps leading down into darkness.

The move saves Henry's life. Unfortunately, it exposes the men who were following him to the full impact of the grenade. One is killed outright and the other has the entire front of his body shredded by steel fragments. His face erupts in a mask of blood and he falls to the ground clutching it in his hands and screaming. Henry steps back out of the dugout and in a reflex action, turns slightly to look at the wounded man.

Thus he is facing away when there is a dull thud of metal on wood and a second grenade clatters onto the duckboards. It explodes instantly, disappearing in a yellow flash and a cloud of dust and smoke and bits of timber and steel. Henry hears the sound of a detonation but it is already very far away.

It is night when James awakes. He is face down with his left cheek resting on the hard earth. The ground exudes a chemical smell and there is a terrible pain all along his right side and arm. But he moves his legs and they respond; they seem to be intact. His left arm also seems to work. He uses it to roll onto his back. Overhead the sky is full of stars. There is the constant rumble of artillery but it seems remote. The crack of rifle fire and the occasional nerve-shredding industrial rattle of a machine gun are closer, though James hears no bee sting buzzing of bullets as he did earlier today.

Mainly, the sounds he hears are the sounds of men. There is screaming – near, in the middle distance and fading off into Christ knows where. Somebody close by is muttering, someone else is weeping and a rather posh voice keeps repeating, 'Mummy, Mummy, oh gentle Jesus'. A voice calls, 'Help me, please help me.' The sounds of some individuals are quite distinct and these rise from a general background of groans of pain and shouts of delirium that seem to rise to the heavens and fill the night sky.

James passes out again so that the sounds are lost to him, just as they cannot be heard at Rawly's headquarters seventeen miles away.

In London Clara has spent the day in bed. Mrs Parsons stayed all day, took care of the girls and saw them off to sleep. Clara's head feels as though it has expanded and that, at any moment, it is going to explode. Earlier in the day, she had tried to work out what was causing this but she has given up on that now. Now all she can do is try to climb to the top of the pain. She thinks that if only she could sleep, she would eventually wake and it would be gone. She knows she should call the doctor but she cannot afford his fee. And anyway, if she is dying, what can he do for her?

Eventually, long after she had given up trying, sleep claims her. The 1st of July is over.

Chapter 51
Sunday 2 July 1916

When James next wakes he is lying on his back and there is a little light in the sky. The sounds of wounded men that he heard whenever it last was, are still there but they are noticeably quieter. He is unbelievably thirsty and goes to find his water bottle. He signals his body to move his right arm and immediately a shattering lance of pain spears its way all down his right side. He becomes dizzy, disoriented and it is some time before he ventures to move at all. He looks down and sees that his right sleeve is completely caked in dried blood. The sleeve also looks strangely collapsed – like there's nothing in it. With his left hand, he reaches down to where his water bottle should be but he is unable to find it.

Clara wakes and lifting herself on one elbow pours some water from a pitcher into a glass. The curtains are open – Mrs Parsons went to close them last night but Clara asked her not to – and Clara reckons that dawn is not too far away. She sips a little water. Is it her imagination or has the pain eased a little? She drinks a little more and then buries her head in the pillow and sleep comes quickly.

James comes to again. It is light. Very early morning to judge by the clarity of the air and the pale blue of the sky. A mound of bodies in khaki lies beside him. There is the sound of distant firing – the usual chorus of artillery and machine gun – but it is a long way off. Around here seems to be unnaturally quiet. He lifts his left arm to check his watch but the instrument has been smashed – presumably when he fell. The glass is broken and one of the hands is missing. He feels terribly weak and is in a lot of pain. But his head is clear enough to know that he needs to get back to the British line. The only question is – which way is it?

He tries to remember what happened. The pile of dead men – was it already there when he was hit? Did he fall behind them or in front of them? The whole question is far too complicated. He gives up trying to work it out.

He tries to see the sun, to work out where east is but it is still too low in the sky. He could stay until it rose higher but he knows he is badly wounded and between that and his raging thirst, chances are he wouldn't last that long. He needs to do something. Weren't they attacking slightly uphill? So if he goes downhill he should arrive at the British line. And downhill should make all this a bit easier.

But he knows too that he can't stand up. He is in no-man's-land. He's going to have to crawl.

James digs the fingers of his left hand into the ground, then pulls with his left arm and at the same time pushes with his feet. The movement triggers fearsome pain on his right side. He makes minute progress and has broken out into a sweat.

Clara is trying to get to the bathroom and again she is on all fours. The distance to the bathroom seems endless. No matter how much she crawls she cannot seem to get any closer. The house suddenly consists of long corridors which she knows she must travel if she is to reach the bathroom.

She can't remember why she wants to get to the bathroom because she knows there is nothing further for her body to discharge. She drifts off to sleep. Or maybe she was already asleep.

In the Gommecourt sector, the area where James' battalion went over the top, the local British and German commanders organise a truce. Tentatively, at first and then with more confidence, stretcher bearers and soldiers from both sides make their way out into no-man's-land and begin to gather in the wounded. By this time James has been several hours making his painful way towards not the British but rather the German line. Every few minutes he has had to rest and sometimes he has passed out. It is a German stretcher bearer wearing a Red Cross armband who finds James.

'Hey, English,' he calls to some British soldiers about a hundred yards away. The German points down to his feet. 'For you – English. You come.'

It is dark by the time James reaches the Casualty Clearing Station. He is brought into the darkness of a tent lit by storm lamps. Ordinarily he would be classed as walking wounded but he has lost so much blood that he is unable to walk. He is given blood and then the stretcher he is on is placed in the pre-operation area. An orderly lights a cigarette and gives it to him. James' left arm is now so weak that he is unable to lift it. The orderly holds the cigarette for him while James draws a few grateful puffs.

He is barely conscious so that he only has a vague impression of where he is. There is darkness above him but yellow light on the edge of his field of vision. There is movement – people coming and going. Quiet voices murmur. Occasionally there is a moan or groan or gasp of pain.

Some time later, James' stretcher is lifted up and he is carried a short distance. There is suddenly a strong hospital smell of chloroform, the sounds of instruments being dropped into metal trays. James is lifted gently from the stretcher onto a table. A face appears above him. Sandy hair that in the lamplight appears almost blonde. Bloodshot eyes. A tired smile.

'Evening, lieutenant. Nothing for you to worry about now. You're in good hands.'

The words sound like they have been specially minted for him. James wants to say something but he doesn't know what. His brain appears to be operating at a very slow speed. He moves his lips in the hope that it will help but they're cracked and swollen. Before he can utter a sound, a mask is put over his nose and mouth and in seconds he knows no more.

In London, Clara wakes to find that it is night time again. She remembers Mrs Parsons telling her that the girls were fine and had gone to bed. Did she dream this? Did it actually happen? She doesn't know. She is very weak and lies on her back, her head sunk into the pillows. She becomes aware that her headache is gone. Tentatively she lifts her head fearfully anticipating that the movement will cause it to return. But it doesn't. It is really gone and Clara realises that she is voraciously hungry.

Chapter 52
Wednesday 5 July 1916

Some time after his operation James is transferred to No. 24 General Hospital at Etaples. He has a faint memory of being moved and of a train journey, but so faint that it could have been a dream. When he wakes he is lying on his back in a long ward with beds stretching away on either side of him. There is still pain in his arm but it is not as bad as it was. He wants to pull himself up and so goes to brace his hands on the bed. But then he remembers his right hand. Gingerly he leaves that one and uses his left hand and elbow to lever himself into an upright position.

A nurse, standing in the centre aisle, sees him and begins to walk in his direction. She is pretty, in her thirties with blonde hair. Something doesn't feel right about James' body. It is as though his balance is all wrong.

'Ah, lieutenant, you're with us,' the blonde nurse says with a smile.

The smile reminds James of Clara's smile. He looks down at his body, to the right and to the left, trying to understand what's wrong. He can't see his right arm and he finds himself turning to the right, stretching, trying to find it. Is it behind his back?

The nurse is by the side of his bed now. She plumps up his pillows and helps to lay him back against them.

'My arm?'

They are the first coherent words James has spoken in days – apart from things he may have said while he was delirious in no-man's-land, in the hospital tent or recovering from the anaesthetic. A momentary darkness crosses the nurse's face like a cloud crossing a landscape. Her smile fades but even then her face is still pretty. Then the smile returns.

She says, 'You're alive, lieutenant. And soon you'll be going home.'

'Soon you'll be going home.' The words reverberate in James' head for the rest of the day. They, even more than the loss of his arm, are the first things that take possession of him. Home. To what? To who? To what home? A house? Is that a home? When he left England, he felt he had a home. It was the one that he was going to build with Clara and her two daughters. Now he thinks of the emptiness he will be returning to. Invalided out of the Foreign Office. That house of his which once was his refuge and once indeed, *was* his home. But not now. Now, it's just a place to sleep, to shelter from the elements, to live out the rest of his life.

It is much later, and darkness has come, when he starts to think about his arm. He is vaguely conscious of the practicalities. He is going to have to learn to write again. How will he shake hands? Lots of things are going to be awkward. Can you tie shoelaces with one hand? He was never much of a one for gardening but he did keep his little patches of ground front and back neat and tidy. How will all that work now?

But it is his right hand. It is the one he used to explore Clara's body and he remembers what he did with it and the pleasure he gave her, so that at times in its aftermath she seemed weak, transported, not quite of this world. By losing his arm and especially his hand, he has lost all of that. By chopping off his hand they have taken memories of her; memories that his body had of her. It was one of the many things he loved so much about the brief time he had with her – how his body remembered her body. Much of that has been taken now.

For the first time ever in his life, James wishes he had died.

Chapter 53
Saturday 15 July 1916

Since Mary is not Frank Richards' next of kin, she doesn't receive any notification of his death. That goes to his parents, both of whom are still alive.

But Mary has been scanning the vast casualty lists that have been appearing in the papers since early July. Today she finds him under the blunt heading 'DIED'. She feels a great sadness for Frank. He was a fine and decent man. She wonders about his parents whom she never met. He was their only son – their only child actually. From what he told her it seemed like he was very close to them, especially his mother. Truly it will be a terrible blow to them. But, as she folds the paper and puts it on the seat of the car, she finds that her overwhelming feeling is one of 'back to square bloody one'.

Chapter 54
Monday 31 July 1916

This terrible July finally comes to an end. However, one great man for whom it hasn't been terrible at all – and who carries a major share of the responsibility for what's been happening – is the former Foreign Secretary, Sir Edward Grey. You may remember, dear reader, that Sir Edward played a major role in the early part of our story.

This month he moves to the House of Lords and becomes Viscount Grey of Falloden. Ever the ornithologist, he will go on to write *The Charm of Birds* and die peacefully in his bed at the age of seventy one.

Chapter 55
Tuesday 15 August 1916

James is on a ship bound for England. He remembers similar journeys he made from before the war. He would be returning to the Foreign Office after his annual two weeks in France. He recalls that while he was always sad to be leaving, he knew he would be back before too long. Apart from his holidays, he occasionally got to travel to France on Foreign Office business. That was almost always to Paris rather than the countryside – but it was France. That was all that mattered. How content he was then.

Today, he is doing just as he used to do then. The day is sunny but there is a stiff breeze on the Channel. Sitting in the lee of the ship's superstructure, he smokes a pipe and reads. He has become quite used to holding a book in his left hand and he no longer notices that he has to put the book down when he wants to turn the page. There is still a low level of pain where his right arm used to be and he tries not to take the pain killers that the doctor prescribed for him; wouldn't be good to get addicted to those damn things. These days, six weeks after what remained of his arm was removed, he tries to keep the pain killers just for the night – so that he can sleep.

His arm was removed very close to his shoulder. There is no stump that he could potentially use. He really is a man with one arm.

He is not concentrating on the book. Rather he is thinking of that arm – how it once held Clara protectively to him. His right hand – how it stroked her, caressed her skin. Where it explored.

The things it was capable of doing to her. He wonders where the arm is now. Burnt? Buried?

What will he do back in England? He will be invalided out of the Army and out of the Foreign Office. He'll have a pension – actually two pensions, he imagines. He could leave England and go to live in France – something he had intended to do anyway when he retired. Of course, he couldn't go now. But the war must end sometime – though how exactly, he cannot see. This titanic effort that the British are continuing to put in seems to be yielding such pathetic results that it is hard to see how the thing could ever end. And supposing the Germans were to win – would this mean they would occupy France and he could never go back? No. That is too unthinkable. Back then, before he met Clara, before the war, the course of his life had been pretty much mapped out. Now, he feels as though he never wants the ship to dock. If he could just stay here on the sea suspended between two worlds.

Clara stands in the hallway of the house in Horn Lane. She rereads the letter she has just received, trying to make sense of it. The piece of buff coloured paper is headed 'Army Form B. 104-83'. It tells her that 'a report has been received from the War Office' that Henry 'was posted as missing on the 1-7-16.'

It is the next few sentences that she tries to make sense of.

'The report that he is missing does not necessarily mean that he has been killed, as he may be a prisoner of war or temporarily separated from his regiment.

Official reports that men are prisoners of war take some time to reach this country, and if he has been captured by the enemy, it is probable that unofficial news will reach you first. In that case, I am to ask you to forward any letter received at once to this Office, and it will be returned to you as soon as possible.

Should any further information be received, it will be at once communicated to you.'

Clara is stunned. Of all the things she had envisaged, she had never imagined this.

Chapter 56
Monday 16 October 1916

James has been to fetch the paper and has read it over breakfast. The day stretches ahead of him. Later in the week, on Wednesday, he has to go for a check up and on Friday he is having lunch with a former colleague from the Foreign Office. Other than that, his week is empty.

James is not independently wealthy so he has always had to work. He remembers how, when he *was* working, he imagined that if he somehow became wealthy and didn't have to work any more, there were so many things that he would do. Now he finds it hard to imagine what these things could have been because right now, no matter how hard he racks his brains, he cannot think of a single one.

Clara is at the kitchen table rereading one of James' letters. He is talking about the Somme – now she knows how it is spelled. 'This is a beautiful country. What a pity I didn't get to come here before the war. I fear it will be very different afterwards.'

She looks out the window. It is a cold, overcast day with a strong wind. Leaves from the beech tree her father planted are plucked from it and scattered by the wind. She remembers a phrase from one of James' other letters – 'blustery autumn days of wind blown leaves'. Yes, it *is* a blustery autumn day of wind blown leaves.

Clara feels paralysed. Is Henry alive or dead? She's heard nothing since she received Army Form B. 104-83. What is she to do? She has told the girls nothing. Sufficient unto the day is the evil thereof. But if he *is* dead? Could she? Find James again?

That's assuming *he* is alive. She has his address. She could write to him. But what would she say? Would he even *read* a letter from her now?

But she could write. It would do no harm. At least she might find out if he is still alive. And if he is, she might get to see him again. To speak with him. To see his face and touch his hand. To just be in his company.

Clara goes into the sitting room, gets some paper and her fountain pen and writes a letter. She puts it in an envelope, seals and addresses it.

But then a wave of doubt washes over her. James won't want to see her again. Not after the way she treated him. If he is feeling as unhappy as she has been, then why would he possibly want to draw that on himself again? And he is in France for Christ's sake, fighting. Maybe he has other things on his mind other than Clara and love and such stupid things.

Clara takes the envelope and puts it between the pages of her diary, which she then locks away in the drawer of her bedside locker.

Chapter 57
Monday 13 November 1916

James is in an armchair in his sitting room having just finished reading today's *Times*. He got up early as he always does, washed, shaved and began reading the paper over breakfast. He finished it in here. His cleaning lady is not due to come in today. He stares out through the net curtains at the world outside. It is a dark, rain-sodden day. There were so many days like this in the trenches. But he remembers they weren't all like this. And it occurs to him that he should be writing down his memories.

Now this is not the first time this thought has occurred to him. And while his initial excuse for not doing anything had been the fact that he had lost his writing hand, he has been doing physical therapy. And part of that therapy has been learning to write with his left hand. With the result that now he can. Admittedly, he cannot write very quickly. The last time he was at therapy, when the nurse praised his progress, he said that he reckoned he was at the same standard he was at when he was in first form in school, forming his letters slowly and with great care. He told her about a boy from his class who would always have his tongue sticking out the side of his mouth when he wrote. It was as though the effort involved required other parts of his body to be put temporarily out of use. James mimicked him and the nurse laughed.

This morning, for a reason that James cannot explain, he goes to a cupboard in his desk and opens it. In it are nearly a dozen empty notebooks, all very attractive, all of different sizes and colours and styles. He laughs at himself. These are books that he picked up when he was out shopping, each time intending to start what he jokingly thinks of as his 'memoirs'. He picks a nice fat one with a black cover and beautifully marbled endpapers. The paper is good quality and an off-white, almost yellow colour.

He places the book on the desk, opens it after the marbling and presses on the line between the two pages to flatten them. Deftly he unscrews the cap of the fountain pen, flips the pen and puts the cap back on at the other end. He hesitates. What title to write? 'My life in the Army'? 'An Officer's Tale'? 'Surviving Hell'?

Finally, he writes simply, 'The War'.

He underlines it and then writes, painstakingly slowly: *'My war began in a serene and beautiful and loving place.'*

The fact that he writes so slowly forces him to think out the sentence before he writes it down. He remembers it was what their teacher told them to do in school.

'It began on Wednesday July 29, 1914. By then I was hopelessly in love.'

Clara wearily begins another week. The children are gone to school and Mrs Parsons is upstairs cleaning. It is raining, as it has been for the last few days, and Clara wonders if it will ever stop. She would really like to get out and do some tidying in the garden.

She thinks about how life goes for most people. They are born, grow up, get married, have children and die. We're alone, we meet somebody else and we have our family. But then, at the end, we're ultimately alone again – even if we die with people around us. But it seems to Clara that she has already reached that point of aloneness – even though she is only thirty four and in theory, has much of her life yet to live.

The girls will rapidly grow up now and start to live their own lives. And even if Henry is alive and comes back, her marriage might as well be over. So she is in that alone place that comes just before death, but she is nowhere near dead. At least not physically.

'At least not physically.'

She actually finds she has said the words aloud to herself.

Of course, she is all too aware that she might have taken a different road entirely with James. But there is no point in thinking about that now.

On the Somme, incredible as it may seem, gentle reader, Duggy and Rawly are still slugging away. The day begins with a mine containing thirteen tons of explosive and detonated under Hawthorn Ridge, a place that already saw a mine explosion on the 1st of July. This time, both Hawthorn Ridge and the village behind it, Beaumont Hamel, are captured.

The Battle of the Somme will finally come to an end this coming Saturday. Dwarfing all previous games in the Group of Death, this one will have cost the British and French about 625,000 casualties – the majority of them British – and the Germans about half a million.

Chapter 58
Thursday 15 March 1917

Russia has not been having a good Group of Death. Nearly six million soldiers have been killed, wounded, captured or are missing. The Army took fifteen million men from the farms and the result of this is that food prices have soared. Butter costs five times as much as it did three years ago. In Petrograd, supplies of flour and fuel have all but disappeared. The severe winter just adds to the misery.

With quite staggering stupidity, Nicholas enacted prohibition to boost patriotism and productivity. Instead, all it has done is to deprive the treasury of alcohol taxes which in turn has damaged the funding of the war.

In February there are food riots and red banners start to appear on the streets. Police fire on protesters. By March the protests have become vast and on Sunday the 11th of March, some two hundred protesters are shot dead.

Next day the army mutinies. The arsenal is pillaged and the Military Government building, police headquarters, the Law Courts and a dozen police buildings are all burnt. By lunchtime the Fortress of Peter and Paul with its heavy artillery is in the hands of the insurgents. By nightfall, sixty thousand soldiers have joined the revolution.

Three days later the Tsar abdicates.

Nicholas wants to go into exile in England and initially, the British government offers him asylum. The British secret service even begins planning a rescue mission. But worried that Nicholas' presence in England might provoke similar unrest to that seen in Russia, George V, who is the Tsar's cousin, withdraws the offer.

Chapter 59
Wednesday 17 July 1918

Since his abdication, the new Bolshevik government has been keeping the Tsar and his family prisoner. They are currently in a house called the Ipatiev House in the city of Ekaterinburg on the border between European and Asian Russia.

After midnight on this warm July night, they are awakened and told to dress. Since they have been moved several times since the abdication, the family assumes that this is yet another move. They are led down into a room at the back of the house. The Tsar's party consists of himself and his wife, their four daughters and son, their doctor and three of their servants.

A squad of ten secret policemen enters the room. The man in charge reads aloud an order for the execution of Nicholas and his family. He then shoots Nicholas who dies instantly. It is probably as well that he does. He would not have wanted to see what happens next.

The other executioners then begin shooting until all of the Tsar's party has fallen. But not everybody is dead and there is much smoke in the room from all of the gunshots. The doors are opened to disperse the smoke and then the executioners go to work on those who have survived the first hail of bullets.

Tatiana, Olga and Maria are stabbed with bayonets. Both Tatiana and Olga also sustain single bullet wounds to the head. Maria crouches against a wall in terror until she is killed. The Tsar's son Alexei is the last to die. Lying on a floor covered in blood, he is moaning when he receives two bullets behind the ear.

As soon as it is light, the bodies are loaded onto a truck, taken and buried in a pit on a cart track twelve miles from Ekaterinburg.

For the Russian manager and his family, the Group of Death has been quite literally that. And just as in the sinking of the Lusitania, the Group of Death has again witnessed something else – the murder of non-combatants, people who aren't soldiers, women and children.

Chapter 60
Monday 21 May 1917

Another great man is about to enter our story, gentle reader. There's a saying that you may have heard. It goes – 'the trouble with common sense is that it's not all that common.' Similarly, I think you'll agree that up to now, many of the great men that we have encountered were … well, not all that great.

However, you'll be relieved to hear that this next man *is* great and that the things he will do will have a profound and permanent – and in some ways, quite wonderful – effect on the Group of Death. Maybe at last, we have found a great man who might actually be worthy of the name; a great man to somewhat restore the pretty tattered reputation of great men.

Let me introduce you, my dear reader, to Major General Sir Fabian Arthur Goulstone Ware KCVO KBE CB CMG, though today he is simply Fabian Ware.

When the Group of Death began, Fabian Ware already had many of the attributes we would perhaps want to see in a great man. He is educated and multilingual, having studied at universities in London and Paris. He is well travelled. He has lived in England, France and South Africa. He has done a variety of things. He has been a teacher, journalist, administrator, newspaper editor, company director.

When the Group of Death began, showing courage and patriotism, Fabian Ware attempted to join the Army. However, by that time he was forty five and so was rejected on the grounds of being too old. Showing yet another trait of great men – perseverance – Ware used a connection of his from his time in South Africa to obtain command of a British Red Cross mobile ambulance unit. He crossed to France in September 1914 and began his work.

It wasn't long before being in an ambulance unit brought Ware in contact with the dead. He saw how there was nobody really responsible for marking the graves of dead soldiers. The soldier's comrades did the best they could. They would make simple wooden crosses from ammunition boxes and scrawl the dead man's name and date of death on it, but often there was very little time or opportunity to do even this. In many cases, the bodies were dealt with as they had always been since time immemorial – dumped into unmarked mass graves and covered over. Ware saw that to take better care of the dead would be both good for the morale of the soldiers and would also comfort those left grieving at home.

In 1915 he set up an organisation within the Red Cross to do exactly this and later that year both he and his organisation were transferred from the Red Cross to the Army where it became known as the Graves Registration Commission. By October it had recorded over 31,000 graves and by May 1916 this number had grown to 50,000.

News of the work of the Graves Registration Commission quickly became public. It began to receive letters and requests for photographs of graves from relatives of soldiers who had been killed. In response, the Commission would send back photographs as well as information on how to locate a particular grave.

But as the Group of Death showed no sign of ending, Ware began to wonder about what would happen to the soldiers' graves after the war. So again using his connections, he submitted a proposal on the subject to the Imperial War Cabinet.

And today, Ware's perseverance has paid off. Today, by Royal Charter, the Imperial War Graves Commission has been created. The Prince of Wales will be its president, Lord Derby the Chairman and Ware will be Vice-Chairman.

Chapter 61
Tuesday 1 January 1918

The New Year sees a new ingredient added to the Group of Death. In the huge British Army staging area and hospital camp at Etaples in France, a flu epidemic breaks out. Due to the massive concentrations and movements of troops, the disease spreads rapidly. This is helped by the fact that many of the soldiers' immune systems are weak due to poor food, the conditions in which they have been living and the appalling stress they are under.

Chapter 62
Saturday 9 November 1918

The German manager in the Group of Death, Der Kaiser, passes the weekend by abdicating on Saturday and going into exile in the Netherlands on Sunday.

In 1919, the Allies will try to prosecute him. King George will write that he views his cousin as 'the greatest criminal in history'. But the Dutch queen, Queen Wilhelmina, will refuse to extradite him.

Der Kaiser or plain Wilhelm Hohenzollern, as he is now known, will buy a country house in Doorn in the Netherlands. Subsequently he will be allowed to remove twenty three railway wagons of furniture and twenty seven wagons of other items from his former palace at Potsdam. The other items will include a boat, Bill Hohenzollern having never lost his love of all things nautical.

Hunting and cutting down trees on his estate at Doorn will be the other passions of Bill's life during his remaining years. He will kill thousands of animals and birds and convert thousands of trees into firewood. He will die peacefully on 3 June 1941 at the quite acceptable age of eighty two, a few weeks before his country invades the Soviet Union.

Chapter 63
Monday 11 November 1918

On what will become famously known as the eleventh hour of the eleventh day of the eleventh month, the actual playing part of the Group of Death finally comes to an end. The after match statistics have yet to be totted up and of course, there is the prize giving. So contrary to what you might have expected, my perhaps slightly puzzled and patient reader, our story isn't over yet.

But we probably should deal with the remaining managers in the Group of Death as well as some of the other contestants we've come across in our journey.

The French manager, Raymond Poincaré's term as *Président de la République* will come to an end in 1920. He will spend the rest of his life in politics with several stints as French Prime Minister. He will die in Paris in 1934 aged seventy four.

Duggy Haig will be made Earl Haig and given a grant of £100,000 to enable him to live in a style appropriate to such an exalted rank. Not bad, you might say, though Duggy evidently didn't agree. He had asked for a quarter of a million. He will die of a heart attack, aged sixty six, in 1928.

Parliament will pass a vote of thanks to Rawly for his service. He will be taken ill after playing polo and cricket on his sixty first birthday and will die a month or so later in 1925.

This memorable Monday finds Clara out shopping. She hears bells suddenly ringing – but it is only when she goes into the butcher's to pick up the week's meat ration that she finds out the reason. As she makes her way home, she is unsure of what she feels. It has been over two years now and she has heard nothing further of Henry. She has a vague idea that there is something about seven years before it can be confirmed that someone is dead. But she wonders whether this has changed because of the war. And if it has changed, is it more or less? If it is seven years, Clara will be forty one then — an old woman.

The girls are ten and eight now and both at school. How much they have grown since the outbreak of the war — and how that sunny summer when it all began seems so very far away. England really was another country then. It seems like history as old as the Battle of Waterloo.

Clara wonders if she is happy that the war is over but of course, she has to be. She feels it as soon as she walks in the door and Mrs Parsons comes and embraces her. The older woman's son was in the Army before the war started at all. He has come right through it, was wounded during the Somme and again at Passchaendale but now, it looks like he has survived. That indeed is reason to be happy. Apart from the embrace, Mrs Parsons is subdued in her celebration. As she sees it, Clara hasn't been as lucky as her.

The ending of the war raises another thought in Clara's mind. If what happened to Henry was that he was taken prisoner, then he will be coming back. The thought is a black one and she feels a sense of panic as it takes hold of her. If he was to return and things went back to the way they were before James — she's not sure she could actually live with that. By which she means she would rather die.

As the day goes on, the panic builds inside her. She cannot sit here and take no action. She cannot wait for that knock on the door and as this thought occurs to her, she pictures it actually happening. A knock on the door. She goes to open it. And when she does there is Henry standing there. Henry — triumphant, having survived the war and now back to resume — as he would see it — his old life and his rightful place in the world. But a Henry even more unbearable than before. A war hero — in his own eyes at any rate and whether he was or not.

Clara must do something. The thought of sitting here day after day waiting for that knock on the door and quaking at every knock that actually comes is too appalling to contemplate. She knows of only one thing she can do.

She hurries upstairs and takes her diary from the bedside locker. Inserted in it is the letter she wrote to James more than two years ago. The envelope has yellowed in the intervening time. She is not even going to read it; she is just going to post it. She has always felt that the gods are mischievous and playful. Sometimes they do grant wishes but more often, it seems to Clara, they do so in a way that the person making the wish had never intended. What's the name of that book of poems by Thomas Hardy? Yes – *Time's Laughingstocks*. Maybe that's what she is and what she has always been.

Well, she will post this letter now and see what the gods do about that.

When the celebratory bells begin to ring, Mary is doing what she has spent a lot of the war doing. She is waiting. This time outside the War Office, for a couple of officers that she brought here earlier. People hurry past heading in the direction of Trafalgar Square. They are smiling, laughing, talking excitedly. Some carry little Union Jacks on sticks.

She wonders what the end of the war will mean for her. She and her fellow women drivers have been speculating for some time about what might happen to them when the war ended. Their contracts say 'for the duration' and while it seemed for so long that the war had become a permanent thing, that duration is over now. Even if so many drivers are still required – and this seems unlikely in a country no longer at war – what about all the men returning from the front? They're going to need jobs.

As for the men in *her* life – well, Frank Richards is dead. She has heard nothing from Henry since 1916 and since she hasn't seen his name in the casualty lists, she has to assume he is alive but has jilted her. She is thirty three now and back to exactly where she was when she first went to work at the insurance company. The years since 1914 might as well not have happened at all for all the good they have done her. In fact she's in a worse position now than she was then. She is well and truly on the shelf and she can pretty much forget about any thoughts she might have had of having a child.

She is depressed beyond belief. How many people are there in the world who have lived for five years and whose lives have not progressed one iota? It's as simple as that – the last five years have achieved nothing. Nothing except that she is older. Older and tired – very, very tired. She is bone weary at the thought of having to go back to the beginning, to rewind the clock of her life, to go over – for a second time – the ground she has already covered.

But she knows that there is nothing else for it. The first thing she is going to have to do is to secure her livelihood. She needs to see if there is still a job for her at the insurance company and she needs to do it quickly – before all these returning soldiers start showing up.

James is having lunch with Lionel Hume, his former boss at the Foreign Office. Hume was fifty when the war broke out and so was too old to enlist. James always got on well with his boss. He remembers the long conversations they used to have about Sir Edward Grey. James recalls those late nights during that long July of 1914. They saw then with the clarity of an imminent train crash how what Grey was doing was leading the country to disaster but they were unable to divert him from the course he had chosen.

'Bastard wasn't there half the time,' says Hume, as though reading James' thoughts. 'Fishing. Him and his damn fishing.'

'Anyway,' continues Hume, sawing at a piece of beef. 'Nothing we can do about all that now.'

Hume is one of those big-in-every-sense-of-the-word men. He is tall, red-faced, built like a rugby forward, with a big appetite and a hearty laugh. When James worked with him it was as though he attacked each day like he was racing for the opposing team's line with a rugby ball tucked under his arm. He hasn't changed.

'So how's that writing of yours going then, James?'

'It's going,' says James.

This is something he has no interest in discussing. He mentioned it to Hume shortly after he first started writing and has regretted it ever since. Every time they meet, Hume asks about what he calls James' 'literary project'.

'Been at it for a couple of years now, haven't you? Must have quite a tome.'

'I've got a lot of pages, there's no doubt about that.'

'So when do you expect to finish?'

Hume has always been like this – goals, results, the end-game. James remembers he was once like this himself. Now, this behaviour just irritates him – even though he knows his friend is doing it with the best of intentions.

'No idea,' says James, trying to kill the subject.

But Hume is relentless.

'There's going to be a huge market for that kind of thing now that the war is over. There'll be a lot of fellers putting out their stories. You should try to get in on the ground floor.'

'A lot of it's pap.'

'You should let someone else be the judge of that. I have a friend or two in the publishing business. You should let me show it to them.'

'One of these days now, I'll get it into some sort of state where someone could read it.'

James is stonewalling. He's listening but he's choosing not to hear. And he's doing it in such an obvious way that he hopes his friend will take the hint and give up on this line of inquiry.

Suddenly it seems like Hume has.

'You'll be able to go back to France now. A pension, all the time in the world. It's what you've always wanted. At least that's what you always told me.'

James shakes his head. A France without Clara. The thought is unbearable.

'I'm not sure I'll ever go back to France,' he says.

'Really? Because I've come across something I thought you might be interested in.'

Chapter 64
Thursday 12 December 1918

It's over a month since Clara decided to post the letter to James. Every day, she was ready to take it to the post office – and every day, something stopped her.

Tomorrow is her birthday. She is going to try and make it a happy and extra special day with the girls. She is just wondering if she has the ingredients to make a cake when there is a knock at the door. Clara breaks out into an instant sweat, just as she has done every other time this has happened. Automatically taking off her apron, she starts heading for the door. She knows – with a terrible certainty she has never felt before – that it is going to be Henry. Just in time for her birthday. The awful symmetry of it. Time's laughingstock. She can hear the gods hooting with laughter.

Heart pounding, hands shaking, she reaches the door and opens it. But it's not Henry. It's just a poorly dressed woman who wants to know if Clara has any old clothes she's getting rid of.

All Clara can feel is a wave of relief.

'I'm sorry, no,' she says, without even thinking.

She closes the door as the woman is saying, 'Thanks anyway, dear.'

Clara is so shaken that she has to sit down. She goes into the kitchen and stays there for she's not sure how long, staring out the kitchen window but not seeing anything. She can't live like this any more. It's killing her.

Eventually, she gets up, puts on her hat and coat and takes the letter to James to the post office. She buys a stamp, sticks it on and then holds the letter in the mouth of the post box. The gods. James. Henry. Time's laughingstock. Divorce. Death.

She lets the letter go.

Chapter 65
Friday 13 December 1918

James is eating breakfast when he hears the metallic clack of the spring-loaded flap of his letterbox and then the soft flop of post falling onto the parquet floor. There is a sheaf of five or six letters. On top is one from the Imperial War Graves Commission. He met with them and was interviewed two weeks ago.

Holding the letter against his chest, James tears open the envelope with his thumb. He extracts a single page and shakes off the envelope which flutters to the floor. He unfolds the paper and scans it rapidly. They've given him the job. Would it be convenient for him … to meet on … details of his travel to France. James feels a warm glow of happiness. It is the first such glow he has felt in over three years.

He rifles through the remaining letters. They are bills but then there is a final one in a hand that seems familiar but that he doesn't recognise. Also, the letter looks very old, like it has lain in a drawer for a long time. Curious, he opens it. It is a single page of cheap writing paper with a date from more than two years ago – the 15th of October 1916. The signature at the bottom is Clara's.

My dear, dear James,
I hope with all my heart that this letter finds you alive and well.
I have just learned that Henry has been posted as missing.
It would be so good to see you again.
Yours ~~affectionately~~ *always,*
Clara.

Holding the letter and reading the words over and over, James returns to the dining room. He sits down and pours himself more coffee. He is quite stunned. He remembers a conversation he had with Clara about how the gods play games with us. Here is such a game now.

James had pretty much made up his mind that if he got the job with the War Graves Commission, he would leave England for good. He has a half-formed picture of himself as the caretaker of one of the cemeteries that are going to be built – tending the graves, mowing the lawns, helping visitors find their loved ones. Now, just when he finds he will be leaving England, Clara re-enters his life.

He tries to decode the letter's meaning. Of course, she doesn't know if he is alive or not. She doesn't know about his arm. When he reads the sentence about Henry being posted as missing, James just has to put the letter down and shake his head. He laughs. He actually laughs out loud. Poor Clara. The gods are having a field day with her. Missing. Henry could be dead, he could be a prisoner. All. Or nothing. Clara gets everything she wants. Clara gets nothing she wants.

This of course, is supposing that Clara still loves him. But if it turns out that Henry is alive, James knows that Clara would never leave him. He thinks it's probably her children, in the end, that are the reason. But it actually doesn't matter what the reason is. It's beyond her. There was a time when James was angry about this. But he's past that now. People do what they can.

And anyway, Clara was being asked to do something he hadn't had to do. There had only been James and his wife. No children. He remembers he said to Clara during one of their first conversations how he wasn't sure he'd have had the courage if he had children. James has been a soldier. He has faced bullets and shellfire, but what he had wanted Clara to do required a different kind of courage.

He wasn't sure if he'd have had it any more than she did.

Chapter 66
Monday 16 December 1918

Clara has been waiting anxiously for the postman. But she doesn't recognise the handwriting. Even after she discovers that the letter is from James, she still doesn't recognise the handwriting. It seems childish, uneducated, spidery, fractured in some way. He had quite nice handwriting, small and rounded, so that there was pleasure to be had in just looking at a page filled up with line after line of his words.

She feels a dart of worry – what does changed handwriting signify? But this is quickly replaced by the joy that he is alive. He is alive. With this, anything is possible. *Everything* is possible.

She thought he might have suggested meeting in the park as they had always done but given the time of year, he proposes Claridge's. The memories she has of there make her almost want to cry. The time of year also means that it will be easy to get away from the children for a day – she will be shopping for little surprises, she tells them. Not that she can afford very much.

She replies to James' letter by return.

Chapter 67
Friday 20 December 1918

James is waiting for Clara when she enters the lobby of Claridge's. When she sees him she smiles. It is three and a half years since they have seen one another. Her eyes are more hollow than they were and there are dark patches under them. The skin of her cheeks seems more taut. She's lost weight and he thinks it doesn't suit her. She's still beautiful though – still the most beautiful woman *he's* ever known.

She comes towards him and extends her hand. He had been turned slightly away from her anyway – it's something he finds himself doing unconsciously – so that when he extends his left hand to take hers, her face registers surprise. And then shock.

'I didn't get back completely in one piece,' he says.

'You got back,' she replies. 'That's all that matters.'

They go in and order afternoon tea. The staff seems extra deferential. Clara wonders if it's to do with James' missing arm. He asks after the children.

'They must be excited with Christmas only a few days away,' he says.

'They are.'

How typical of him, she thinks, that the children would be his first thought.

'Did you go back to the Foreign Office?' she asks.

He shakes his head.

'I thought I'd done enough damage there. The war, I mean.'

'It was hardly your fault.'

'It wasn't yours,' says James. 'Or most of the other so-called ordinary people in this country. And what about you, Clara, how have you been?'

'Oh, you know – just muddling on.'

'The years have been good to you. You've hardly changed at all.'

She smiles a feeble smile.

'Thank you.'

They both fall silent. Neither of them can think of anything to say. To fill the gap, James takes a scone from the tray. Clara wonders if she should offer to help him but says nothing. Then she is glad that she didn't when she sees how he manages, cutting it by holding it between the blade of the knife and his thumb. He butters it, adds some jam and cream. He looks up to find her watching him. He is reminded of that day they first met when he caught her staring at him. He wonders if she is remembering that too. They speak together.

'So what are you –?'

'You've had no word of –?'

'You go first,' he says.

'I was just going to ask what you were doing. You know – if you're not at the Foreign Office any more?'

'I've got a new job. Just about a week ago. There's an organisation called the Imperial War Graves Commission. Have you heard of it?'

She shakes her head.

'I shall tell you all about it,' he continues. 'I'm very excited about it. But first tell me, is there any news of your husband?'

James never referred to Henry as Clara's 'husband'. She is struck by the fact that he does so now.

'Nothing,' she says and then, after a pause, 'I think he must be dead.'

She says it almost as a question – as though asking him to agree with her.

He does anything but that.

'You don't know. It's only been a month since the Armistice. It's going to take quite a time to sort everything out. Just getting all those men demobilised and back into civilian life, never mind finding out about prisoners in Germany. It's far too soon to give up hope.'

It is not at all what she wanted to hear.

'Why did you want to meet?' he asks.

The question is so blunt it's like a slap in the face.

She knows she should have worked out the answer to this question. It was something her late father used to say to her when he was going off to a business meeting. Always know what you're trying to get from the meeting. What was she trying to get from this meeting?

'I just wanted to know you were alive,' she begins.

He says nothing and just looks into her eyes. She knows he knows that's not it. His silence makes her continue.

'And I thought … we might … that we could … establish our friendship again.'

She knows he knows that's not it either.

'Our *friendship*?' he asks. At best, he says the word with disbelief. At worst, there is anger in his voice.

She responds with a flash of anger of her own.

'Legally, I'm still a married woman.'

'I know that only too well, Clara.'

His use of her name seems to distance her rather than bringing her closer.

'And will be for seven years,' she adds.

She's not a hundred percent sure about this statement but she adds it for good measure.

'Assuming your husband is dead,' he says, as if completing the sentence for her. 'If he's alive, you're a married woman and that's that.'

Clara suddenly feels like she is going to cry. What does he want her to do? Beg?

'Couldn't we wait and see?' she blurts out.

She now knows that *this* is what she was trying to get from the meeting.

'Life's so short. Look at all the people who have died. You might have. Instead, we're both here. Shouldn't we make the most of it?'

'And if your husband turns out to be alive and comes back?'

'We'll cross that bridge when we come to it.'

There, she thinks – it's said. Clara feels exposed, naked. Here she is, in a hotel, offering herself to a man.

The sounds of the room seem to become very distant. The room itself, the animated people, the busy staff – it is as though they move, fading into a distant background. Clara notices that James missed a bit on his upper lip when he shaved. How difficult has that been, she wonders – changing the hand with which he shaves. It seems to take hours before James speaks.

'If we did,' he says. 'Re-establish our relationship, as you put it. And then your husband came back. What would happen?'

'We'd talk about that if it happened. I'd have to –'

'You'd have to what?'

'I'd have to think about … the girls. I'd have to –'

'I don't think that was the right answer,' says James.

Clara thinks that this must have been the way James was when he worked at the Foreign Office. She could imagine him saying exactly this in a negotiation. She responds with irritation bordering on anger.

'So what *is* the right answer, then?'

Very quietly, James says, 'You know the right answer, Clara.'

Clara feels her eyes smarting. She can't cry here in public. And she's afraid that if she tries to say anything, she will either cry or the words won't come. James seems to recognise her distress. His tone softens.

'Clara, I love you. I love you as much now as the first day I saw you. Yes, we could pick up where we left off. I want to do that so much. But for us to do that and then for your husband to return. Can you imagine what that would be like?'

Clara's urge to cry has receded a little. She goes to speak but James says, 'Please – let me finish. I would be finding you only to lose you again.'

'But he may not *be* alive,' replies Clara. 'And then think of what we are wasting, the opportunity for happiness we are going to let pass us by.'

'Don't think I haven't thought about that every day since I received your letter.'

It's the first hint that Clara has heard that James might be for turning.

'So how would it be – this relationship of ours? If we went ahead?' he asks.

Clara hasn't really thought about this. Or rather she has thought about nothing else but it was always from the point of view of Henry dead and she and James together. She has never considered the details of how their relationship might work until such time as Henry was either pronounced dead or returned. She curses herself for that now as James asks her the questions she should have asked – and answered – herself.

'Would I meet your children? In what capacity? Would I be "Uncle James"? Would we live together? And if not, how often would I see you? Would it be just the same as having an affair? Would – ?'

'I don't know, James,' sighs Clara miserably. 'I haven't thought about any of this. I know. I should have. Before I came here. Before I wrote to you.'

'It wouldn't work, Clara. We would have some stolen hours of happiness. And then it could all come crashing down.'

'Aren't some stolen hours better than no hours at all?'

'Are they?' he asks.

They go silent again. Then James says, 'I ought to tell you about what I'm doing.'

Clara takes a deep breath. There is something very bad coming here. But she is determined not to cry.

'This organisation that I mentioned. The Imperial War Graves Commission. It's been set up to make sure all the men who died get a decent burial and then to manage the cemeteries afterwards. I interviewed with them a couple of weeks ago and this day last week I learned I got the job.

They want people with managerial skills and a knowledge of French to coordinate the building of their cemeteries in France. So that's what I'm going to be doing. I'm going to France early in January.'

'So you got your wish?'

'My wish?'

'To go to France.'

'Yes, I suppose I did. But under very different circumstances from those that I had ever imagined.'

He pauses as though wondering if he should say something and then continues.

'It's the perfect job for me. To be among the dead, I mean. Part of me has been dead these last three years.'

Clara knows she's lost but she tries anyway.

'Maybe I could see you when you're back in London.'

'I don't think that would be such a great idea. Anyway, I probably won't be back here that often. And who knows – if I like the work and the work likes me, I'm thinking I might stay in France.'

'You mean permanently? Go to live there?'

He nods.

'I could sell my house here and with the money I'd probably be able to buy quite a nice place over there.'

Clara has one last throw of the dice.

'In five years, Henry could be pronounced dead.'

'My dear, dear Clara,' says James. 'Who knows where we'll all be in five year's time?'

Chapter 68
Wednesday 1 January 1919

Somehow Clara gets through Christmas. She does it by going machine-like from one task to the next – cooking, cleaning, dealing with Mrs Parsons, the girls, presents, Santa Claus – all the things that have to be done. The time she looks forward to most is when she can go to bed and sleep claims her. Then, at least, she can dream. And she does – rich dreams, full of the most bizarre and wonderful happenings that seem so real. One night she dreams she has sex with a man younger than herself and has an orgasm. She wakes remembering the sensation of his lips on hers. It is so long since anyone apart from the girls has kissed her, held her or even touched her.

The task of getting out of bed each day seems overwhelming. But somehow she manages it. Today there is something she must do that she has been dreading. But she wants to start the New Year without this particular thing around her neck.

When she was notified that Henry had gone missing, she told the girls that he had been taken prisoner by the Germans and that when the war ended, he would be home. It seemed like the best thing to do at the time. If nothing else it put off the day when she would have to tell them that he was dead. Since the war has actually ended, Ursula and Virginia have been constantly asking about their father. In December it was whether he would be home for Christmas. When that date passed, they said that surely he would be home in the New Year. Clara has overheard Ursula who is ten, explaining to her younger sister how it must take a lot of time to get all of these prisoners back from Germany and how that country is a long way away. Clara knows this can't go on.

The girls are sitting at the breakfast table, one on either side. Clara pours herself some tea and sits down at the head of the table. It is a ritual they have every day and it is one of the times when she feels closest to them and when she can sometimes put other thoughts out of her head.

'Remember I told you how Daddy had been taken prisoner by the Germans?'

'He's coming home?' says Virginia.

'Well, you see my loves, it's a bit more complicated than that. The letter I got from the Army said that he had gone missing.'

The girls are listening intently. Clara can see from Ursula's face that she knows there is something bad coming.

'There are two reasons why a soldier might go missing. One is the one I told you – that he was captured by the Germans. But the other one is that he just ... well, that they couldn't find him after the battle.'

'But why wouldn't they be able to find someone?' asks Virginia.

Clara has hoped that the conversation wouldn't take this turn but the girls are too intelligent for that.

'Even if he was shot,' continues Virginia. 'He'd be lying on the ground. And even if he was knocked out and couldn't shout for help, the men with the red crosses on their arms would find him. Our teacher told us about them,' Virginia says to her sister.

'Yes, you're right darling. That's usually what happens. But sometimes it could still happen that they mightn't be able to find somebody.'

'Because he was in some place where they didn't look?' asks Virginia.

'Yes, exactly,' says Clara. 'That's exactly it.'

Virginia frowns.

'But then he would die, wouldn't he? If the doctors couldn't find him.'

'Well this is what I'm trying to tell you,' insists Clara. 'Your Daddy could be a prisoner and he could be coming home. Or –' she falters, 'or he might not be.'

'You mean he's dead, Mum?' asks Ursula.

'Yes,' Clara replies. 'He could be.'

Virginia begins to cry. Clara pushes her chair back and puts her arms out.

'Come here, my darlings.'

Virginia comes first, burying her head against Clara's breast as she sobs.

'And how will we know?' asks Ursula, as Clara puts an arm around her and draws her to herself.

'That's just the thing,' says Clara. 'If your Daddy is alive, he'll come back. If he's not then … well then he won't come back.'

Tears are sliding down Ursula's face now too. Clara clutches the two of them to her. She thinks that there are some things that it is just not possible to bear.

Chapter 69
Saturday 28 June 1919

With a rather nice piece of symmetry, five years to the day after the Archduke Franz Ferdinand was assassinated in Sarajevo, the treaty marking the end of the Great War is signed at Versailles outside Paris. It is the prize giving in the Group of Death.

England, France and Russia are declared the winners; Germany and Austria are the losers.

That same day, Clara is at home baking bread. Like most other 'ordinary' people in Britain, she is unaware of and mostly indifferent to, what this latest collection of great men is doing at Versailles. She plans to finish kneading the dough and while it's rising, she'll sit in the sun for a while. Clara is thirty four. She feels much, much older.

Knocks at the door haven't in any way lost their ability to scare her and there is one now. She leaves the dough, wipes her hands and hurries to the door. Her heart races as it always does. Will this be the one? When she opens the door, it is a figure in uniform. It is a much thinner version of the man she remembers. It is Henry.

Henry has come home with plenty of money. The bulk of it is the part of his army pay which didn't go directly to Clara. It accumulated for more than two years while he was in the prisoner of war camp. He has been given some of it now and the rest of it will come in three further payments over the next few weeks. He gives Clara money to go and buy food and drink. She buys the kind of things that Henry hasn't tasted since he was taken prisoner and Clara hasn't had since before the war.

Once Clara's shopping is delivered, Henry drinks beer as he tells them about his time as a prisoner. The girls listen, fascinated. They have wine with dinner and while Clara does the washing up, the girls play joyfully with their father and the things he has brought them. Henry brings a French silk scarf for Clara and she thanks him but not in the profuse way he would have expected.

Henry has had a lot of time to think about things. Indeed, in the prisoner of war camp, he had little but time. Some men are bitter about having been taken prisoner but not so Henry. He knows that he owes his life to the fact that he ended up in enemy hands. Had that not happened and given that the war ran on for two and a half more years after his capture, he is certain he would have been killed or blinded or maimed or castrated or turned into a vegetable. He finds it funny that he should be so grateful to the Germans. Of course the conditions weren't that great and, particularly towards the end, the food was shit and there was little of it. But that's all behind him now. A couple of weeks of Clara's cooking will soon fatten him up and have him back to normal.

One of the results of Henry's thinking is that he has a very clear vision of how he wants things to be from now on. This vision is not new. It's actually the same one he had before the war broke out. But now, more than ever, he feels he's earned it. He's fought for his country, he's risked his life and come through. Things are going to be good from now on.

The first piece of his plan – for there are three pieces – is already in place. After he was released, he was shipped, along with all the other prisoners from the camp, to a base depot near the French coast. Here they had several weeks of doing very little other than eating and sleeping. While he was there, Henry wrote to Mr Faber, the managing partner of the insurance company telling him that he was alive and inquiring about his old job.

Faber had said he would keep his job for Henry but that was nearly five years ago. Henry is not that optimistic about his chances.

The reply he receives back at first seems to confirm his worst fears. The letter is from someone called Stewart and begins by explaining that Mr Faber has passed away and that Stewart is now in charge. Henry liked Faber and he has no recollection of anybody called Stewart so they must have brought him in from the outside. This looks ominous. But then the letter goes on to say that as Stewart is an ex-Army man himself, he will be honouring all of the commitments made to returned soldiers who were former employees of the company. Henry is overjoyed. A further exchange of letters sets up an appointment for Henry to go in and meet with Stewart. That appointment is tomorrow.

The second part of Henry's plan concerns Clara. The last time the pair of them was together was when Henry confronted her about James. Shortly afterwards, Clara wrote to Henry claiming that she had broken up with James but Henry had no way of finding out if that was true. But now he knows.

He knew, the minute that Clara opened the door, that her other man was no longer part of her life. When the door was pulled back and she was revealed, Henry knew that this wasn't a woman in love. There was nothing bright, girlish or happy about her. Rather, in that instant before she recognised him, he saw a great emptiness and sadness. The shock on her face, which he enjoyed tremendously, didn't so much obliterate happiness; it just added to what was clearly an already heavy load.

Henry's original thoughts had been for another huge argument which he would win. He wanted to show her who was in charge. He rehearsed the clever and hurtful things he wanted to say to her. But gradually, he began to have second thoughts about this. There was a better way and after dinner, when Clara comes down from having put the children to bed, Henry is eager to get started.

But he is in the sitting room and Clara goes into the kitchen. She spends ages there until Henry concludes that she is avoiding him. He gets up and goes out to her.

'Would you like some tea?' she asks, her back turned to him.

My god, she is well and truly beaten down, he thinks.

'No thank you,' he says reasonably. 'I'd just like to talk.'

'What about?' she asks and this time, she turns to face him. She stands with her back to the sink and folds her arms.

She has lost weight. There is a hint of hollowness in her cheeks and even though her arms are folded beneath her breasts, they too appear to have gotten smaller. And the sadness that surrounds her, the weight she looks like she's carrying seems to make her smaller anyway.

It is over four years since Henry has had a woman. This is another thing he has had plenty of time to think about. It was the time of his last leave in 1915. He spent a couple of nights with Mary before going home and finding out that Clara had a lover. (The thought still has the ability to make his blood boil.) After that he returned to France and from then until the Somme offensive there was nothing. Several times he was tempted to go off with a prostitute but he always balked in the end. The shame of catching something would have just been too great.

So tonight, Henry wants more than anything else to give Clara a good fucking. How often he has thought – and dreamed – about her blonde hair, her perfect little breasts, her sturdy thighs. She always tended to be a little cherubic, which he adored, and even though she may have lost some of that, he is still hugely physically attracted to her. And she is his wife, godammit – she has no right to refuse him. But he tries to put that thought to one side. He will take a different approach.

'I want to put the past behind us,' he says. 'I just want things to go back to the way they were. You, me and the girls.'

'And what about that fancy woman of yours?' Clara replies, but she does so with a weariness that surprises Henry. The words may be combative but her mood doesn't seem to be.

'That's over,' says Henry. 'Has been for years.'

Clara gives no reaction but Henry knows that the message has registered. Neither of them says anything. The silence lengthens. She looks at him expressionlessly and he returns her gaze.

Finally, Henry asks, 'So what about it?'

When Clara still doesn't respond, Henry says, 'I love you, you know. I thought about you all the time I was in Germany.'

Slowly he goes to her and puts his arms around her. At first she doesn't respond and Henry is very close to losing his temper. But then he feels her arms close around him tentatively. He smells her familiar fragrance and the sensation arouses him. He feels a sudden erection and he wonders if she notices. They stand like this for a long time. Henry wants her to know that he is aroused.

Finally he says, 'Shall we go to bed?'

Tonight, Henry undresses Clara. She stands there, allowing him to remove her clothes. She is wearing a brassiere underneath her blouse and Henry kisses the skin of her breasts that shows above the brassiere. Then he kisses her nipples through the fabric of the garment. Finally, he reaches behind her back and removes it. He kisses her nipples again teasing them with his tongue.

Henry moves on to the lower part of her body. He has undone her skirt and she's stepped out of it. She would like him to have picked it up and placed it over a chair but he just leaves it there. Quickly he removes the rest of her under things and then he buries his face in her groin. At this stage he is kneeling before her. It is a pose of utter submission but strangely, she is the one who feels defeated.

He begins to probe with his tongue between her legs and she moves her feet apart to facilitate him. He holds her buttocks, pressing her to him.

'Come on,' she says, breaking away and moving over to climb into bed.

She wants to get the thing over with as quickly as possible but he doesn't interpret it that way. Instead he takes her words for eagerness. He quickly undresses while she lies in bed watching him. His body is bony – unrecognisable from the pudgy Henry she remembers. As he takes off his trousers and underpants together, his erection springs clear of them. He gets into bed and immediately lies on top of her.

She spreads her legs and realises that she forgot to moisten herself with cream. It's too late now as he tries to enter her. But she is too dry and after several failed attempts, she says, 'Just a minute'.

She takes a jar from the bedside locker and does the necessary. Henry then resumes and is quickly inside her. The thought of *The Pickwick Papers* crosses Clara's mind for an instant but she puts it away. After a dozen or so quick and silent strokes, Henry climaxes inside her with a huge, quite unbelievable shuddering and a deep, dying groan.

He collapses onto her and lies there for several minutes. Neither of them says anything. Eventually he rolls off and out of her and lies beside her. Within moments he is asleep.

Clara gets up and goes to the toilet and then into the bathroom. She douches with the solution of baking soda. She's still capable of having children and that's something she absolutely couldn't countenance. Then, returning to the bedroom with its heavily breathing Henry, she takes a fresh white nightdress from the drawer and puts it on. It is not the one she wore with James. She has stopped wearing that. She climbs back into bed and turns on her side away from Henry. She draws herself up into a foetal position.

And this is how she falls sleep.

Chapter 70
Monday 30 June 1919

His appointment with Mr Stewart, the new managing partner goes far better than Henry could possibly have wished for. The company is indeed honouring its pledge to give pre-war staff their jobs back. The thing is that there are so few of the pre-war staff. It turns out that of the more than sixty men who joined up in 1914, only a handful has come back. Of these, Henry is the only manager. In addition, as luck would have it, the head of New Policies has just retired. Henry lands the job.

As he walks out of Stewart's office, Henry wonders if Mary still works in New Policies but a quick visit down there establishes that she doesn't. He discovers that she left to become a driver for the Army in 1915. Henry wonders if she is still at the same address. Sitting in his new office for the first time, Henry writes her a letter and posts it on his way home. It is the third and final part of his plan.

Chapter 71
Friday 4 July 1919

Henry meets Mary a few days later at the ABC that was one of their old haunts. She too has lost weight and her face has a grey pallour to it. But her breasts are still full and Henry remembers her body and the things they used to do. He has had sex with Clara every night since he returned but it's not enough. He hungers for more. The three years he spent without sex have made him like a man who has crossed a desert and now found an oasis. He feels like he will never be able to drink enough. He feels aroused now simply looking at her.

Just as he was magnanimous with Clara, he takes the same tack with Mary now. He opens the conversation by apologising for his behaviour the last time they were together.

'So how have you been?' he asks, with the apology out of the way. 'What are you up to?'

The tale she tells is a sorry one. Her job with the Army finished just before last Christmas. The insurance company wouldn't take her back and since then she has been looking for work.

'But it's impossible,' she says, shaking her head. 'There are so many returned soldiers, nobody's going to hire a woman. Unless it's to be a maid or something like that. And even then.'

'So how have you been surviving?' Henry asks.

'I got a small payment from the Army, I get a tiny pension and I had some savings, but they're nearly gone now. I've paid this month's rent but then there's no more. If I don't find something in the next week or two, I'm sunk.'

If Henry had tried to imagine an opening, he couldn't have come up with a better one.

'How would you like to come and work for me?' he asks.

'Are you back in your old job?'

'Better than that.'

He pauses for effect.

'I'm the Head of New Policies.'

And another pause.

'You'd be working under me.'

Along with the *double entendre*, he looks Mary in the eye. He wonders how she'll respond. Most of all he wonders what he will do if she wants the job but doesn't want what comes with it. It is something that has been worrying him since he got back in touch with her and arranged this meeting.

But he needn't have worried. After a few moments' thought, she smiles and says, 'I'd like that very much.'

Henry goes home on the open top of an omnibus, enjoying the summer sunshine. Everything has worked out as he intended. He is back in a new job on a higher salary. Clara has clearly been living on a shoestring for the last five years so she'll be happy to have things back to the way they were. Mary is due to start on Monday and Henry expects to have his first night with her next week. He will use the usual excuse that he has to stay up in town for a meeting – not that he feels he has to explain himself to anybody, least of all Clara. He doubts too if he'll hear a squeak out of Mary about him leaving Clara. Mary is lucky to have her job back – and she knows it. He expects to see a lot of gratitude from her over the months to come.

Despite all of this, Henry finds that there is something nagging at him. Did Mary only come back to him because of her need for a job? He was on the point of asking her but mercifully, he wasn't quite that stupid. There was only one answer she would have given him – that she was happy to be back with him because she loved him. This, whether it was the truth or not. And he would have seemed like such a fool to have asked.

Chapter 72
Monday 15 December 1919

Extraordinarily, in a world where pretty much everything has changed and been turned on its head, for some of the people in our story, very little has changed.

Henry is back working at his old company, albeit in a new role. His marriage to Clara is back to the way it was before she 'strayed', as he thinks of it. The girls are older of course, eleven and nine now, healthy and happy and beautiful. They are looking forward to Christmas. Henry finds it remarkable that after all he has gone through, so much has survived intact. Indeed, he believes that his marriage will be even stronger than it was. What he means by this of course is that Clara is unlikely to stray again.

Mary was the first to notice that she was back to where she had started except she doesn't see it in quite the same positive light as Henry. 'Back to square one' is how she thinks of it. But still it could be a lot worse – and for the first half of this year, it was. At least now she has a steady income and she has her relationship with Henry. It isn't marriage, of course, but he treats her well and doesn't expect all that much in return. Given that she doesn't foresee marriage at all now, she has decided she will squeeze as much as she reasonably can from him. Accordingly, she steers a fine line between asking and taking on the one hand and not upsetting him on the other. She has a fine nose for this kind of thing and it is no real trouble to her.

Mary will spend Christmas with her family. Henry has told her that they will get some time together between Boxing Day and New Year's Eve. And of course she has given him enough hints to let him know that she is expecting a substantial present. She wants jewellery – an asset, something she can sell if times ever get hard for her again.

Clara's life is now centred on the children. She fusses over them – their hair, their clothes, what they're eating, whether they're getting enough sleep. She helps them with their homework. She walks them to school every day and meets them in the afternoon. She is glad too to have a little money to spend after the five really terrible years of the war. Henry stays 'in town' at least once a week, something that he no longer bothers to find an excuse for. Shortly after he took up his new job, he told her that he would have to do this and this statement has served as a sort of blanket justification for those regular absences.

Mrs Parsons still comes to Clara's house. As soon as he returned, Henry was adamant that she should go but this was a battle that Clara actually won. Given how generous Mrs Parsons had been during the war, Clara wasn't going to sack her now. She and Henry had a row of biblical proportions. Eventually Clara stopped screaming at him and said in a quiet voice, 'Please give me this one thing. It's all I'll ask.'

'Do what you like,' Henry had responded before storming out of the house. So Mrs Parsons still comes, working the old hours she used to work before the war. However, Henry no longer speaks to her and consequently she tries to be gone before Henry gets home from work.

He also still takes Clara to dinner most Saturday nights and has sex with her afterwards. The thought that he was inside a different woman a few days earlier revolts Clara but she has managed to put it in a place in her mind, where apart from Saturdays, she can mostly forget about it. As Christmas approaches, Clara is focussed on making it a wonderful one for the girls. It will be the first one they have had with their father in six years and she wants it to be truly special.

Today is Monday and Clara plans to ice the Christmas cake she has made. Tomorrow she and Mrs Parsons are going to begin giving the house its Christmas cleaning. Friday, Henry is 'staying in town' so at least she will have the house and the bed to herself.

The only person whose life has changed dramatically is James. He has rented a small house in Amiens and using this as his base, he is one of a team of people whose job is to identify where the Imperial War Graves Commission will build its cemeteries. His territory is primarily the Somme. He has a French driver, Maurice and large scale maps of the area. Every morning, five days a week, the two of them set off early about their work. For the moment, their task is simply to map all of the existing spots where men lie.

Their work brings them across terrain that has been flayed by years of battle. They find mass graves and small clusters of roughly made crosses and often, a single cross or two. They find themselves in ruined orchards and woods and meadows, along streams and rivers, beside or on former railway lines and roads, on low scatterings of pulverised brick that were once villages. Every grave or collection of graves that they find is duly marked on a map and directions to its location are recorded in a book.

James finds the lone crosses particularly moving. The soldiers who lie in these isolated graves will be brought together in larger cemeteries. James thinks back to the camaraderie of that time. While he hated the Army and his time in it, he remembers how men helped each other, looked out for each other, and in some cases gave their lives for each other. It was the noblest and most tender thing in the vilest of circumstances. It is fitting that these men who lie in lone graves should be brought together with their friends and comrades. The men would have wanted it that way and for once, it seems like the authorities have actually done something sensible.

James buries himself in his work. He uses the weekends to plan the journeys he will make the following week. At nights, he eats in one of the small family restaurants that have sprung up in devastated Amiens again. These restaurants are usually little more than somebody's dining room with the food cooked in the kitchen. But the cooking is good – even if food is still a bit scarce – and there is wine. Most nights he drinks a bottle.

Sometimes it is more. On the weekends he'll finish up with a couple of Armagnacs. He was tempted to buy a bottle of Armagnac and have it at home. So far he has resisted.

James loves living in France and his missing arm is always a passport to hospitality, conversations with returned French soldiers and more offers of free drink and food than he can possibly accept. He is reminded of something Clara used to say about nothing being all bad.

He tries not to think about Clara but he finds it almost impossible. In his wallet he carries a photograph that she gave him of herself, taken before she got married. The Clara he knew was a good ten years older than the nineteen year old in the photograph. But the beautiful adult face that emerged from the teenage one was already there.

It is the last working week in December. He and Maurice will stop work on Friday the nineteenth. James would happily have continued right through December but a letter he received at the beginning of the month told him that he was entitled to holidays. The nineteenth will be their last day and then they don't return until Monday 5th January. The IWGC is assuming that James will want to return to England to be with his family for Christmas. Maurice is delighted as he will be paid for the two weeks that he is off. James won't be returning to England and the two weeks that lie ahead seems like an infinity. He thinks that maybe he will just spend them drunk.

When Henry hasn't come home by half past six, Clara gives the girls their tea. Seven and eight o'clock pass and Clara is irritated. It means that she won't be able to relax – when Henry comes in she'll have to make tea especially for him. She gets the girls to bed and at nine o'clock settles down by the fire with a book. She is tempted to drink some sherry but is afraid that if she does she will just empty the bottle. She decides she will have some on Friday. Simultaneously, she is appalled that this is what her life has come down to – decisions like this. There is still no sign of Henry. She makes tea.

By eleven o'clock, Clara is starting to worry. It's not so much that she cares what happens to him, though somewhere there is a tiny part of her that remembers she once loved him. Rather, she can't bear the thought of her life being thrown into turmoil again because Henry was involved in an accident or the victim of some random crime.

At one o'clock, as Clara is taking the tea things out to the kitchen, her mind has moved on. No longer is she thinking about the bad things that might have happened to Henry. Rather, it is the thought that he is more than likely with that slut. (Clara still doesn't know Mary's name.) Tonight, more so than usual, Clara is appalled at the thought that Henry is inside that woman and inside Clara a few nights later. Is she clean? Or is she some pox-ridden cow? And is it even the same woman every time now? When Henry enters Clara, is he carrying some awful disease that he is about to infect her with? And she doesn't know which is worse – that Henry does this or that she allows him to do it. Is that all she has become to him – a receptacle for his spunk?

The thought revolts her. She is a condom. That is what she has become. A human condom.

And this is the moment when Clara knows that she cannot go on. It doesn't matter about the girls. She had hoped to live until they were grown up and married to good husbands. Then she would happily have died. But she understands now that she has become so worthless that there is no point in her continuing. She is dying. That's what it is. Her body has become fouled and even if Henry hasn't infected her with some ghastly disease, that foulness is eating away at her.

She is going to die. What's more, she wants to die. She doesn't want to live this life any longer. It is so far away from the one she pictured when she was a little girl and a teenager and a single woman.

In the kitchen, Clara puts the tea things on the draining board. She is overtaken by a terrible weakness. It is the weariness of her life, the weight of a world that she no longer wants to be part of, pressing down on her. She tries to steady herself against the sink but finds herself collapsing slowly to the floor as her legs buckle. Her dress puddles out around her. She cries out – a wordless howl of pain. She does it again and again and again until eventually the individual cries merge into one loud wailing. She draws in great gurgles of air like one who is drowning. She wonders if she *is* drowning – drowning in her tears.

She rests her cheek against the cold ceramic of the sink. She draws her knees up to her chest and wraps her arms around her legs. She rocks backwards and forwards, keening. It is a lament for herself – for her lost childhood and youth. For the death of all her dreams. The death of all hope. The death of everything.

Chapter 73
Tuesday 16 December 1919

It is still the middle of the night when Clara stirs from the kitchen floor. It is the chill of the room that rouses her. She hasn't been asleep; she's really not quite sure where she's been. Her eyes feel swollen from crying. Gingerly she pulls herself up onto her feet. She is exhausted but knows that if she goes to bed she will not sleep. She feels so small. Why has there been nobody to take care of her? To defend her? Why has she made such terrible decisions? She is just stupid. A stupid little woman is all she is.

All she has tried to do all her life is to be happy and make the people around her happy. Was that so bad? Did the gods really have to punish her like this? And for what? What has she done to deserve this? Clara holds the edge of the table to steady herself. What a waste her whole life has been. All this love she had inside her that she just wanted to share. Where will it go when she is dead?

There is so little in her life now that it is really not worth continuing. Now she has to find a way out. She doesn't think she has the courage to kill herself – not with a knife or by stepping under a bus or jumping off a bridge. But there are other ways. Clara reckons her mother decided to die; just decided she'd had enough of the world and was able to gradually whither away and eventually disappear. This is what Clara will do. She will think herself to death; invite death in, welcome it with open arms, embrace it. The girls will be fine. Henry will marry his fancy woman or some woman. They'll have a mother. Henry loves them. They'll be fine.

And it is as Clara thinks these thoughts that she finds that something else has started inside her. She's not sure whether it's a thought or a feeling or a sensation in her body. In her imagination she sees a tiny flicker of flame as though from a candle. It wavers as if it was being buffeted by the wind. It seems almost to go out. For a moment it is not there but then it returns and it grows the tiniest bit stronger.

She feels this sensation, whatever it is, inside her somewhere in her stomach or maybe it's in her womb from where her children sprang. And now it slowly dawns on Clara that there is only one course open to her and she knows what she has to do.

Henry comes in at six thirty that evening. Even though he looks a bit the worse for wear, he is in great spirits. Ursula and Virginia are laying the table. A shepherd's pie cooks in the oven.

'How are my girls this evening?' he asks.

The two children run to him and he kisses them. Then he goes to kiss Clara on the cheek but she turns away from him.

'Oh, I'm sorry about last night,' he says. 'Stewart called an impromptu management meeting that turned into dinner that turned into a celebration of a good year at the firm.'

As it turns out, dear reader, this is a rare occasion when Henry is actually telling the truth – well, sort of anyway. Mr Stewart is one of those bosses – haven't we all come across them? – who isn't particularly good at thinking ahead. He will suddenly come up with an idea and then, without thinking it through, will act on it. Sometimes these ideas are remarkably good – or lucky – which explains the height to which his career has reached. Sometimes his ideas are atrocious – not that anyone will ever tell him that. Last night's idea was probably somewhat neutral although it did annoy several of the managers who had plans to be with their families in the week leading up to Christmas. Henry was happy to go along with it – a good meal, plenty of good drink and a night at a hotel. He could – as most of the managers did – have sent a message home to his family using runners that the company arranged. But Henry used his runner to send a message to Mary asking if she cared to join him in his hotel room later.

Mary had already arrived home and was preparing dinner when the message came. Nonetheless, like a good trouper, she bathed, dressed up, put on makeup and perfume and went out to the address of the hotel that Henry had given her. She never liked arriving at these places with the 'I'm meeting my husband here' line. She felt the desk clerks never believed her. However, the young man this evening was courteous and professional, she was taken upstairs and she ordered dinner in her room along with a half bottle of wine.

It was late when Henry eventually showed up and he was quite drunk. After he attempted to fumble Mary a few times, he sat on the bed to untie his shoelaces and promptly fell asleep. She undressed him and put him to bed and in the morning he was too badly hung over to think about sex. Mary said, 'I hope my Christmas present is going to make this all worthwhile' to which Henry responded by sulking.

Clara says nothing but takes warm plates from the oven and puts them out in four places. She takes out the shepherd's pie and cuts out sections for each of them.

'Mmm, this looks good,' says Henry. 'I'm starving. I could eat a horse.'

'Or a shepherd,' says Virginia and the girls and Henry laugh. Even Clara smiles.

Later she puts Ursula and Virginia to bed and kisses them goodnight. Then Clara goes into the bathroom and looks in the mirror. Even though Henry hasn't said anything – and probably hasn't even noticed – her face looks gaunt from her tears during the night. She brushes her hair and puts on some lipstick. Then she takes several deep breaths, a final great gulp of air and goes downstairs.

Henry is in the living room in his armchair engrossed in his newspaper. He doesn't look up as she comes in.

Clara says, 'I want you to go upstairs now, pack a suitcase, leave this house and not come back.' She speaks evenly, slowly, saying each word with great care.

For a moment there is no reaction from Henry. It is as if he hasn't heard. Then he lowers his paper.

'What did you say?'

He asks the question like a teacher who has just heard a pupil swear.

'You heard what I said. Legally this is my house and I don't want you living in it any longer.'

'Don't be ridiculous,' he says, folding the paper and putting it beside his chair as though he'll be picking it up again in a short while. She looks at him steadily. Clara's heart is pounding and her mouth is dry.

'The law is on my side,' she declares. 'Apart from the house, you're an adulterer. I'll be pursuing a divorce just as soon after Christmas as I can.'

'Now listen here, Clara —'

As menacingly as she can, Clara demands, 'Get out of my house now.'

She is standing and Henry is sitting down. But now he stands up and comes towards her. She recoils from him, wrapping her arms around herself.

'Don't you come near me,' she says. 'Don't you touch me.'

Despite trying to keep herself under control, Clara's voice has risen so that it sounds – even to herself – hysterical.

'Whatever you say,' he replies, putting his arms out with his hands up, palms facing her.

Henry feels that he needs this like he needs a hole in the head. The headache from his hangover finally cleared on the way home from work but he is tired and feeling quite seedy and had been looking forward to an early night. Clara has a mad stare in her eyes. Henry says, 'Look, let's just sit down and talk about this like adults. It's Christmas. Think of the girls. Why don't we all just go to bed now and in the morning we can talk about it reasonably.'

'I don't want to ever spend another minute in bed with you.'

It is as though she spits out the words. Her eyes are blazing with anger. She is rarely like this but when she is, Henry finds her quite frightening. His eyes move around the room trying to ascertain if there is anything there she might conceivably use as a weapon. He notes the poker by the fire.

Henry tries to be reasonable. He is having great difficulty doing this. He would really like to scream at her. Actually he would really like to slap her hard across the face but he has never hit a woman before in his life and he doesn't want to let himself down by starting now.

'Look,' he suggests. 'I'll sleep in the spare bedroom tonight. Tomorrow we'll talk. What about that?'

Clara's voice becomes murderous – it's the only way Henry can think to describe it. She looks to be having great difficulty keeping herself under control. He is afraid that at any moment she is going to become completely unhinged. She looks like a malevolent witch.

'I want you out of this house tonight,' she says through gritted teeth. 'Fuck off out of my house and out of my life.'

Henry goes to speak but now Clara does explode.

'Get out, will you. Just get out. Get out! Get out! Get out!'

The repeated shouts eventually dissolve into unintelligible watery gurgling which in turn becomes tears. Clara collapses onto the floor, her back against an armchair. He moves as if to come towards her but she looks up at him from hooded eyes. A strand of her hair has become dislodged and hangs in front of her face. She really looks quite mad.

Through huge sobs, she hisses, her voice full of menace, 'Don't you come near me. Don't you *dare* come near me.'

Henry is at a loss for what to do. But he acknowledges now that if he stays here tonight, there will be no sleep. What's more, it's a miracle that the girls haven't heard all this and come down to see what all the fuss is about. He will do as Clara says and come back tomorrow when hopefully she will be in a more rational frame of mind. When she will be sane again, is what he actually thinks.

Angrily, he turns out of the room. He goes upstairs and packs an overnight bag, swearing aloud while he is doing this. He leaves drawers open and slams the wardrobe door several times. Going back downstairs, he takes his hat, coat and scarf from the hallstand and wraps himself up carefully. It is nearly ten o'clock and bitterly cold outside. He is exhausted and his headache has returned. Jesus, she's going to pay for this.

He goes back into the living room and Clara is still on the floor where he left her. Her skirt is spread out around her and she hunches forward, head bowed and sobbing.

'I'm going now,' he says.

He repeats it several times, each time louder, but if she hears him, she gives no sign of it. Eventually, he gives up and goes out into the freezing London night, slamming the front door loudly after him.

After Henry leaves, it is all Clara can do to drag herself up the stairs, take off her blouse and skirt and pull the covers over herself. She falls asleep in her underwear and sleeps the sleep of the dead.

Chapter 74
Wednesday 17 December 1919

Henry had thought of spending the night at Mary's but he felt it would be too humiliating to appear at her door looking for a place to stay. Instead he finds a cheap hotel and spends a restless night. In the morning, things look brighter. He will go to work and then go home as usual. Perhaps this will all have blown over and if it hasn't − well, it's Christmas. He'll appeal to Clara's better nature. And if that doesn't work, he'll just stay there anyway. That bitch is not throwing him out. Yes, the house may be hers legally − he believes she's right there − but that isn't going to stop him.

Clara doesn't ever want to get out of bed again but has no choice when she finds Virginia shaking her shoulder and saying, 'Come on, Mummy, it's time to get up'. Clara tries not to think as she gets dressed, splashes some water in her face and brushes her hair. She gets the girls' breakfast ready and walks them to school. There are just two more days before their Christmas holidays. After she has left them at the school gates, Clara knows what she needs to do.

She never did see the solicitor that James had intended her to see nor can she remember the name of the firm. James had described him as 'the best there is' and way back in those days, she had a sense that James would help her pay for the man's services. It's all different now. Clara is on her own and she will have to take what she can afford − that's if she can afford anything.

Leaving the school, she goes to the shops. It is a bitterly cold day. There has been a heavy frost overnight which doesn't look like it's going to thaw. It actually feels like it's going to snow. The clouds are low and grey and brooding. The streets are filled with a grey light like that of pre-dawn even though it is nearly ten o'clock. A few doors along from the butcher's there is a brightly painted red door. A brass plate on the wall beside it says, 'Robin & Company, Solicitors'.

Clara is not sure if she should knock. She does but the sound of her gloved knuckles is so tentative she hardly hears it herself. She knocks again, this time more loudly but there is no answer. She pushes against the heavy door and opens it about halfway. She steps into a hallway. On the left an open door reveals an office and a perfectly made up young woman in her twenties clacking away at a typewriter. The woman's clothes are as impeccable as her hair and makeup. She wears a white blouse under a dark green jacket. As Clara steps closer, she sees that there is a fire burning happily in the grate. The room is warm.

'Can I help you?' asks the woman, looking up.

Her tone is neither friendly nor hostile – just business-like – but Clara wishes it had been warmer.

'I was wondering if it would be possible to see Mr Robin. Or if not today, to make an appointment.'

'Just a moment, please. I'll check,' the woman replies.

She gets up and goes through a door behind her. Clara realises she is shaking and she doesn't think it's from the cold outside. The woman returns.

'Please come through,' she says. Again the tone is business-like and Clara feels completely intimidated.

The woman holds the door for her and Clara steps past her into the inner office. She hears the door click shut behind her.

Mr Robin turns out to remind Clara exactly of the bird which is his namesake. She judges him to be in his early forties with a modest paunch pressing against his waistcoat and watch chain. His suit is well-cut tweed but may last have been fashionable before the war. He is of medium height with bright eyes. 'Dumpy' is a word that could be used to describe him. Clara could imagine a miniature version of him sitting on a branch watching while she dug her little vegetable patch in the back garden. A bird.

He comes round the desk to greet her.

'Noel Robin,' he introduces himself, shaking her hand. 'Mrs –?'

Clara wonders if he was born at Christmas. Inwardly she is smiling. It seems like a good omen. And his use of his own Christian name relaxes her a little.

'Jordan. At least that's my maiden name. My married name is Kenton.'

'Please, sit down, Mrs Jordan and tell me what can I do for you?'

'I want to get a divorce,' says Clara, bluntly.

The next words take her completely by surprise.

'Mrs Jordan, I wonder if you'd like a cup of tea.'

The woman in the outer office, whose name turns out to be Elsie, brings in a teapot and tea things on a tray. Noel Robin plays mother and after Clara has taken a sip of her tea, she tells her story of Henry's repeated infidelity. Clara cannot think of the man opposite her as Noel or Mr Robin. He is Noel Robin – the Robin sitting on a snowy branch on a tinselly Christmas card. He listens intently, ignoring his own cup of tea.

'You have grounds,' he says, when she finishes.

He asks her some questions about Henry's circumstances, particularly his financial ones. Clara explains about Henry's army pension, his new job and the fact that she really has no idea what he earns.

'Will … will it cost a lot?' she asks. 'I believe I would own the house – that's right, isn't it?'

'From what you've told me, yes, so it would appear.'

'But I don't have a job or an income. I thought I would sell the house to pay for it … the divorce … your fee.'

Noel Robin smiles. 'That's a little bit drastic perhaps. Anyway, let's not think about that for the moment. Maybe we can get your soon-to-be ex-husband to pay – at least for some of it.'

'Would that be possible?' Clara asks.

'Who knows?' replies Noel Robin. 'It might be. Lots of things are possible.'

He pauses for a few moments and then asks, 'May I inquire what it is you want, Mrs Jordan? Apart from a divorce, I mean. Financially.'

'I just want what I'm entitled to,' Clara says. 'If the house is mine, I want that. And then just a little money for myself and the children.'

'When you say "a little money"?'

'What we managed on during the war. Part of his army pay and the separation allowance. He earns far more than that now, I imagine.'

'He'll fight it.'

It's a statement, not a question.

'Tooth and nail,' says Clara.

As she says it, she wonders if the apparently gentle Noel Robin is the man for this. Henry will use some City lawyer and won't care what it will cost. She could see Noel Robin being eaten alive.

'So that's what *you* want. What does your husband want?' he asks.

'Things just to continue as they are, I imagine. Me to look after him and his children and his bit on the side.'

Clara feels a great sense of bitterness as she says this.

'I'll look after his children and he can have as many bits on the side as he wants. I just want to be done with him.'

Noel Robin nods.

'Of course. Of course,' he speaks soothingly. 'And may I ask, Mrs Jordan, what's he like, your husband? What's his temperament?'

'He likes things to be just so. He gets angry if they're not.'

'Is he a bully, Mrs Jordan?'

Clara thinks back over the last few years. Yes, in a way, Henry is. He doesn't hit her or anything like that but their relationship has never been a balanced one. He has always dominated.

'Yes, I think he is,' she replies.

Noel Robin shakes his head.

'Never liked bullies,' he states. '*Never* liked the blighters.'

After a thoughtful pause, Noel Robin continues, 'Are you familiar with Sun Tzu, Mrs Jordan?'

'Is it something legal?' she asks.

'No, it's not,' he smiles and Clara is embarrassed, not that Noel Robin seems to notice.

'He was a Chinese general. Lived – oh, a long time ago. He wrote a book called *The Art of War*. Lots of good advice in it about what to do when going into battle.

He says for example, than rather attacking the enemy's cities and armies, better to upset his plans. If we'd done a bit more of that over the last four years, then a lot more young men might be alive today.'

Clara can't help but ask.

'You were in the war, Mr Robin?'

'I was.'

He looks off into a very far distance.

'I was.'

Then he appears to snap back to the present.

'The other thing Sun Tzu says is that "If your opponent is of choleric temper, seek to irritate him." And that, my dear Mrs Jordan is what we shall try to do. Do you mind if I ask you a few more questions?'

'Not at all,' replies Clara.

'What did you do before you got married?'

'My father ran a stationery shop in the City. Jordan & Co. I worked there.'

Clara wonders what relevance this could possibly have. Is Noel Robin just asking questions for the sake of it?

'He'll probably hire a big City firm,' Clara says and the words are out of her mouth before she can think how insulting they might be to Noel Robin. Her hand begins to fly up to her mouth and she has to stop it.

'And you're wondering how a little David like myself will be able to grapple with those Goliaths.'

'I'm sorry. I didn't mean –'

'Think nothing of it, Mrs Jordan.'

Noel Robin seems quite unperturbed.

'I should perhaps explain. Before the war I worked for one of those big firms. I wanted to climb the ladder, become a partner, all the usual sort of thing. Then I went to war. I came back a different man, Mrs Jordan. I had seen how precarious life is. And my passion was *never* the law. I wanted to travel. See something of this amazing world of ours. So that's what I decided to do. I could have had my old job back but I set up here instead. Elsie makes sure I don't book too many cases and now I take half a dozen trips a year. This place keeps me in beer and baccy – and travel tickets. Just came back from Canada a month or so ago. Too cold for me, I'll tell you, Mrs Jordan.

So trust me – I believe I can get you what you want.'

'There's one other thing I probably should tell you,' says Clara.

Noel Robin steeples his fingers and looks over them into Clara's eyes.

'And that is?'

'I was unfaithful to my husband too.'

'After he was or before?'

'After.'

'And he knows about your … indiscretion?'

'He does.'

For the first time since she has come into the room, Noel Robin frowns.

'Hmm,' he says. 'That could make things a bit more tricky.'

When Henry finishes work that evening, he goes home as usual. He's hoping the whole thing will have blown over. When he arrives in the front door, he makes as much noise as possible to signal his arrival. By the time he reaches the open kitchen door, he finds himself blocked by Clara. Over her shoulder the children are doing their homework. They both say hello to him but carry on working. Clara takes a step forward and then another and another so that she moves him back out into the hall. He is so surprised by this that he complies meekly.

'What are you doing here?' she hisses.

'This is my home,' he says, and he feels his anger starting to rise. This has gone too far.

'Not any more,' she replies.

Her face is ugly with anger.

Henry is really fighting to keep his temper under control. It is his best option.

'Look, let's have tea, get the girls to bed and then we can talk.'

'There's nothing to talk about. Don't you understand? This is not some little tiff we've had. Our marriage is over. I can't say it any clearer. I saw a solicitor today. I'm divorcing you.'

Now Henry *does* get angry.

'How could you afford a solicitor? You'd better not be paying him with *my* money.'

'I haven't used any of your precious money.'

Clara almost spits the words at him. She is not showing any sign of relenting. For the first time Henry starts to think that this may not be as easy as he thought. He plays his trump card.

'Look Clara, you can't do this to our children. It's Christmas. Of all times.'

'Pity you didn't think about that before all of this started.'

'It's still Christmas,' he argues. 'What kind of Christmas are you going to give them? Their first one with their father in Christ knows how long.'

This time Clara doesn't respond immediately. Instead she says nothing and Henry can see, from the expression on her face, that his question has scored a direct hit. She slowly folds her arms as though hugging herself. She had been looking into his eyes but now she looks away. Henry is tempted to say something more but wisely he shuts up. The silence goes on and on until finally, Clara pronounces, 'Here's what I'm prepared to do. You can come and stay here for three days, Christmas Eve, Christmas Day and Boxing Day.'

Henry is appalled.

'But where will I go?' he blurts out before his brain has a chance to tell him not to. It is that pathetic schoolboy voice that he hates so much about himself.

Clara looks at him again and there is pure hatred in her eyes.

'Do you really want me to tell you?' she asks.

'Look just let me stay here tonight as well. I'm here now. What's to be gained from sending me away?'

He doesn't mind how pathetic he sounds now. In fact he thinks it might be having an effect on Clara. She is wavering. He can see it.

Clara unfolds her arms and holds up the first three fingers on her right hand.

'Three days,' she states. 'Now say goodnight to your children, get whatever you need and get out of my sight.'

Soon afterwards, standing on the doorstep having shut the door behind him, Henry pulls the collar of his coat up and hunches his neck down against the bitter cold. He still can't believe he allowed her to do this to him. He is tempted to go back in and to be physically violent if necessary. But he wouldn't want the children to see that. That really is the only reason. Otherwise he would happily give Clara a good slapping around.

But he has never seen her quite like this and, if he is honest with himself, he is a little afraid of her. Not that she could do anything to him while he was awake. He is taller and stronger than her. But what might she do while he was sleeping? He has heard of wives stabbing their husbands – or worse. And by worse, Henry means his cock and balls.

He counts the days on the fingers of his gloved hand. There are eight nights before Christmas. He can't afford to stay in a hotel for all that time. He has only one other alternative.

Mary opens her front door and is astonished to find Henry standing there with a suitcase. He has never come here before. She asks him in and shuts the door. Standing in the hall, he hurriedly explains what's happened. One of the three girls Mary shares the house with looks out of the kitchen, sees Mary with Henry and shuts the door quickly with an 'Oh sorry, Mary.' A few moments later, there is laughter from the kitchen.

'I'll have to check with the others,' Mary says. 'Wait here.'

Chapter 75
Wednesday Christmas Eve 1919

Henry leaves work and makes his way home – or at least to what he used to think of as home. Working on Christmas Eve. Faber always gave them Christmas Eve off but not the new man. Henry curses him. But that is only one of a long string of things that Henry curses. He curses that bitch of a wife of his. He curses those girls that Mary lives with. They have been charming and sweet and welcoming to him but he knows that they are laughing at him behind his back. It has been the most humiliating week of his life. He curses the fact that Clara normally bought all of the Christmas presents for the girls but now he has had to buy things for them. He has no idea what they like and so in the end he has spent much more than he intended to spend, buying doll's houses for both of them. The articles should have been delivered to the house yesterday. Of course it would be just his luck if they hadn't been.

Then Henry tried to make contact with his solicitor but the fellow had taken an early Christmas holiday. According to his secretary he wouldn't be back until the 5th of January. Henry is dreading the next three days. And in her current mood it seems most unlikely that Clara will let him stay a minute longer than she has said. In fact, Henry is slowly coming to the conclusion that this is not just a mood – Clara is serious and intends to go through with all of this. She has ruined Christmas for him and for all of them – for now and for all time.

But he'll be damned if he's going to make it as easy for her as he has since this started. His solicitor is one of the best or so he's been led to believe. Henry is going to fight Clara with all the resources at his disposal. That bitch, sitting there in that big house, spending *his* money. Well, he's going to see about all that. By the time he's finished with her, he'll have her out of that place and living in a tenement. And she's not going to see a penny more. Yes, the law may be on her side – Henry has a hunch that she does indeed own the house and is also entitled to money to pay for herself and the girls – but Henry has seen how the law drags its feet. And if Clara is destitute, Henry will make the case that the girls should live with him. If necessary he'll bring Mary into it. They'll seem like an ideal couple in comparison to Clara with her raging anger. How will she like that when her children are taken off her?

Clara is dreading the next three days even more than Henry. She knows that the only way she can get through it is to try and forget all of this business and just do what has to be done – the food, presents, decorations, the Christmas tree and all the rest of it. In a funny way, the fact that it is Christmas helps. There is an almost endless list of things to be done and Clara can just keep busy working her way down the list. Nobody yet knows about her and Henry. Her story is that with his new job, he has been away on business and the girls and Mrs Parsons have all accepted that.

Most of the time, Clara cannot believe that she has done what she has done. She cannot believe she has kept her nerve and brought things this far. And she has done it by herself. Noel Robin – Clara smiles whenever she thinks of her little Robin Redbreast solicitor – has said he will begin his work in early January. He will write to Henry – that's how this will all begin. Clara doesn't know how she will pay him. Nor does she know where she will get money for food or any of the bills, once the Christmas supplies have been consumed. Luckily she had done most of the buying by the time she threw Henry out – Clara has always been well organised for Christmas. She even has a present for him – a new shaving kit in a nice leather case.

But what will happen after this, when he leaves on the day after Boxing Day, she has no idea. She knows she will have to ask him for money. But what will he say? Presumably he'll only give her money in return for staying in the house. And what she'll do then? She doesn't know and is very fearful.

Another person who is fearful is Mary. Initially, when Henry had appeared at her door, she had been delighted. It looked like at last something was starting to come right for her. Henry's wife had kicked him out and by bringing Henry in, Mary had, for the first time ever, some kind of hold over him.

But Henry has *hated* every minute he had to spend in the house. Apart from their initial amusement at his predicament, the girls have been nothing but kind to him, but he doesn't see it that way. For some reason, he's gotten into his head that they're laughing at him and he's been going around the place all embarrassed and humiliated. And of course, this is something they *are* starting to find very funny indeed. And his sleeping on the couch in the sitting room is disrupting their preparations for Christmas not to mention their general routine.

So now Mary knows things are at a critical point. Henry is going home to spend Christmas with his wife and children. According to him, his wife is giving him three days and then he has to leave again. Mary doesn't know if this is true or not. But what she does know is that Henry is hoping he can get all this sorted out during his three days. If he does, then things will go back to the way they were; but if he doesn't then Mary knows that she will be Henry's only option. Now she won't just have a hold on him. She will *have* him.

Long ago Mary had decided that she would never go to live with Henry until he was divorced and they were married. But now she is happy to give way on this. If Henry comes back after the three days, he won't want to live with Mary and the girls a moment longer than is necessary. This means that he will want to find a place to live with just her. And she is happy to do that now because apparently it is the wife who is divorcing Henry. Bizarrely, Mary now finds herself on the same side as Henry's wife, Clara. (Mary has, for the first time ever, begun to think of Clara by her name.) She prays that Clara *will* throw him out again after the three days and that she will go all the way through with the divorce.

'Good luck, Clara,' Mary breathes as she hurries from work.

This Christmas Eve James is getting very drunk. Before he met Clara he had a rich social life in the days leading up to Christmas. And there were always plenty of women around to flirt with or go further with, if he chose to. This year the thought of being in London for Christmas has just saddened him beyond belief. So he has stayed in France. His driver Maurice invited him to spend Christmas with his family, but James declined, telling Maurice he was probably going to go back to England. He is hoping that he and Maurice won't run into each other over the next few days and that Maurice will see that this was a lie.

James was tempted to do a Christmas dinner for one but the prospect of that, of sitting alone in his house, eating a Christmas feast, seemed too pathetic for words. He thought there was a very real danger that he would spend the two weeks in an alcoholic stupour, so James has decided to do what he intended to do the year that the war broke out. He is going to walk at least some of the Somme from its source. He will take supplies for a week or so and a tent. He will begin tomorrow, Christmas Day and return on New Year's Day.

In some ways, he sees it as a pilgrimage. A way of remembering the people who died. He spent today packing and has just returned from dinner at a restaurant. Tonight he wants to get very drunk. He has a bought a bottle of very good Armagnac – his Christmas present to himself – but tonight he wants to remember all of those British boys and men who died. So he will drink a British drink. Single malt.

He throws some logs on the fire that he banked up before he went out, and lights a few candles, so that the room is a warm cavern of shadows and flickering yellow light. Then he pours himself a large tumbler of whisky that smells of the damp turf of the Highlands.

He feels truly homeless. Yes, he has his house back in England and there is here, where he is tonight. But if home is where the heart is, then his heart is in a place of hopelessness. Maybe, he thinks, his home is on the Somme, with the men who died. The Somme. It's such a strange word. Before 1916, it was merely the name of a river. But now – now, it is a world. A world of the dead. He repeats the word aloud, over and over, 'Somme. Somme. Somme'. It reminds him of some other word which he can't remember and which maddeningly lies just beyond his consciousness.

He pours more whisky, a good inch and a half into the glass. He looks at a candle through the amber liquid. What the hell is that word? 'Insomnia,' he says aloud. 'Somnolent. Sombre.' He drinks more whisky. He is knocking it back in large mouthfuls, like water. 'Immolate.' It's not the word he was looking for but there are those two 'm's. Yes, the Somme was an immolation.

'Consommé.' A watery soup. There must have been times when the River Somme was like a watery blood soup.

'Consummate.' Except that James says it as 'consommate'. Yes, that was the word.

'Well, it's not quite really a word,' he finds himself saying aloud.

But it was the word he wanted. Consummate. That's what they all did here. What does that word mean exactly? Suddenly it is vital that James knows. He goes to his little row of books on the bookshelf, selects his dictionary and quickly finds the word. Consummate – the verb. Accomplish. Complete. Fulfil. Finish. Make perfect.

Yes, that was what they did here – the living but especially the dead. The heroic things they accomplished. James squats down holding the book, tilted into the candlelight with his finger under the word 'accomplish'. He is conscious that this is an action he hasn't done since he was a schoolboy.

He moves his finger to the next word – 'complete'. Yes, they completed. They completed their duty and many of them completed their lives. 'Fulfil'. If ever a group of men fulfilled the mission they were sent out to accomplish, it was these men. And that, despite things like that unspeakable first day. 'Finish'. 'Make perfect.' Maybe this was what 'Somme' really meant.

This terrible, unselfish sacrifice. 'Made perfect.' Yes, the sacrifice couldn't have been more perfect.

Putting the book down, he returns to his chair and sprawls into it. He drinks more whisky. The candles burn down. It has just become Christmas Day when James either falls asleep or passes out. He will wake several hours later when the fire has burned down and the room becomes cold. But the chill isn't enough to overcome the drugging effect of the whisky. He sleeps again and when he eventually wakes, light is peeping through a gap in the curtains and James is chilled to the bone with a raging headache.

Chapter 76
Saturday 27 December 1919

Somehow Clara gets through Christmas. Afterwards she will find she doesn't actually remember that much of it. Memory can sometimes be merciful, she thinks.

She had hoped Henry wouldn't have a present for her – it would have made it that much easier for her to see him off the premises the day after his three days were up. But he did – and strangely enough, it was something she liked. It was a page a day diary for 1920 with beautiful blue, grey and black marbling on the inside front and back covers.

The day after Boxing Day, she finds herself in the kitchen with him at breakfast time. The girls have eaten and are in the living room playing with their new toys. Henry sits at the table having tea and toast. He looks like he is ready to go some place – he just has to put his jacket on and he will be fully dressed. Clara stands with her back to him, arms folded, looking out the window at the frost encrusted lawn. Birds are hopping around on the bird table pecking at the little pieces of bread that she put out for them earlier. She longs for him to be gone. She has a first faint feeling of how this could be a happy house without him – happy at least for her, whatever about the girls, she thinks blackly.

She takes a deep breath and turns to him, arms still folded.

'I'm going to need some money for food for the children, Henry.'

He puts down the cup he was about to drink from. The clink of the cup on the saucer is loud in the icy silence of the room.

'So you still intend to go through with this?' he asks.

'I do.'

Then she adds, 'I'd also like that, before you go this morning, we tell the girls what's happening.'

'Dear god, have you no pity? Not even at Christmas.'

There is so much Clara could say but she is very deliberately trying for this not to develop into a row. She says nothing. Neither does Henry. They stare at each other. She sees hatred – real hatred – in his eyes. The silence lengthens.

Finally, he takes his wallet from his inside jacket pocket and extracts five pounds which he puts on the table.

'Make it last,' he says.

'Thank you.'

'And for your information,' Henry adds. 'I'm not talking to the girls about this today. And I forbid you to. Is that clear?'

Clara says nothing.

'Is that clear?'

'I heard what you said,' replies Clara.

Henry gets up and walks out.

Clara breathes a deep sigh of relief. Her strategy worked. She asked him for something, and then asked him for something bigger so that the first thing seemed small by comparison.

She takes the banknote from the table and puts it in her apron pocket.

'We live to fight another day,' she breathes to herself.

When Mary hears the knock at the door, she knows that she has won. She opens it to see Henry with suitcase in hand.

'Are you by yourself?' he asks hopefully.

Mary shakes her head.

'Florence is here.'

Henry looks up to heaven.

'Come into the sitting room,' Mary says. 'I'll make some tea.'

When Mary returns with the tea, Henry tells her, 'We'll have to get out of here.'

'What do you mean?' she asks innocently.

'You know what I mean,' he says with irritation. 'Find a place of our own.'

'But you're married,' replies Mary. 'How can we –?'

She leaves the sentence unfinished.

'Look, I'm getting a divorce.'

Henry's irritation goes up a notch.

'You know this. Once it comes through we can be married.'

It is the second time that she has had this conversation with Henry. The last time, she got him to ask her to marry him. She does exactly the same thing now.

'Are you asking me to marry you?'

Henry comes ever so close to losing his temper but he just manages not to.

'I asked you before,' he says. 'Don't you remember?'

'Of course, I remember,' she responds. 'But that was a long time ago.'

Then, playfully, she adds, 'Ask me again?'

She can see she's really annoying him. She loves it.

'Mary, please would you do me the honour of becoming my wife once I'm divorced?'

Mary ignores the weary tone in his voice.

'I will,' she says. 'And what's more, I'll come and live with you until then.'

Mary has thought all this out carefully. They will rent a place for now but she wants them to start looking for a home to buy. With both of them working, they should be able to get a mortgage and the house will be in both their names – Mary will have some property. She will insist on a half share, even though Henry, with his salary, will pay the lion's share of the mortgage.

As they drink their tea, Mary talks about all of this excitedly. Of course, what she is actually doing is explaining the terms of their agreement to Henry, just so that he can be in no doubt. He sits opposite her almost – but not quite – managing to look happy.

Chapter 77
Monday 29 December 1919

Back at work, Henry is still shell shocked by the speed with which everything has happened and with which his life has unravelled. Going through his mail on this first day back, he finds a letter postmarked 'Acton'. He opens it and what he finds delights him.

The letter is from Clara's solicitor, a Mr Robin and informs Henry that Clara is instituting divorce proceedings and that further communications will follow. Henry has pretty much gotten used to the idea now that Clara is doing this and so there is nothing particularly surprising about the letter. What delights Henry though is the appearance of the letter itself. It has been typed on cheap, almost flimsy paper. As well as that, the letter 'y' of the typewriter that was used to type the letter must have been missing because the 'y's have been written with a pen. And if all of that weren't bad enough, there are several misspellings. All in all, it is a pretty amateurish – no it's worse than that, Henry thinks – it's a shoddy job.

It's marvellous news. If this is the calibre of the man Clara is using, then Henry's man, Smithson, will have him for lunch. Henry cheers up enormously. It is the first good thing that has happened to him since the sixteenth of December. (Henry refers to the day Clara threw him out as 'the sixteenth of December'. He doesn't like to think of it as the day that Clara threw him out.) That bitch is going to pay for all the havoc she has caused. Henry sees that he now has the potential to wreak great destruction in *her* life. Revenge will be sweet.

A short while later Mary looks in and tells Henry that, over the next few days, she is going to arrange for them to see some places where they might live together. Henry can't wait to move out of Mary's place and that, coupled with Clara's solicitor's letter puts him in high good humour. Not only will he be getting his revenge on Clara, but he'll be setting up house with Mary and he won't have to think about his commitment to marry her for several months, at the earliest. It may not be quite what he had envisaged but there's still a lot to be thankful for.

Just after lunch, Henry's secretary looks in to tell him that there is a Mr Robin downstairs to see him. 'He doesn't have an appointment,' she says.

Henry knows instantly who it is and smiles. So – Mr Robin who can't afford a new typewriter and doesn't know how to spell. It occurs to Henry that he shouldn't meet Robin without Smithson being present, but he quickly dismisses the idea. He is curious to meet Robin and give the fellow a first sense of what he might be up against.

'That's alright, Miss Campion,' Henry replies. 'Ask them to send him up.'

Henry had been expecting a short, diffident fellow in a shabby suit, with an ancient satchel stuffed with papers. What he actually gets is a very prosperous looking man of medium height in what could very well be a brand new suit. The trousers have a knife-edge crease, the shirt is immaculately white and the expensive looking shoes gleam. The fellow walks confidently into Henry's office, shakes his hand and says, 'Mr Kenton – a pleasure I'm sure.' Then he sits down without being invited.

Henry had hoped to take charge of the conversation but he finds he is already hurrying to catch up.

'Mrs Jordan tells me you were in the Army,' Robin begins brightly.

It takes Henry a moment to work out that the 'Mrs Jordan' to which Robin is referring is actually Clara. The bitch is using her maiden name already. Outrageous. Henry is surprised too by Robin's matey manner.

'You made it all the way through,' Robin continues. 'There's not too many of us can say that.'

Henry grasps that Robin is talking about the war. What's that got to do with anything?

'I was taken prisoner on the Somme,' says Henry and immediately regrets it. He shouldn't have fallen for Robin's chumminess and being taken prisoner makes Henry sound as though he cheated in some way. Robin sees the opening and goes for it.

'You missed some of the best bits, then. By the middle of 1918, old Duggy Haig and Rawly and the rest of them seemed finally to have worked out the difference between their arses and their elbows.'

Henry is shocked by the man's coarseness but instead of diminishing Robin in any way, it only seems to add to his stature. Henry feels quite intimidated.

'Those last few months were quite invigorating – at least we were on the move instead of skulking in holes.'

Feeling like he has gone several points down, Henry knows he has to strike back. He goes for Robin's obvious weak point.

'You really ought to get a new typist,' Henry suggests. 'Her spelling is atrocious. And maybe a new typewriter wouldn't go amiss while you're at it. And you could spend a bit more on your stationery.'

Three shots. Henry is pleased with himself and is a bit taken aback when Robin appears not to have noticed.

'Did you find, Mr Kenton – when you were in the Army, I mean – that appearances could be deceptive? You know, you might have a fellow in your platoon who was strong, a big hulking sort of chap, loud, brash, full of bluster. And then when it came to the crunch, the same man fell apart. And similarly, it was the ones that seemed weedy that were often the bravest under fire.'

Henry wonders where this is leading.

'Was there a reason you came to see me today?' he asks. 'Other than just to reminisce about old times?'

Henry feels it's a nice barbed shot. However, again Robin ignores the question, something which Henry is starting to find infuriating. But Robin answers Henry's previous jibes.

'I should tell you, Mr Kenton, that Elsie, my typist is excellent at spelling and her grammar and punctuation are impeccable. It always pains her when I ask her to do that.'

'Do what?' asks Henry.

'That business with the spelling mistakes. And that terrible paper. Not to mention that typewriter without the "y" which she truly detests.'

Henry is nonplussed and doesn't know quite what to say.

'Let me get to the point,' says Robin and suddenly all of the chumminess is gone to be replaced by a steely look and voice.

'I wish you would,' Henry just about manages to reply.

Robin looks Henry in the eye.

'I came here today, Mr Kenton to tell you that if you intend to make this divorce difficult for Mrs Jordan, then sir, you had better have very deep pockets indeed.'

'What do you mean?' asks Henry. Too late he realises, he should have said, 'Are you threatening me?'

'Perhaps I should explain a little of my own background,' offers Robin. 'Before the war, I was a partner in a City firm. Why who knows, it may be the very one that you have employed or are intending to employ? If not, it will be one of their competitors. After the war, I could have gone back there but that wasn't what I wanted to do, Mr Kenton.

I had my major's pension –' with the mention of Robin's rank, Henry feels he has just gone another point down – 'and I thought I'd work less and enjoy life a bit more. So now, I run a small one man firm and only take on the cases that interest me. And this one, Mr Kenton, this one interests me very much. Shall I tell you why?'

'Why?' Henry asks, not knowing if he managed to keep the nervousness out of his voice.

'Mrs Jordan is an old friend of mine –'

'How?' The word escapes Henry without him intending it to. He didn't know that Clara had any friends – least of all, a solicitor.

'I'll tell you how, Mr Kenton. I knew her father – when he ran that stationery shop. I don't know if you knew them then?'

It's a question.

'I did.' The words just about escape Henry's lips.

'As a result I got to know your wife – or Miss Jordan as she was then.'

Henry suddenly wonders whether Robin is Clara's lover. He wants to say something but doesn't really know how to phrase it. Robin continues. His voice is steady – almost conversational, as though he were discussing his garden or the weather.

'So you need to understand, Mr Kenton, that your wife is not paying me any fee. I am doing this out of respect for our old friendship – especially the friendship I had with her father. I don't want to see Mrs Jordan hard done by or done down in any way. Not that I'm for a moment suggesting that you would. Just that – well, I care for my friends, Mr Kenton. As one should. That was another thing the war taught me.

So I hope you can see what this means. Your wife essentially has limitless legal resources at her disposal. For you to have any chance of getting whatever it is you want, you will have to match these resources. The only trouble is that you'll be paying for yours, she won't. You could have a very long and very expensive few years ahead. I don't know how much you earn here, Mr Kenton but if I were you, I'd start looking for a more lucrative position.'

Henry can't quite believe what he is hearing.

'This … what you're saying … you can't …'

Finally, he manages to string a coherent sentence together.

'You can't come in here and make threats like this. This has to be illegal. Unethical. If my lawyer were here. I shouldn't have –'

'You shouldn't have met me without your solicitor?' Robin finishes the sentence for him and then shrugs.

'Maybe,' he continues. 'Though to be honest, he'd just advise you to fight me. Why would he suggest anything else?

He'll be dining out on you for several years to come. And as for it being unethical, Mr Kenton, I mean, really. You fought in the war. Both we and the Germans used poison gas. They declared unrestricted submarine warfare. We blockaded them and starved their children to death. I think you'll find that our ethics have changed quite a bit in the last few years.'

'What do you want?' asks Henry.

'I can tell you what Mrs Jordan wants, if that's what you mean.'

Pedantic fucking shit, thinks Henry.

'Go on,' he says.

Robin tells him.

Henry is simultaneously relieved and furious. She gets the house. He has to keep on paying her money. What – until the girls are grown up? Forever?

'I'm going to have to think about it,' says Henry.

'Naturally,' replies Robin.

'Why don't you take until the end of the year? Thursday's a holiday. So you could telephone my office on Friday morning and let me know what you've decided to do. Here's my card.'

Robin hands Henry a heavily embossed card with gold lettering. It is clearly expensive.

Robin concludes, 'I know feelings are running high for everybody involved now, Mr Kenton. But a new year, a new start. Best for everybody in the long run, don't you think? Anyway, thank you for meeting me and good day to you.'

Robin gets up, sweeps out of the office and is gone.

Chapter 78
Friday 2 January 1920

Clara has an appointment with Noel Robin at two thirty in the afternoon. She arrives and is shown into his office. Again he offers tea but this time she declines.

'The reason I asked you to drop in, Mrs Jordan, is that I think I have some rather good news for you.'

Clara looks at him quizzically.

'You see, it appears you've won your case. Mr Kenton has agreed to give you what you want.'

Clara is dumbfounded.

'But there hasn't been a case,' she says.

'No, of course not, you're right. There will have to be some legal formalities to go through, but they will be just that – formalities.'

Clara's mystification gives way to laughter. She laughs in a way that she hasn't laughed in years.

Noel Robin smiles.

'You're pleased, I take it.'

Clara nods as her laughter subsides.

'That's one word you could use.'

Clara has laughed so much that her eyes are wet and she needs to blow her nose. She takes a handkerchief from her bag. Then she is suddenly anxious.

'So this must have cost a ... how, how much do I owe you for this, Mr Robin?'

'Well, next to nothing so far. I wrote a letter and attended a meeting. That was all.'

'A meeting?'

'With Mr Kenton. There will be some legal fees as we go through the formalities but rest assured, Mrs Jordan – they won't be anything you can't handle. Trust me.'

Clara has recovered her composure somewhat.

'And this meeting?'

Noel Robin's face is a mask of innocence.

'I merely explained what you wanted and how I proposed to go about getting it.'

'And he just agreed?'

'Once he was in full possession of the facts, yes, he did.'

'The facts?'

Noel Robin's smile becomes a grin. He really *does* look like a cheeky little robin.

'Well mostly facts.'

'Mostly?' asks Clara, raising an eyebrow.

'There *was* one thing I told him that wasn't strictly true.'

'And do you mind me asking what that was?'

'Ah, Mrs Jordan. If I gave away all my trade secrets then nobody would employ me any more. You wouldn't want that now, would you?

Let me just say this. I don't know if I mentioned that I fought in the war. I saw a lot of fighting, Mrs Jordan. A lot of fighting. And remember I told you about Sun Tzu?'

'The Chinese gentleman.'

'The Chinese gentleman, indeed. Well, he always reckoned that if you could win a war without fighting at all then that really was a better thing indeed. How's that he put it? "The supreme art of war is to subdue the enemy without fighting." And that, my dear Mrs Jordan, was what we did.'

As Clara comes down the steps from Noel Robin's office, there is a vision forming in her head. The gods are having a meeting.

'What's next?' one of them asks.

'This woman. She's had a difficult few years.'

'How many?'

'Five and a half.'

'Mmm, that's long enough. Time to send her something good. Will you see to it?'

'Of course.'

It hasn't happened since that July day she met James all those years ago. But this time it looks like she hasn't been time's laughingstock. This time, something really good has happened to her. She feels tall. Strong. Courageous. She sees that a doorway has opened up to her. Whether James lies beyond that doorway or not doesn't seem to matter right now. At this moment, she just knows that she has been given another chance. And dear God, she is going to seize this with both hands. Who knows what terrible things still lie in wait for her? And of course she is delighted with what Noel Robin has told her but there is still a tiny voice in her head advising caution. But now she feels she can face whatever gets thrown at her. She is going to savour each day of this new life starting today. She is going to make plans for the future. It's the start of a new year and the start of her new life. She is young. Or at least not that old. There is plenty of life still to be lived. She is going to make the most of it.

Clara goes along to the grocer's to do her shopping. In the window, Mr Evans the grocer is in the process of putting up a sign. On an impulse Clara stops. Mr Evans sees her and smiles through the glass. As he straightens out the paper sign with the palm of his hand, Clara sees that it reads in big letters, 'Help Wanted'.

She doesn't really think about what she does next. Afterwards, she will marvel at her own confidence but at the time it just seems like a perfectly normal thing to do.

She goes into the shop and approaches Mr Evans as he turns away from the window. Clara realises she didn't even read the sign. Were they looking for a delivery boy?

'Oh, I'm so silly,' she says, and she thinks she is sounding quite flirtatious. 'Your sign, Mr Evans – I didn't even bother to read it, other than that it said you had a position available.'

'Somebody to serve behind the counter, Mrs Kenton,' Mr Evans replies in his Welsh accent.

'Ah,' says Clara. 'So I wonder if I might apply?'

'You, ma'am?'

'Yes me, Mr Evans. I love food. I love cooking. I think that with a little instruction I should be able to give a good account of myself.'

'It's only a part-time job, ma'am – just mornings.'

'That would suit me down to the ground, Mr Evans. Down to the ground.'

Clara walks out of Mr Evans' shop with a job and an arrangement that she will start tomorrow. She cannot believe her luck. She's also bought a bottle of wine to celebrate. She feels like whistling. Laughing.

'Why isn't Daddy coming home every night like he used to?' Ursula asks.

They are having tea. Clara bought Cornish pasties and opened her bottle of wine. The red wine is velvety in her mouth. The girls had seemed a little sullen this evening and now Clara understands why. There is nothing else for it. May as well get it out of the way. And she's already had two successes today. Maybe how the girls react to this will be number three and round her day off.

'There's something I need to tell you, my darlings,' Clara says.

Clara has never spoken to the girls like this before. They sense it too. There is something in her voice and now they look at her anxiously. Ursula is eleven and Virginia is nine. They are too young for this, Clara knows.

'When people get married,' Clara explains. 'They hope that it will make them the happiest they have ever been. Just like in fairy stories when the princess marries the prince and they live happily ever after. But sometimes it turns out that getting married didn't make them happy at all.'

Virginia looks mystified. Ursula doesn't. Clara has a sense that the older girl sees where this is heading – or if she doesn't know exactly, at least that it's nothing good.

'And I'm afraid, my loves, that's the way it's turned out with your Daddy and I. We –'

'So what are you going to do?' asks Ursula.

There is nothing else for it. There is no easy way to say it.

'Your Daddy and I are going to get divorced.'

'What does it mean?' asks Virginia and her eyes have already filled with tears. One runs down her cheek.

'We won't be married any more,' says Clara and of all the terrible moments she has experienced over the last six years, she feels that this has to be the most terrible of all. Before she can say anything else, Ursula asks, 'So he won't be living here any more?'

Ursula isn't crying. She looks angry and is interrogating Clara. 'No, he won't.'

Virginia has burst into tears now and is crying loudly.

'He will live in a different place and you will live here most of the time – during the school term and that sort of thing. At weekends and during some of the holidays you will spend them with him. It will be like having two homes.' It is the only selling point and Clara tries to make it sound like one. She fails.

'But I want us to all be together,' bawls Virginia.

Ursula looks at Clara and she sees contempt in her daughter's eyes.

'At least he never hit you,' says Ursula.

Later Clara lies in bed staring unseeing at the ceiling. She got the girls to bed about an hour earlier. Virginia had stopped crying and Clara stroked her hair and said soothing things. Ursula refused to kiss her goodnight.

But Clara has a sense that the worst part has been done and is over. Of all the things she has feared – not having enough money, being alone, losing the house – telling the girls was surely the worst. And now that's done.

Who ever wants anything bad to happen to their children? Like all parents she wanted to protect them forever – that their lives would be uncomplicated and simply happy. But when has the world ever been like that? They will get over this just as Clara got over the poisonous relationship between her parents. Her girls are in pain now but like all pain that will ease and eventually become a dull ache and eventually a memory. At least this is what she hopes.

As she thinks all of this, Clara wonders if she has just become heartless. Has she lost all of that love that she felt was so much a part of her and that she wanted to share with the world? As the thought occurs to her she feels her own eyes pricking with tears. She will be leading her little platoon forward from here. But she will be as she has always been. Her natural state. Alone.

Chapter 79
Tuesday 29 June 1920

It is early morning and Henry lies awake in a single bed in a room in a house in Lewisham. It is the house that he and Mary are renting and share. They are actually married though very few people know this yet. The same day that Henry's divorce came through, Mary insisted they arrange to get married. Since Henry felt in no position to stall any further, they were married a few weeks later.

Henry's daughters are staying with them for a week. They have stayed before. Henry has explained to his girls that Mary is his landlady. Whenever they stay, Henry sleeps in this room, even though he will often make his way to Mary's bed during the night. He then gets back to this bed before the girls wake in the morning. So far the system has worked. This is the first time Henry has had to keep up the landlady-lodger pretence for a whole week. It's only Tuesday and he's already finding it a bit wearing. He hopes there won't be any slip-ups, either by himself or Mary.

The girls don't know that Henry is married. At some point he's going to have to tell them. It's not something he's looking forward to. But he has been enjoying them staying this week. He has taken holidays and today the four of them are going to Brighton. It is the first time that Mary has come with them on one of these jaunts. Last night, Henry asked the girls if they would like Mary to come along. Virginia was delighted while Ursula said, 'Whatever you like.'

Henry's intention is to do the landlady-lodger act for at least several weeks more. Maybe then, when the girls get used to

Mary, he will tell them about the wedding and that they have a stepmother. He'll also have to tell Clara. That's something else he's not looking forward to.

Henry is relatively happy with his lot. (He is thinking this as he lies in bed on this sunny morning – he has some more minutes before he will have to call the girls.) Of course this whole divorce business has been terrible. Terrible for the girls, but also terrible for him. It still galls him how much he has to pay Clara every month and how that blasted solicitor of hers behaved. (Every time Henry thinks of this he becomes – quite literally – hot under the collar. His face becomes red, he can feel anger rising and it's all he can do not to explode at whoever happens to be nearest.) But with both Mary and he working, they have quite a decent standard of living. Mary is a bit more demanding than Clara – she won't just settle for dinner out once a week – but in return, the sex is good and plentiful and varied.

Despite this, Henry still can't keep his eye from wandering. There is a pretty thing called Louise who has just come to work in Claims. She really has quite the most gorgeous face framed by thick chestnut hair. If she is not a virgin, Henry senses she hasn't done it very often. When he is about to enter Mary, Henry finds himself wondering what it would be like to enter Louise in Claims. He feels the sensation of gently parting her lips with his fingers; then the head of his cock finding her interior very moist; finally a gentle push and that wonderful sliding feeling as he goes hard into her. She would be tight – of that he is almost certain. Tighter than Mary. And it is that feeling of the dampness and inner flesh dragging on his cock as he enters a woman that Henry finds perhaps the most exciting thing in the world.

So far he has only flirted with Louise in Claims. And of course, it's complicated that Mary works in the same office as him; that wasn't the case with Clara. Anyway Henry hasn't made up his mind one way or the other yet. He remembers how complicated things were when he was married to Clara and seeing Mary. There were times when that was really almost too much. Things are nice and simple now. Still – if Mary was at home or didn't work in the office then that would be different and would certainly make things easier. But never mind, he's not in any hurry. He has plenty of time to think about all this.

In the adjacent room that she normally shares with Henry, Mary is nursing a secret. Not that it will be a secret for much longer. She will tell Henry as soon as his girls go back to their mother. Mary enjoys having Henry's two daughters to stay. They are very sweet and always impeccably polite to her, even though the eldest one is clearly nursing a huge grievance about her parent's divorce. Mary enjoys her weekends of being a stepmother – cooking and baking for the girls and talking with them. There have been occasions where the three of them have ended up laughing together about something and Mary finds these moments especially nice. Even the eldest one, Ursula, seems to enjoy these.

But today Mary knows that she is not going to be just a stepmother all her life. Mary is certain that she is pregnant.

Clara is on a ferry on her way to France and the ship is about mid-way through its passage. It is six years to the day since she met James and she hopes that this is auspicious. She stands on deck leaning on the railing and looking across the sun-speckled sea. The sea is calm, the day hot and with a steady breeze that drives the black smoke from the funnel in a long ragged banner away over the stern of the ship.

This is the first time Clara has travelled by herself and the first time she has been outside England. She is excited and apprehensive at the same time. She takes comfort from the fact that there are many women on board the ship – far more than there are men. Almost all of the women are dressed in black. They are clearly going to visit the graves of loved ones – or try to find then. When Clara compares her mission to theirs, she is thankful. But she is still worried. She is thinking that she probably should have done things very differently.

Clara is thirty-seven – and divorced. The children are with Henry for a week. She feels free in a way that she hasn't been since before she was married. Once her divorce was finalised, Clara did two things. The first was that she contacted the Imperial War Graves Commission and got James' address. The other was that she enrolled in French lessons. While she has only had a few weeks of them, she thinks she has enough French to get by. And anyway, the lessons were more about wanting to surprise James than anything else.

She should have written to him, of course. But she chose not to do this. For some reason that she cannot fully explain, she wanted this – wants this – to be the biggest gamble of her life. It is something about having lived in fear for too long. She lived a small life with Henry and she never wants to have that feeling again. Yes, she has been lonely – terribly lonely – since she threw him out but that is still better than the mouse-like existence she lived while she was with him.

Of course, there are times now when she feels mouse-like or even smaller. Sometimes the enormity of what she is doing – raising two children by herself, working in Mr Evans' grocery shop, even if it is only part time, running the house – threatens to overwhelm her. Fear threatens to engulf her like an avalanche. But today she feels like she has reached a new place in her climb to the top of that mountain of fear.

She knows that she may find James married or with a woman – Clara believes the French are more relaxed about these things. Worse still, she could find that he is no longer interested in her or wants to have anything to do with her. But she doesn't care. She wants to make this journey and see him – even if it is for one last time. And who knows, even if he no longer cares, maybe she will meet somebody else. She is out in the wide world and that's all she cares about right now. The little voices of fear that call to her are inconsequential this gorgeous summer afternoon.

Clara catches a train to Amiens and arrives in the late evening. She wants to be refreshed when she goes to find James so she checks into a small hotel she previously booked through the travel agent. The hotel is in the Rue Amiral Courbet. The woman behind the desk is young, in her twenties but wears widow's black. Clara would love to talk to her, to find out her story, but Clara's French isn't good enough and somehow, it doesn't seem right to ask in English. She eats a delicious dinner by herself and drinks some red wine. Clara can't get over it. She is in France. She feels she is starting to love the country already. It is so different from England.

Chapter 80
Wednesday 30 June 1920

Next morning, for breakfast, Clara has wonderful coffee and gorgeous pastries shaped like pairs of horns. They're called *croissants*, she is told when she asks. Afterwards she makes her way through a city that is full of the sights and sounds of rebuilding. There is scaffolding everywhere with men swarming over it. Wagons carrying bricks or timber or sacks of building material pass through the streets. The air is full of hammering, sawing, shouts, laughter, whistling and singing.

Clara had expected herself to be anxious about her meeting with James but she finds that she isn't. She feels a quiet confidence that everything is going to be all right and will work out for the best. She finds the correct street and finds the door. When she knocks there is no answer. For a while she is puzzled but then she decides that she has been silly – he must be out working. He will be home towards evening time. She will explore the city and try again then.

She visits the Cathedral and is stunned by its beauty. She has lunch in a little restaurant that is really just somebody's front room with the food cooked in the kitchen. Again, the meal is delicious. She wanders some more after lunch and about four she finds a little pavement café where she orders some coffee and sits outside in the sun.

She is just killing time and now she starts to worry. What if he *is* married or living with a woman? It will be so humiliating. Like a great weight falling on her, Clara suddenly realises what she is doing. She is chasing a man. That must make her little more than a slut. Certainly that's what her mother would have said. And given everything that has passed between her and James, how is he likely to react?

And it isn't just that. All the newness of the past two days has blinded her to a very simple fact. She still loves James and the future, the life that she has been envisioning for herself, assumes that he will be in it. This is why she has learned French. This is why she has come to France. This is why she has put her children in a position where they only get to see their father once in a while. It is so that she can be with James. And the thought that this might not now happen is so crushing that for a while she finds she cannot think. She cannot remember where she is or what she is doing here. It is only when the moustachioed waiter with one leg and a crutch, comes out from the café's shady interior and says, '*Encore un café, Madame?*' that she returns to the present.

'*Oui, si vous plait,*' she says though she doesn't actually want it.

She has arranged to stay in Amiens until Saturday when she must catch the train for a ferry on Sunday morning. What will she do if James doesn't want her? Wander the wreckage of the city as she ponders the wreckage of her life?

The bells are ringing five when she decides she had better go. She retraces her steps and knocks again on the door. Again there is no answer. She remembers that James was always quite strict about his hours. Maybe he doesn't stop until five and it will take him some time to get back here. She is tired now but walks down to the river, finds a bench and sits down.

So here it is. The Somme. That terrible, terrible name.

At six the bells ring again and she returns once again and knocks.

This time the door opens and James is standing there in trousers, braces and a shirt without a collar. He is tanned and fit looking. For a moment she can see that he doesn't recognise her. Then he does. And the lack of recognition is replaced by shock.

'Clara,' he says.

'Hello James.'

Chapter 81
Wednesday 30 June 1920

Clara is not sure how long they both stand there, James on the doorstep, she looking up at him from her lower position on the pavement.

'I'm divorced,' Clara says simply.

And then, 'I wondered if you –'

Chapter 82
Wednesday 30 June 1920

There are times, dear reader when it seems that the gods *do* play tricks on us and they make us – in Hardy's memorable phrase – into 'time's laughingstocks'. We ask for something, we appear to receive it, but then it turns out to be not at all what we had been picturing. A poisoned apple.

A by passer sees a woman standing in summer clothes on a sunny street in Amiens, France all that time ago. A man stands in shirtsleeves in a doorway. The woman looks up into his eyes. It is perhaps the most ordinary and unremarkable of scenes.

Except that now – somewhere – the gods have to decide. Do they roll a dice? Perhaps. It is certainly one way to imagine it. And so they do.

And James says, 'Clara – my darling – you came back.'

Chapter 83
Wednesday 30 June 1920

Clara freshens up and she and James go out to eat. Once they are seated, Clara counts on her fingers. She has the rest of today, then Thursday and Friday before she has to leave on Saturday.

'What are you counting?' James asks.

'Measuring the amount of time I have with you. It's less than I had with you in Teignmouth.'

'We have the rest of our lives,' James says.

This restaurant has menus. The waiter comes with a basket of bread and hands out the small handwritten single pages.

'Shall I tell you what's what?' James asks.

Clara shakes her head.

'I think I'll be able to work it out. If I need help I'll ask.'

'You've learned French?'

'A few weeks' lessons,' she replies, with a smile. 'But it's a start.'

Once they have ordered, Clara says, 'I thought I should like to come and live in France – that's if you'd like me to. And your work is going to keep you here. Well, for a few years anyway. And then we could see.'

'Do you mean it?' he asks in delighted surprise.

'Yes, I mean it. Of course, you know I'd have to bring the girls. But I thought it would be good for them – finish their education in a different country. Learn a new language. A new culture. Exotic new friends. I haven't told them yet and Henry will probably kick up a stink but I think I can convince him that it will be a good thing. What do you think?'

James reaches across the table and takes her hand.

'There's nothing I'd love more.'

Later, as the waiter is about to take away their empty plates, the power fails. It is a frequent occurrence in a city, large portions of which still lie in ruins. He raises his hands dramatically in a '*qu'est-ce que on peut faire*' gesture and emits a sound like escaping steam. He takes the plates and navigates his way to the kitchen in the pitch darkness. James and Clara hold hands. The waiter returns bringing candles to each of the tables. As he lights their candle, he says something in rapid fire French that Clara has no chance of catching. In the resulting little cavern of flickering light from the candle, it is suddenly like they are alone.

James tells her, 'You're amazing, do you know that?'

'Why is that?' Clara smiles.

'This big life you're living. These huge decisions that you're making. You're incredible.'

'I lived a small life for long enough.'

Chapter 84
Thursday 1 July 1920

Sometime during the night Clara wakes. It is the first of July. Both she and James lie naked, he spooned against her, his left hand on her right breast. James is sound asleep but his cock is hard – she can feel it pressing into the cleft of her buttocks.

Clara moves up and forward a little. Then she parts her legs just enough so that she can press herself onto him. He slips deliciously into her. He is still asleep. She wants to laugh out loud. In the morning, she will tell him what she did.

And this is how she falls asleep – two people as close as two people can be.

Epilogue
The Group of Death

And this, dear and faithful reader, is where our story ends. Those two pistol shots that rang out on that sunny Sunday in Sarajevo all those years ago, along with the decisions which followed, would eventually claim the lives of some seventeen million people, seven million of which were civilians. It was the single biggest reduction in population since the Black Death six hundred years earlier.

But of course, the cruelest irony of all was that this was not the end of the Group of Death. Because of the botched peace at Versailles, the Group of Death would restart less than twenty years later with even more horrifying consequences. This time it would kill one fortieth of the world's population, some sixty million people. The figure would include two thirds of Europe's Jews – in Eastern Europe that number was over ninety percent – not to mention the removal from the face of the earth of one of the richest and most vibrant cultures in Europe. More than half of the people who would die in the second half of the Group of Death would not be soldiers at all. They were civilians – men, women, children, old people. We can only try to imagine how different Europe and the world would be now, had all of these people, soldiers and civilians alike, with their intelligence, creativity, potential and love, not died.

In August 1920, Clara and her daughters moved to Amiens, where she subsequently married James. About a year later, Clara gave birth to a son, Alain.

When the Germans invaded France in May 1940, Clara and James were living in one of the Somme villages that had been rebuilt after the war. James, aged sixty, continued to work for the Imperial War Graves Commission while Clara ran a small bed & breakfast whose main clientele was relatives of soldiers who had died during the battle. Fearing that the Germans would imprison them or worse, Clara, James and Virginia managed to flee to England. Ursula, who had married a Frenchmen, opted to stay in France as did Alain who by then, was nineteen and saw himself as completely French. In time, all three would join the Resistance and survive the war.

Clara was not surprised when Virginia, the little girl she had always regarded as an old soul, chose to do something dramatic for the war effort. With her accent-perfect French, she joined the Special Operations Executive as an agent and was parachuted back into France. She was eventually betrayed, captured, tortured by the Gestapo and was shot in Ravensbruck Concentration Camp in 1944.

Clara and James decided not to go back to France after the war. For Clara the memories of Virginia and the life the five of them had led there were too unbearable. Both she and James had often talked of living by the sea and that was what they did, moving to Cornwall. They lived into their nineties.

Lightning Source UK Ltd.
Milton Keynes UK
UKOW05f0218300714

235991UK00001B/6/P